Dedication

Sometimes survival looks like waiting for your soulmate to come home again.

TRIGGER WARNINGS

The MMC is in a relationship when the FMC returns to her home town. There is OW drama in this book.

There are references to cheating and one scene (First base where MMC cheats on his now GF with the FMC - Chapter 14)

This book includes a character who is an SA survivor (although not graphic, there is a flashback in chapter 18)

Playlist

Broken Roots - Michl
Youth - Daughter
Berlin - RY X
Mr. Sandman - SYML
Stone Heart - Elijah Woods x Jamie Fine
Fix You - Sam Smith
Arcade - Duncan Laurence
If You Ever Want To Be In Love - James Bay
Secrets - Regard, RAYE
Adore You - Jessie Ware
Lost - Dermot Kennedy
Wish You Well - Sigale, Becky Hill
Contaminated - BANKS
War - Chance Pena
Don't Hurt Like It Used To - Grace Carter
I'm Tired - Labrinth, Zendaya
Don't Watch Me Cry - Jorja Smith
Bleeding Out - Chance Pena

DAN'S HOUSE
VILLAGE HALL
DANIELLE'S BAKERY
RISE HILL
MEMORIAL
HILL TOP FARM
COLLEGE
HOLLY'
HOUS

CAMERON'S HOUSE

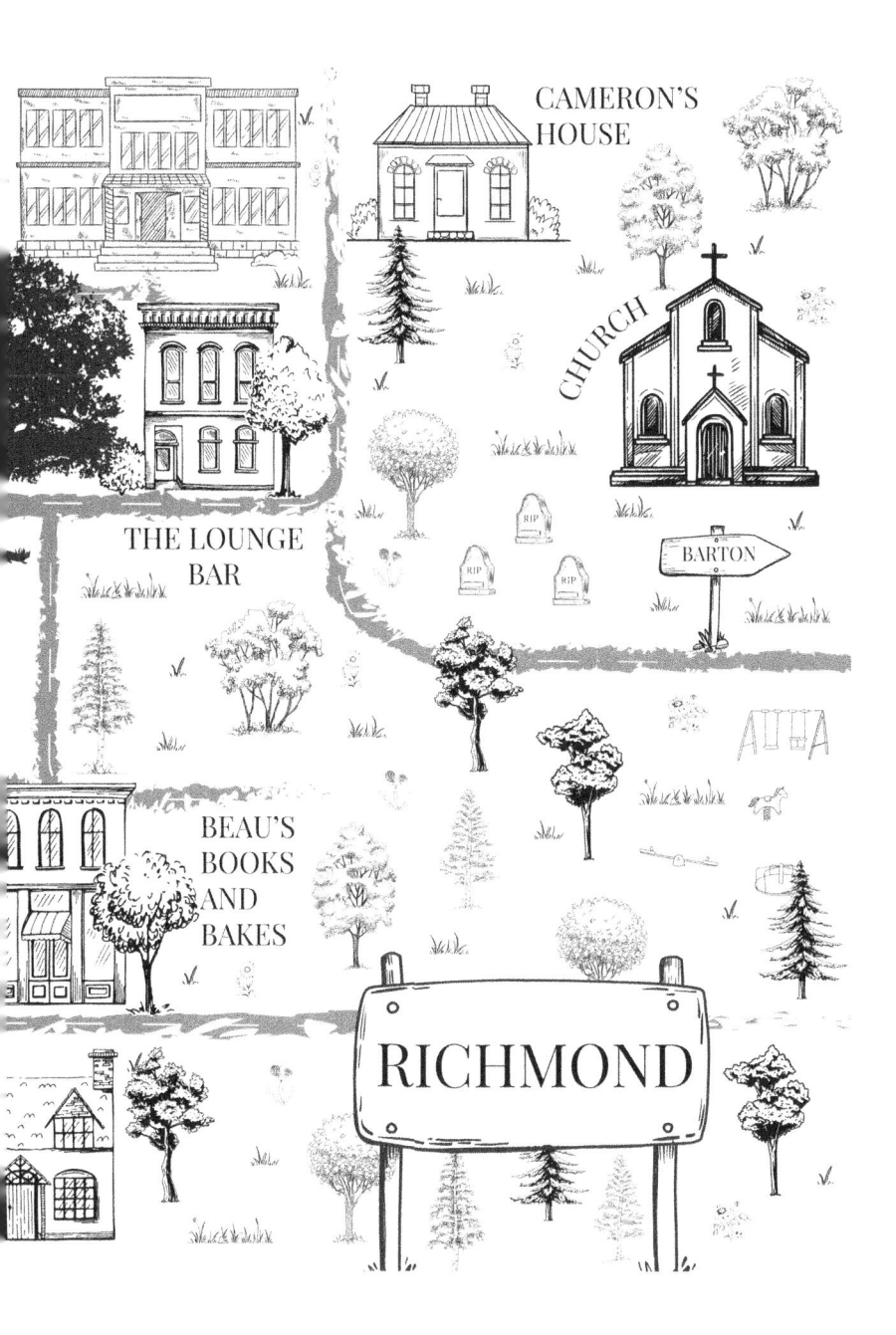

CHURCH

BARTON

THE LOUNGE BAR

BEAU'S BOOKS AND BAKES

RICHMOND

Chapter One
Cameron

My phone rings for the third time in ten minutes, and like before, I ignore it. It will be one of the guys wondering where I am. Not at the Richmond village fete, that's where. I'm not against the celebrations, but after last year's drama, I'm all too happy to sit this one out. I can catch up with the guys later. Resting my head on my hands, I get myself comfortable and close my eyes against the beating sun. My broad chest is on full display, and for a moment, I contemplate getting up and carrying on with the decking. I've worked through the last five weekends, so I owe myself some downtime. I glance back at the house and the newly made wrap-around I've built and installed myself. It leads down to a half-finished decking, and my hands itch to complete it, but I turn away. I can carry on later, let the sun drop, and do another hour or two. It's a conversation I've had with myself more than once today, and I keep reciting it, hoping I actually listen, but the truth is I want it finished now. I've still got heaps to do on the house, but my plan was to have it all done by the end of summer. The only problem is, summer is here, and I want to enjoy it. Rarely are we graced with decent weather.

My back door bangs shut, and I spin around. Dan shakes his head at me. "You sly bastard, you're not leaving me to deal with Brant and Cole alone." He jogs down the steps, and I laugh, going back to my sunbathing.

"I can't be arsed to deal with Mandy bloody Jacobs. Is she there?"

"Of course she is; she organises it every year." He scoffs. He helps himself to a beer out of the cool box and drops into the lounger beside me. "Come on, Cam, it beats sitting at home alone."

"I'm not going. Mandy still tries to corner me in any shop." I shudder. One night, one stupid night of beer-fuelled fun and the crazy woman was practically planning our wedding. She was the drama I was avoiding.

"Cam, you knew she was crazy, so you only have yourself to blame. Nadine is there with Kerry." Dan slugs a mouthful down. "Don't be a whiner; it's a good laugh." I know it is, and I'd have fun any other time, but I really can't be bothered with Mandy coming onto me again. "Nadine seemed pretty bothered that you hadn't shown up. I thought things with you two were good?"

"Yeah, they are," I say, scratching my abs.

"She's hot and the group likes her." He sits and places his arms on his knees. "I thought you wanted to make it more serious?"

"I like her. Sex is good," I say, necking my beer. "I think I'm ready to give it a go."

"That's great, Cam, she's decent. You could do far fucking worse."

"Like Mandy Jacobs," I mutter.

"How could you, Cam!"

I throw my bottle lid at him, and he laughs. Mandy is hot if you go for the Stepford wife look; she's the village busybody and a rhetorical pain in my arse. The sex wasn't worth the shitstorm I've dealt with since. "Just come down for a few hours. It'll be good for you. You're working like mad. The house looks amazing, but take a break." His tone is soft but adamant. I know my friend well enough to know he will not leave until I go. With a huff, I push myself up, and he whoops, "Cole owes me twenty quid." I shake my head as he finishes his beer off, and I pull my t-shirt on over my head.

"Where's Grace?" I ask, finding it odd that he has come without his daughter.

"Kerry is watching her whilst I collect your stubborn ass." I throw him a wide grin and follow him back through the house so I can lock up and grab my wallet. "Looks heaps better since you knocked those walls down." Dan eyes the open plan space, and I nod.

"Opened the snug up too." I point over his shoulder to where there was an arch from the kitchen through to a small living room. I've knocked it all out into one large living space. I've still got my man cave, but this space is for entertaining.

"It's a shame you've still got that shitty sofa." He pokes, making us both laugh. It's the most hideous sofa I've ever seen, but it was here when I moved in and it fills a space for the time being.

"Trust me, bonfire night, that thing is gone!" I chuckle, following him out of the house and down the path to his car. We drive back to his place so he can ditch his car, then head back to the village green. I don't know why we call it a village. In the past ten years, the small, humble setting has doubled in size. It's busy and most people buy locally to support the neighbouring trades and shops. Dan heads towards the enormous oak tree in the far corner, and I follow along. My eyes sweep the green as families and visitors mill around and music plays in the background. It's picturesque to any outsider, but I've looked at it so many times that I'm indifferent to it now. That, and I know first-hand how awful the residents can be.

We reach the group and Grace runs towards me. "Uncle Cam!" she squeals, throwing herself in my arms. She pats my cheeks and pulls back. "I don't like your beard." Displeasure scrunches up her little face, and she wriggles to be put down. I laugh and rub my stubble against her. "No!" She giggles, and I gently pin her to the ground, tickling her like crazy until she's in a wheezy tight ball.

"What's that? You love my beard?" I joke, grinning as she jerks against the grass, squealing. I blow a raspberry on her cheek, then lift her to her feet.

"I love your beard," she huffs dramatically. I fold my arms with a wide grin. "Your beard is stinky!" She laughs and runs off before I can grab her again.

"You cheeky little madam!" Sticking out her tongue, she hides behind the tree as I grab a beer off the side whilst Dan and Cole argue about twenty quid.

"Hey, mate." Brant drops into a seat beside me. I take the other one and chug my beer. I give Kerry, his wife, a wink, and she smiles briefly, her attention fixed on their newborn, Darcey, who's rolling around on a mat. "Mandy has already walked by three times looking for you. I don't think she'll be back for a while," he leans in to murmur.

"Jesus," I mutter, ignoring Kerry's snort of laughter.

"You took her to bed," he replies with a shrug.

"It was a moment of stupidity," I grumble, looking up to see Mandy across the green in five-inch heels and a ridiculously tight dress on. She flicks her straight blonde hair over her shoulder, and I twist away before she clocks me. "Where's Nadine? Dan said she was here?"

"She did come over, but I think she felt weird without you here," Kerry says, lifting Darcey up. I had told her I was coming but changed my mind last minute. No wonder she feels awkward. I pull my phone out and send her a quick text. She comes back almost instantly, and I know it's because she has probably been checking her phone constantly. The thought makes me smile.

> I'll catch up with you in a bit. With the girls.

SHE ENDS it with a cheeky wink, and I know for a fact tonight will end how I want it to. She's a little shy, but I kind of like that in a woman. I shoot her a simple kiss back and tuck my phone in my back pocket. Dan cranks up the barbecue, and we all settle in, chatting away. The guys laugh at something Brant has said, and I twist my head around.

"Oh, come on, that goal was legendary!" Dan exclaims, his face tight.

"Just like how legendary you were when you made out with Lacey O'Brian in high school behind the science block?" I quip, lifting my brow. The group breaks out in laughter, and Dan does a quick sweep to check Grace isn't in earshot of the incoming insult I expect he plans to throw at me.

"Fuck off!" He gives me the finger and clips Cole around the ear when he belts into more laughter. "I didn't make that up," he grumbles defensively. Kerry mocks him, and the poor sod pinches his nose to stop from losing his shit.

My stomach aches from laughing, and I'm glad Dan dragged me out. As I take a swig of my beer, my eyes zero in on someone over my friend's shoulder. I cough, choke, and spit my beer out, almost drenching us all.

"Cam, you dirty bastard!" Cole flinches as beer trickles down his bare leg.

"Fucking hell, someone grab him a bib." Dan's face creases with humour, but it slowly turns to concern when he focuses on me.

"Swear Jar. Swear Jar!" Grace shouts at her dad.

"Kerry, babe, pass that cloth, Cam's making a right mess," Brant huffs, grinning my way, but I'm paling by the second.

"No, I need it to mop up Darcey. Last thing I want is her drunk," she mutters.

"Cam, what's up?" Dan walks to me, his wide shoulder momentarily blocking *her* from my view, and I move without blinking.

"Did you know?" I ask him. "Did you know?" I can't look away from her moving quietly as she looks at something on one of the cake and toy stands circling the green. Her blonde hair has grown. Fuck me, has it grown! She used to wear it to her shoulders, but now it's halfway down her back.

"Know what?" Dan pulls back at my low bark.

"That Holly was going to be here?" I say with a ragged breath, and my friends swing to look where my eyes are trained.

"Fucking hell." Dan has the decency to react.

"That's a naughty word!" Grace huffs, tugging on his arm to reprimand him.

"When did she get back?" I'm looking around at them all, trying to get an answer and find some explanation as to why she is here. Is she staying?

"I don't know," they mumble collectively, seemingly as shocked as I am. Some sixth sense must alert her to being the centre of our attention because her head lifts and her deep blue eyes knock me on my arse. She's even more beautiful now than she was all those years ago. Her eyes do a quick sweep of us, and her lips flatten briefly before her attention drops away to someone behind her. It all happens so fast to prepare me. Holly bends and lifts a girl up into her arms. She is a carbon copy of her, blonde curls, big blue eyes, and a wide smile. Pain splinters my chest, and I suck in a gutting breath. The boys are looking back at me, and Dan thrusts another beer into my hand.

"Drink," he instructs, and I neck the entire bottle. How is this happening? Any minute now, I will wake up and find myself back at home and not slipping into that painful void again, where she left me.

"I should go speak to her," I say with uncertainty as that horrible ache spreads through my body and gives me a headache.

"Erm, no. Absolutely not." Brant puts a hand on my chest. "I can guarantee after everything that happened, she won't want you approaching her."

"Nothing happened," I grit, eyeing them all. Their concerned faces turn hard, warning me to stay away. I know they believe me; they had my back throughout the whole shitstorm of my breakup with Holly and the aftermath. I'm not sure what I found more painful—her leaving or the hell that followed.

"It did, though, man. It's shit, but it's history. She's obviously moved on, and you need to as well," Cole murmurs. My throat closes, and I choke back a growl. I drop my gaze, and before the boys can stop me, I'm moving.

The love of my life is metres away, so how can they expect me to ignore her?

I've not seen her in years. Ten, to be exact, but I'm not letting this moment slip away.

Not this time.

She ran from me before. Not again. It's not history. I still feel like it happened yesterday. Those ten years have consolidated into a mere blink for me, and my girl is *here*. My lungs open for the first time, and my heart flutters. I recognise the sensation, the emotion. Hope.

That's not all that I am feeling. I'm too shocked to recognise the slow simmer of anger beneath the surface. The swirl of deeply buried anxiety.

I'm a few feet away when a mouse of a man walks to her

and squeezes her shoulder. He's everything I'm not, and it feels like a vice is around my throat. I'm athletic and a little rough around the edges, and this little weasel is sporting a comb-over and fucking sandals. "Pick me up?" the little girl asks him when Holly puts her down, but he ruffles her hair instead.

"You know I can't. I have that bad wrist, sweetie." The staid prick must know he is punching above his weight, punching hard, because Holly Matthews is every man's dream. She's beautiful, smart, respectful and fun. She's sexy as damn hell and innocent too. She's the whole package. Long flowing blonde hair, a knockout body, and unusually demure, given how stunning she is.

His presence doesn't stop me, though. I make it to her quickly as the little girl whines, "I want the unicorn, please!"

I'm at the stall now so I pick it up. "Here you go." I smile and drop down, holding it out to her. She stops and looks longingly at the toy before flicking an unsure look at her mum. Holly's smile is brittle. Her body has gone stiff, and I feel like a twat; I should have listened to Brant.

Holly nods, and the girl takes it. "What do you say, Beau?"

Beau. It needles into my heart, and I force a swallow down. She had said time and time again that if we had a child, she wanted to call them Beau.

"I like your name," I say gruffly.

The girl smiles cautiously. "Thank you." Her eyes go back to her mum. "Please, can I have this unicorn?"

I stand tall and take all of Holly in. She has a floaty summer dress on and a little gloss. For once, she is wearing make-up. It's minimal, but she doesn't need it. Never has.

"Hi, Holly, how are you?" I swallow thickly. "When did you get back to Richmond?" I add right away. The pipsqueak bristles and puts a hand on her arm, but I ignore him. My eyes are on my girl and she is exactly that. Mine. Always was. Always will be. My chest expands with a deep sigh as her face sets into a neutral look.

"I'm good, thanks. We moved back a few days ago." Her smile is polite but uncomfortable, and her eyes slip to the man beside her but quickly come back to me. I take great pleasure in that. But it's momentary. *We.* She means him too. I don't recognise the weasel of a man. I don't get it. Holly is incredible, and the guy looks like he'd ask her to push the car if it ever broke down. He's a wet fish.

But she's finally home.

Here. Near me.

I'm soaring and falling, headfirst back into that painful void. Several residents are watching, and my gut starts to cramp with unease.

"That's great, you look great, and Beau, wow, how old is she?" I mostly hate that Holly has moved on, especially with this schmuck. I hate she has had a kid with him, and I wonder if there are more children. If they are married. I feel nauseous at the thought.

"I'm five!" Beau pipes up, shoving the unicorn at her mum. "Pleeeease, she is the most glittery pink one!" Her tiny teeth are gritted together as she pleads her case, and I laugh lightly. "I have pockey money," she begs passionately.

"Yes, okay." Holly laughs. "But you don't need to use your pocket money," she replies softly, calmly, like I expected she always would with any children we had. Because that was our plan. Marriage. Kids. My heart squeezes, and I look at the wormy man beside her and smile.

"Hey, sorry. I'm Cameron." I hold out my hand to be polite and repel the image of me crushing his hand as he lifts it to shake it back.

"Marcus." I notice he doesn't stake his claim and say he is her husband, nor do I check if there is there any ring. It'd be too obvious. I feel a heavy slap on my shoulder.

"Hey, Hol!"

"Hi, Dan." She moves slightly, and I see a glimpse of the awkward teen I became so fascinated with.

"You're looking good. How's things? Who's this?" He drops to Beau, who holds her unicorn up.

"This is my unipony," she declares proudly.

"She looks like candy floss," Dan says and sniffs it. "She smells like it too!" His eyes widen, but my eyes are on the woman looking lovingly at her daughter.

Beau grins and sniffs the unicorn. "Mummy smell, she's candy!" Holly sniffs, and I want to scoop her up and carry her home. But that fatal night comes crashing back, and I remember the bone-crushing hurt on her face. She'd shut down on me and left.

Completely vanished from my life.

This is the first time I've seen her in years, and I know for a fact that it has taken her everything to face me after what she believed happened. I broke this woman's heart. I know she has put every piece back together, slowly and securely, until she felt strong enough to come home.

But she broke mine too.

Broke it with every ounce of power she had over me and left me, shattered and bruised, to pick up the pieces. Pieces that others continued to kick around, knocking them further away, out of reach until I no longer recognised myself.

She thinks I broke her heart, but she never allowed me to explain the truth.

All that hurt, pain, and despair shift in my mind, but shock alone holds it at bay. Shock and my misplaced love for this woman. I hate her as much as I love her.

She must sense my appraisal as her feet shift, and she clears her throat. "We should probably get going," she says quickly. Her smile doesn't reach her eyes, and her posture is stiff. I want to grab her and plead with her to listen, to hear me out and understand what happened that night. To shout at her for abandoning me. She has no idea of the hell that followed or how crushed I was when she left me.

"See you around," I say with a heavy breath as Beau takes Holly's and Marcus's hands and skips away with them.

That was supposed to be me.

"You okay, man?" Dan asks, and I shake my head.

"She's back. I need her to know."

"Give her time, mate. She just got here, and no matter how many ways you try to swing what happened, the truth is, you slept with another woman. That's all that mattered to her."

"It wasn't like that!"

"Hey, whoa." Dan holds his hands up. "I know that, Cam, I fucking know, but give her some space. Let them settle in. And I hate to break it to you, but she's already taken." He looks back over his shoulder at the family walking away, and I sigh loudly.

"Taken by *him*. Grace could take him out with one punch." I scoff angrily, internally fighting the thought of him and Holly together.

"He is kind of puny." He frowns.

Holly slowly walks away when Nadine breezes over. She passes Holly, all the while grinning at me. I know that look. My heart sinks, and I feel terrible because this woman has got it bad for me, and I'm now torn up about the woman walking away.

"Hey, you." Nadine blushes and pecks my mouth. It's the first display of open affection between us. Usually, we are holed up in my house or some town over eating dinner. My eyes falter across her shoulder, where Holly is looking at me. Her expression falls, and she picks up her daughter and smiles at the little girl. My heart slams repeatedly against my chest, and I force my eyes down to Nadine. "You okay?" she asks. Her brow furrows when I don't respond. She looks embarrassed, and I know it's because it took a lot for her to kiss me just now.

"Yeah, good. You look nice," I tell her because she does. Her creamy legs are on show and her ample chest is tucked in a small wrap dress.

"I thought you would like it," she purrs, and I pale inwardly because what I like is walking further away from me, and it's the closest Holly has been to me in forever.

Marcus places a hand on her lower back. *She's definitely in a relationship.* I've refused to think of her for years, but knowing she is here, back in Richmond... I'm so screwed.

"Yeah," I mutter, not hearing what Nadine is saying. "Drink?" I offer quickly and look away. My friends are eyeing me avidly, and I have to force a smile. It's not just Holly, though; a thousand sickening thoughts have brutalised my mind and I want to punch something.

Nadine slips by me to grab us both a beer and Dan takes it upon himself to wrap an arm around me. "I know that can't have been easy, but we'll figure it out. Don't do anything rash."

I grunt, wishing I had stayed home and chased after her.

Holly Matthews is back in Richmond with her perfect family.

I'm officially in hell.

Chapter Two
Holly

I almost throw Marcus out of the house when we make it home, feigning a headache. "I could watch Beau for you whilst you take a nap?" he offers kindly.

"That's so kind, but I'm tired, plus Beau has her first induction at the summer club tomorrow morning. We could do with an early night," I remind him.

"Are you sure? You seemed pretty quiet this afternoon." He rubs his nose out of habit.

I point to my head. "Too much sun." I placate him with a smile. "Thanks for coming to visit us."

"Of course, just checking you're all settled in. The city is pretty boring without you both." He's so sweet, but I'm ready to stick my face into my pillow and scream after bumping into Richmond's finest. None of the men have changed, except they all have because it's been so long. They have obviously settled down here and continued with their lives, unlike me, who had to start over after the painful encounter all those years ago, with Cameron and his bit on the side. I force another smile and wave Marcus off. The minute the front door clicks shut, I walk past the living room to check on Beau and then go in search of wine.

I never asked my dad about Cam when he was alive, and I never expected him to stay in Richmond. He'd planned to go to London and be a banker like his father. It's disconcerting to learn they are all still here. *Maybe they commute.* I pour my glass almost to the rim with my favourite pinot. "He's an unfaithful pig," I remind myself. I need to, because seeing him again after all of this time almost had my knees collapsing. He's filled out so much. He always was fit and athletic, but now he is broad and muscular, his jaw covered with a little stubble and vivid green eyes a complete contrast to his dark blonde hair. He is a liar and a cheat. It doesn't matter how nice they are now. I know how unkind his friends can be. I still remember their mocking laughs and the soul-crushing humiliation I faced. That's what I got for being naive enough to think the popular kids actually liked a plain buff like me. Cam had always playfully picked at me for having my nose in a book or losing me to the library when I had agreed to meet him. Little had changed about me, other than having Beau. That little bundle of blonde curls has given me more confidence than Cameron Stone ever had.

This time would be different.

I know first-hand what they were capable of and I'm not about to let them manipulate me a second time.

After I've bathed Beau and settled her down for the night, I grab a hoodie and sit out back with a wine. I knew if I ever came face-to-face with Cam again, it would be hard, but I had never expected just how deep the pain would burrow. My chest aches, and my eyes have filled more than once this evening. I'm annoyed at myself for feeling so emotional, but I remind myself that this past year has been difficult with Dad passing. Dealing with his loss, Beau's grief, moving back home, and starting a business alone, it's easily been the hardest year of my life. I overcame it all ten years ago, and I can do it again. The initial shock will have worn off by tomorrow. That and the nasty fact that he is dating a ridiculously beautiful woman.

I'd secretly wished he thought I was dating Marcus, and as much as I respect the man and how much he has supported Beau and me, he's no Cameron Stone. I pull my phone out of my hoody and gear up my music, choosing acoustic artists, and relax back in my chair. My mind wants to drift off to my college days, but I don't allow it, as they were a lie. I was a sick joke to them all, a weird experiment.

Who could make the nerd fall for the hot guy?

I had fallen fast, then even harder when I'd caught him with Sarah Daniels. I'd fallen into a humiliated depression. I blink my eyes shut and force my mind to focus on work. I've got so much to do tomorrow after I drop Beau off for her induction. I need to head over to the shop and stack the rest of the shelves and inventory before I open at the end of the month. I sit out for another hour, lost in thought, worrying about the shop, but mainly I'm imagining Cam in his polo shirt and tan legs on show. I force myself up and lock the back door before heading straight to bed. The wine helps me sleep.

"Mummy!"

I groan loudly, then paste on a smile. Beau stands at the side of my bed. She scrambles on, and I pull her in for a squeeze. Her little hands push and pull at my hair strewn everywhere.

"Where are you?" she huffs, and I laugh, lifting up and pouting for a kiss. She giggles and kisses me quickly.

"Let's go to the park," she suggests, pulling my arm. I prise my eyes open further and see that it's only a quarter to six.

"At six?" I mutter.

"Oh." She flops down on the bed and sighs.

"We just need thicker curtains," I tell her sleepily. "Mummy will order you some curtains, okay?"

"Unicorns!" she squeals, and I pull a pillow and cover my eyes and ears. The pillow lifts and her little giggle makes me smile. "Hello in there!"

"Boo!" I jump, and she screams before dropping back on a loud laugh. I tickle her and pull her in so I can kiss her cheek. "Come on, early bird, let's get up. Waffles?" I ask, yawning. We take it easy and eat breakfast out in the back garden on the old table that was my dad's. It reminds me of when I was a child. I tell Beau stories of me when I was her age, and she eats it up like her sticky breakfast.

"A swing in the tree... Can I have one?" she asks. I nod over my fruit. Her little face drops. "I miss Pop Pop," she says quietly.

"Me too," I say, rubbing her hand. "He loved you lots and lots, Beau. He misses you too. It's good to miss people because then we remember how much we love them."

"And I love Pop Pop as much as I love unicorns!" Her grin is infectious and with syrup dripping off her chin. Losing my father has been so hard on us both. His death gave me the push to fight for what I want for my little girl. Even if it means facing my past, I owe it to Beau as much as my father.

"Are you ready for summer club?" I say excitedly. I plaited her hair on request, and she is wearing her favourite sequin t-shirt and denim shorts.

She nods, licking the spoon clean. "Can I have a clip in my hair?"

"Sure, let me wash up, then we can find a clip."

"This one." She holds up a unicorn one. I laugh and take it from her, leaning over to clip it in. Her smile is wide, and I sigh happily. I've got my little girl, and that's all that matters.

We arrive a few minutes early to the summer club at the village hall, so I quickly check over the paperwork, my eyes staring long and hard at the parent guardianship details. It's just me in there, always has been and more than likely always will, but I know the questions will linger when I drop her off, but I'm not ready to discuss my life and personal choices with them. Beau unclips her belt and we exit the car, excited for her first session. I help her put her backpack on, and she grips my hand, throwing me a nervous smile. "You will do great. Everyone will love you," I say honestly. It's busy inside but not too loud, and most children are already sucked into an activity. Beau points at a huge doll house. "You'll have the best day," I tell her.

"This must be Beau?" Claire, the summer club owner, smiles and waves at Beau, who thrusts her face into the back of my knee.

"Yes, this is, and she's not nearly this shy. We have a unicorn fan here. Do you have any unicorns at the club?" I ask.

"Hello Beau, I'm Claire. It's lovely to meet you."

"Hello." My daughter's soft voice melts my heart.

"We do have unicorns here, in fact, one just like your pretty clip," she tells Beau, who lights up. "Let's go and have a look and your mum and I can have a quick chat." Beau takes my hand, and we follow Claire through to a quieter area where my girl is given a big fluffy unicorn toy. She drops down on the floor and begins chatting away to herself.

"Here are the forms. No known allergies and she is pretty good with most foods," I say, handing them over.

"Most snacks are fruit or vegetables. This is great." Her eyes skim the form, and she takes a second look. I know she is wondering why I have listed no family or father on the emergency contacts. I am the only parent Beau has. My mother lives too far away to help in emergencies.

"So I just stay for a few minutes, then leave you to get on?" I ask her. I have a moment of indecisiveness where I worry about leaving Beau, not because I don't trust Claire or the club, but because since we lost my father this year, she has become quite clingy. I say as much to Claire under my breath, who nods in understanding. I have prepped Beau, so I do what I planned and kneel down. "I'm going to pop to work now for a little bit, but I will be back soon, okay, just like we spoke about?" There is a flash of panic on her little face, and my body goes stiff with concern, but as soon as it was there, it is gone when a ruckus behind us has Beau standing up and peering past me. Children are screaming excitedly and laughing, and my eyes lock on Cameron growling and stomping after a little girl I recognise from the fete.

He pins her down and showers her with kisses, and my heart clenches painfully. "Right, squirt, I love you. Be good, and I'll come to get you later." He ruffles her hair playfully, and she tickles under his chin. He drops down on a fake whine, and the girl pounces on him, as do a few others. I'm smiling before I realise who I'm smiling at, but I drop my gaze and kiss Beau. "See, you'll have the best time!" I repeat. Beau nods, and I get away whilst she seems relaxed. I slip by and stiffen when Cam clocks me. I walk faster, but he is hot on my heel. I try not to look back, but when I do, Beau's little lip is quivering. I rush out and head for my car.

"Hey, Hol, everything all right?" His deep voice sends a spray of shivers over my body. I keep my face forward and unlock my car, trying to get in, but his hand captures my wrist and pulls me his way.

I pull free. "Sorry, Beau's first day." I sniff. "I've got to go."

"Do you want me to check if she's doing okay?" he asks, his attention now fixed over his shoulder. He looks at me earnestly, and I frown, unsure whether to trust him or not, but the fear of hearing him say that Beau is upset makes my stomach clench. "Claire is great. I'm sure Beau will quickly adjust." With that, I get in the car and snap the door shut. I'll call the club when I get to the shop.

I drive straight there, rounding the memorial before I pull

into a small side street. I'm expecting a late delivery, but head round the back of the shop and let myself in. The light scent of baked cinnamon still hangs in the air. I'd first wanted to open a small bookstore. The old newsagent was empty, and I'd had my eye set on that but then the old bakery went up for sale and another idea occurred, so before I or anyone else could talk me out of it, I was buying the place and opening a bookshop and coffee house, two of my favourite loves. Danielle Hind had moved premises and had agreed to stock me with some baked goods, a fresh delivery each morning. I'd only ever wanted to be surrounded by books, but this business had never been on my radar, so now that it was happening, I couldn't think of doing anything different.

I quickly call the summer club, and I'm relieved when they say Beau is fine. I get started at the shop. I have a few boxes of books my supplier had dropped off yesterday morning, so I spend the next few hours filling the shelves, sorting the books into genres, and alphabetically lining the walls. I'm moving my way round the room until I'm back at the front, filling empty spaces and adjusting other authors, when the demanding sight of Cameron walking across the memorial gardens has me stalling. Safe in the limits of the shop, I watch him, soaking him in, every lean long inch of him. From his strong jaw and wide shoulders, where he has filled out to his unnervingly green eyes. Then some mean bastard poured a ton of sex appeal on him, added a confident walk, sexy smile and ta-da... Cameron Stone, everyone.

My first love, my only love.

His face lights up, and I remember all too well that look he'd stupefied me with, made every naive cell twist in on itself and combust because he was that hot in college. As a man, he's catatonic. I suck in a breath and swallow harshly as the brunette from the fete walks straight up and kisses him. His hands fall to hang loosely around her lower back. I look away when his head lowers and jump a mile when the door bangs. I rush to open it, seeing a courier with my last delivery of books. Stepping out, I hold the door wide. He lifts the box and nods behind me. "Want this in there?" But my eyes are focused on Cam, who is looking at me.

"Please." I follow the courier in and instruct him to put my parcels on a table.

"Place is looking great. I thought it was going to be empty forever."

"Oh, thank you. I just have a few bits to sort before I open."

"When's that?"

"A few weeks," I tell him. It gives me time to smoothen everything out and secure staff. Marcus helped me look over the resumes.

"Good luck, see you round." He smiles, walking out, and I follow him and scan the village green, but Cameron is nowhere to be seen.

Closing the door, I check over the invoice for all the items. The coffee machine is being installed tomorrow, and I need to bulk buy from the nearest wholesalers. I look around, debating on whether to have fresh flowers. I'm not the greatest with them, and if I start, I will need to keep it up. I take a seat and Google house plants instead to give the interior some greenery.

I wander about the shop making notes and end up in the stockroom. I jot down wicker baskets so I can store items in them rather than shoving them on the shelf. At least it will look nice and organised. After that, I set my laptop up in the small back office, which would give most airing cupboards a run for their money. I pin the calendar up I got in the post this morning and place a picture of Beau and me on the small thin desk. My father would be so proud of all this. I can't believe he has gone. A heart attack out of nowhere, but he knew he wasn't well, and he had kept it from us. I still have no idea why he did that. We had such a close relationship, and he knew it would shatter me if he died, so why did he never prepare me?

I'm due to collect Beau soon. I promised her a treat from Danielle's bakery afterwards. Locking up, I head straight to the club, finding her locked in conversation with another child. The boy has a head of curls and is laughing with Beau, and I smile watching them, seeing Cam's daughter approach. She says something and joins in. I almost don't want to interrupt their fun. The boy taps Beau on the shoulder and points at me. She drops everything and runs to me. "Mummy!" Her happiness soon fades, and she bursts into tears.

"Hey, it's okay. I told you I would be back." I wipe her face. "Less of that. Where is my smile?" Her adorable cheeks pull into a soft grin. "There she is."

"I missed you." She sniffles, still holding her quivering smile.

"Me too, pickle. Are you ready for our lunch date?"

"My daddy is coming soon!" Cam's daughter says excitedly. "We are having a movie night because my Barbie film came in the post." Beau looks at me with shared excitement.

"That sounds like lots of fun. We have lots of ice cream with our movies," I tell her, picking up Beau's bag hooked on a peg.

"That's what I have too!" she shares confidently, looking at Beau.

"Bye, Grace." Beau smiles. "Bye, Sammy." She sucks back a sniffle and shoves her head into the dip of my neck. Pecking her head, I wave to the children. It's surreal being here waving goodbye to Cameron's child while leaving with my own. At one point, I had honestly thought we'd have a family together. I always knew what I wanted to name my first child, since we spoke of it often. I nearly chose something different, but I refused to let him change any more of my life than he already had.

Claire rubs Beau's back. "You did so well today, Beau. We

had lots of fun with you, and I hope you come to play again soon," she says softly.

"I can play with the unicorn?"

Claire nods, and she settles back into my neck.

"Thanks, Claire, we'll see you soon."

Chapter Three
Holly

I've done it. I survived my first full week back.

If surviving consists of too much wine and running myself into exhaustion, then so be it. Beau is settling in well and making new friends and has even arranged two play dates, the little diva. I knew the first week back would be tough, and that was before I came face-to-face with my ex. Luckily, the business is taking up all of my time and shaping up to be the perfect distraction. Marcus has agreed to visit and help out whilst I begin interviews. I'm hoping two extra pairs of hands will do the trick. At first, they can job share or alternate shifts and then when things pick up, I can take them on.

I can do this.

Marcus arrives late Sunday afternoon, and Beau is so excited about her new unicorn bedroom set that she drags him off upstairs.

"Beau, make sure you wash your hands before you come down. Dinner is almost ready!" I call up the stairs after them. Marcus is staying in the spare room; it's still sparse, but it's free. I can hear them chattering away to one another. No doubt she is filling him in on summer club and her new friends. I serve up the lasagne and toss the salad as they make their way downstairs. Marcus grins. "Please tell me you made garlic bread?"

"I helped!" Beau shouts, jumping up into her seat. "We melted the butter and put the garyic in," she states proudly, using her arm to move some hair out of her face.

Marcus leans over and pats her hand. "It's garlic," he says slowly, and Beau frowns.

"I like garlic and garyic," I tell her. She giggles, and Marcus' cheeks burn a little. He's a huge help so I don't want to pick at him for correcting her. He does it often and it's good for her, but it's more the way he does it that even I feel patronised. I place the offending item on the table. "Who is ready for garyic bread?" I laugh.

"Garyic, garyic!" Beau chants and helps serve the salad, dropping pieces as she does. Dinner is comfortable and easy. Marcus and I get along well, and Beau never allows a moment's silence. "Can we go for a walk?" she asks, pulling the buttery bread apart and licking any drips from her fingers, it's the kind of thing my father would say, 'Let's go for a walk to help our dinner go down,' and hearing her voice, it makes me smile sadly.

We have visited his grave twice since returning home, but I don't want to hold Beau back from moving forward with his death. She knows he is gone; she just doesn't understand the full depth of it.

"Of course we can." Clearing my throat, I finish my meal and avoid Marcus's eyes when he rubs my arm in a gesture of comfort. "When we get back, we can have ice cream!" I state, lifting the mood. Beau whoops and snags the last slice of garlic bread before asking to get down from the table.

"I'll clear up." Marcus stands, collecting plates and cutlery into a neat stack. "Why don't you go grab a cardigan? It looks like the air's chilly."

I see a few clouds. My jean shorts and sleeveless blouse are fine. Beau has a summer dress on, so I leave him to clear up and find her an extra layer. He's an orderly man, everything well thought out, calm and logical. When I landed my first serious job, Marcus was the one person to make me feel welcome. He has been so supportive with Beau, he's always on the other end of the phone to help if needed, and although we never really discuss feelings, he is probably my one and only friend. When my father passed away, he helped with the funeral arrangements, and my decision to move back to Richmond was heavily discussed with him. Both he and my mother were against the move, purely as it would mean Beau and I were further away from them, but they understood my desire to bring Beau up in a small village. She loved Pop, and I missed this house.

The incident with Cameron was never discussed with my father. He never so much as even whispered his name. After I left Cameron, I became as good as a ghost. Until this week, I hadn't laid eyes on him or heard his name in ten years. My father had been my hero, and leaving all those years ago had left a bitter taste in his mouth towards Cameron for more than one reason. My father never asked why I refused to return to the village but simply agreed to meet me in neighbouring towns. He'd loved being in Beau's life and I'd loved being back in his when I could be. That's why I could never give this house up. It meant too much; all my memories were here. Beau had given me a strength I didn't know I had, and I owed it to her to be brave and not only face my demons, but to conquer them. I never expected Cameron and his entourage would still be living here. Richmond offered a safe community environment not too far from London but far enough away that you felt hidden in the country.

Beau comes charging in, her hair like a sheet of gold sand behind her. "Are we going?" She is breathless and excited. I grin at her and take a seat on the edge of her bed.

"In a minute. Come and put this on." I hold the cream

cardigan open, and she shrugs it on, tugging at the buttons to keep it in place.

"Marcus says we can go on the swings if we walk by the park," she tells me, grappling with the buttons before giving up and leaving it to hang open.

"Sounds like a great plan." I follow her downstairs, where Marcus is waiting for us.

"Ready?"

"Let's go," I reply, unlocking the door and pulling it wide open as the evening air hits me. It's so close, muggy, Beau will probably get too hot herself.

"What about your cardigan?" he asks, rubbing his nose.

"I don't need one," I say, seeing him frown at my blouse. It is a little low in the front, but it's been so oppressive today I don't want to be cooped up in clothes. "I'm too hot as it is," I tell him. With a brittle smile, he steps out, calling for Beau to be careful as I pull my hair up into a big bun to stop it from sticking to my neck. We set off down the street as Beau races ahead. "Thanks again for coming back to help. I really need to get my head around all the business stuff," I admit on a tired sigh.

"You know I love Beau; it's great to see you both." Marcus rubs my back. "I checked on your mum. She is still angry at Mavis for changing the starter at the golf club."

I snort, recalling the horror on my mother's face when she told us about it over Sunday dinner before we moved here. "Oh, she was so mad, I don't think I've ever seen her so angry." I giggle loudly, and Marcus rubs his watering eyes. Beau is zigzagging her way down the street until she comes to the park, her small hands push open the heavy gate and she is grunting her way in.

"Wait for us!" I yell, walking faster to catch up with her. We round the line of trees and I almost slam into Cameron's chest. I let out an unladylike *oomph*, and he grips my arms to steady us both.

"Whoa!" He laughs, letting me go and taking a healthy step back. His eyes drop to the petite brunette beside him now cupping his bicep possessively. I almost want to roll my eyes and tell her she can have his arm and the rest of him because my heart can't withstand another round of Cameron Stone.

"Sorry," I croak. Marcus gives Cam a tight smile, touching my back to encourage me round them as a dark-haired girl bounds towards us. He catches her mid-air, laughing deeply, and swings her up onto his shoulder in the most effortless display of maleness I've ever seen. My smile falters and I twist away, moving round them. I'd been naive enough to believe I would have been that woman, that my child would have been ours. I would never change Beau, not for anything or anyone, but her conception was not how I pictured it. I wanted it all: a brood of children after years of wistful marriage to a good man. My life had unravelled in a way I'd never expected or chosen, yet it was all worth it for the little girl hoisting herself onto a swing.

"That's my friend, Grace!" Beau tells me proudly. Cameron and his family hang back and Grace waves excitedly from up high. Cam has a smile a mile wide, yet his wife watches me closely.

"That's Beau." Grace giggles, and I start to wonder things I have forced myself to not think of, like how they met. How long have they dated? What was their wedding like? Will they have more kids? What does he do, what does she do? But worst, the one crushing question that has me almost tripping over a root is what is it about her that he loves enough to be faithful for? I hate that I've allowed myself to sink so low as to compare myself. To allow those thoughts in. I quicken my pace over taking Marcus and begin to push Beau, her screams of laughter blocking any lingering thoughts.

Grace hops onto the swing next to Beau, their little voices chiming together. Marcus looks green around the gills. He knows little about what happened in Richmond, and what I haven't told him, I suspect my mother has. I keep my focus on Beau and smile at the little girl beside her and seeing their friendship blossom. Cameron and his wife join us, and she takes the last swing, smirking at Cam. Grace interrupts their moment and asks him to push her. "High to the sky like a bird!" she says, grinning at Beau. Cameron steps behind his daughter, making us opposite one another. I focus on Beau and not the gorgeous man across from me. As I hold my smile in place, I can feel it becoming strained. An ache starts to form as my resolve wavers.

"Right, are you ready?" he asks, pulling her back and holding her elevated. Her little hands are gripping the chains and Beau is watching wide-eyed. Cam pushes hard, and Grace swings high, her feet kicking to the clouds.

"Me now!" Beau laughs over Grace's screams. "Me, please?" She looks expectantly at Cameron, who falters and turns to me for guidance. There are a thousand reasons I want to shake my head, but only one has me nodding. My little girl, smiling happily at me. Soon, both girls are giggling into the sky and his wife is laughing as she gets swung out into the open air too.

Beau screams for a high-five, holding her tiny palm out to Cameron. He eyes me briefly, but not long enough to see my breath catch. He pats Beau's hand, grinning. It lights up his whole face and my daughter's too. "Thanks!" My little girl giggles, kicking her legs and reaching for another. "High, go high!" she squeals, her hair swishing as the wind catches it and Cam pushes her higher.

Cameron is broad and athletic. His top is tight and shows off ample muscles as he pushes all three swings, his legs toned. His wife looks buff too, so they are probably health nuts and always at the gym. Working out together. I want to be angry at him for moving on with his life, but I have too. And more importantly, I shouldn't be thinking any of this, or wishing

Marcus resembled a Viking and not the buttoned-up conservative guy he is. He must feel the underlying tension as he suggests we move to the slide. "Remember, we are going home for ice cream." He moves to help Beau out of the swing.

"Can I have ice cream?" Grace twists to Cameron.

He frowns at her. "Better wait for your dad to get back." He's not her dad?! Cam catches me eyeing him. My confusion must be written all over my face. I dip my head and move away with Beau, hearing his wife tell Grace her dad will be back soon. I'm guessing she and her ex split, and Cameron has taken on her little girl. It makes my gut clench.

"I'll race you to the slide," I tell Beau, allowing her a head start before I run after her. I catch her just short of the slide and she begs me to go down it with her. We reach the top of the grassy mound, and I take my spot on the slide. Her little frame nestles in my lap and we're whizzing down to the bottom, laughing. I catch Cameron smirking at me and blush, dusting myself off whilst Beau heads to the grassed area. Why did he have to be here?

Beau runs back over, handing me the flowers. "These are for you!" She grins.

"Thank you, pickle. Let's get home and we can put them in water," I say, taking her hand. When I look up, Cam is leaning on the swing frame, watching me cautiously. "Say bye to your friend," I tell her, embarrassed he is staring at me.

Beau races off and hugs Grace. It's so cute that I stop and watch. They are chatting quietly, so I barely hear much until she says, "Come to my mummy's new shop!"

No, surely, he wouldn't come, right?

Beau holds her hand out for another high-five and Cam drops down and lifts his hand out for her to pat. "Bye, Beau." He reaches to tuck a strand of her hair away and his eyes meet mine over her little head. "See you soon." I turn away, too disturbed by the emotions I am feeling. We leave quickly after that, Beau chatting away rapidly as Marcus, and I answer her each time she throws a question at us.

As soon as we make our way up to the house, Beau pushes inside, diverting to the kitchen. "Ice cream and unicorn sprinkles!" I make up three bowls of ice cream and Beau sets about decorating them with sprinkles and wafers. We roll out a blanket, drag the pillows to the floor and watch a movie. It's a perfect way to end the weekend and forget about a certain man.

BY THE TIME I reach the shop, it's nearly nine a.m. I left Beau and Marcus making Playdough castles. My first interview for a shop assistant is at ten, so I get stuck in and file bits away, tidy up and place the fake plants Beau and I chose around the shop. Books line the shelved walls between each window looking onto the village green, to the far end of the room is a snug with sofas, armchairs and coffee tables, all situated to allow groups to come in and relax. The place smells of new paper and polish. I've finally mastered the coffee machine and worked out the main database after having uploaded inventory incorrectly twice. I'm ready to open the doors and let people in.

By the third appointment, I'm ready to sob, since only one of the applicants seems appropriate for the role and that's only because I compared her to the first two people who were horrendous. I stand tiredly, worrying I will not find anyone. I have a small window for lunch and Marcus brings Beau in so we can spend it together. They've made us a small picnic, which we eat on one of the coffee tables in the snug. She is enlightening me on her morning, making a unicorn den, when the door opens, and a young woman walks in. "Hi, sorry to interrupt, but someone mentioned you were hiring?" she asks, blushing.

Covering my mouth, I nod. "Yes, I am," I say around my small bite, swallowing it quickly.

"I can come back later?" She grimaces, then she spots Beau leaning past Marcus and waves at her. "Hello, Beau."

"No, now is fine." I smile and see Beau watching her. I've not seen the woman before, so I have no idea how they know each other.

"I'll take Beau to the park for a bit." Marcus smiles. "Come on, little one, let's go find some more flowers for your mum." Beau snags up her cookie and leaves, giving the woman a little wave on the way out.

"I'm an assistant at the summer club," she tells me. "I met Beau last week. She's a lovely girl."

"Thanks, she seemed to enjoy her first few sessions," I reply, picking up my pad and pen.

"Yes, she was so quiet at first, but after a few books and snacks, she loved it. I'm Emily." She sticks her hand out and I silently beg that she will fit the role. After a short interview, hearing she is an avid reader and a quick walkthrough of the business and coffee machine, I hire her on the spot. I also learn that when the summer club closes, she may work full time. I didn't think I'd be able to get someone full time at such short notice and decide to offer the part time position to Keeley, the younger girl from earlier. "Beau will begin school the week after next. I can hopefully train Keeley up, and then you can start when summer club ends if that's okay with you?" I say, looking up from where I had jotted a quick timetable out.

"That sounds amazing, thank you."

"No, thank you. I was ready to make a sacrifice to the gods." I roll my eyes, and she laughs.

"Once Beau is at school, I can do longer hours, and occasionally, I will bring her to the shop with me after school. I think the first two weeks will give me a good indication of what we are to expect." For all I know, the village could show little interest and my dream will be washed away.

"Well, I can help in any way you need. I'm sure Keeley and I will get along well too. I'm pretty sociable." After giving me her personal details, I find she is only a few years younger than me.

We chat longer, with Emily telling me she only moved to Richmond about two months ago. She's new and due to her role at the summer club, and she hasn't made many friends as most parents like to keep it professional. "I can imagine Claire wants that too, so I can see how that's been hard. Well, hopefully, being here will change that for you." I smile, following her to the entrance.

"Yes, thanks again. I'm really looking forward to it."

"Me too, thanks for stopping by." I'm thrilled she dropped in. Everything finally seems to come together. Emily leaves, and I call Keeley back, feeling lighter than I have all week. By the time I step out of the shop, it's mid-afternoon. A few people are milling about, others are on the green. I see one woman, Mandy, who I recall meeting her at the fete. She is scowling across the grass, and my eyes follow until they land on Cam and his wife kissing. My chest aches, my eyes returning to Mandy stomping off, and when I look back, Cameron's eyes are hot on mine. I twist away, my heart beating frantically, and rush to my car.

After all, no one likes to see an ex with their new partner, right?

Chapter Four
Cameron

I'm going crazy. My head is a concoction of inaccurate thoughts and desperation. Then there's the guilt, guilt my friends have slowly but surely dampened down. Shame they have helped push away so I no longer felt the sickening burn of dread in my stomach because of one disgusting moment I had no control over. Guilt that had buddied up with a loss so profound I had tasted it daily for the last decade. I thought I had mastered how to forget it, but I could feel it all coming back. Haunting me.

"Are you okay?" Nadine asks.

No, the love of my life witnessed me kissing you, and for the second time, it felt wrong to do so. I don't want to be a prick to yet again another woman, and I don't want to break her heart, but I don't know if I can be with her. Not now that Holly is back.

The thought rushes to the forefront of my mind far too quickly for my liking.

Dan had phoned me late last night. He knew where my head was at, and he told me I had a good thing going, that Holly being back didn't change anything, but for me, everything has changed. This could be it for me. I could finally get my woman back, finally be at peace. I doubt peace would ever find me, not with the curdling anger biting into my chest. Nadine is a decent woman and I feel like the world's biggest tool for wanting to drop her just because my ex is back. An ex that won't look at me or even talk. An ex that has grown even more beautiful over the years. She still has an innocent aura about her. Her blonde hair and shy eyes have my heart lancing with pain each time I catch sight of her. She's incredible and her daughter is this miniature little clone of her. I envy and hate Beau's father.

What does she even see in him?

Holly Matthews is undeniably gorgeous, but she has this fragile quality about her, which makes her look petite and vulnerable, and it makes me hot as fuck.

"Hey?" Nadine calls again.

"Yeah, sorry, worrying about the weather. I need to finish the decking," I lie.

"I can help. I'm not sure I will be of much use, but I can pass you a hammer." Her smile is cheeky, and I allow one of my own to fall free. She's a good woman. Even though I can think of nothing else but Holly.

Holly who is taken.

Holly who has a child.

My Holly.

My chest hollows because the truth is she has moved on and is back in Richmond, she's settled and happy. She has a beautiful daughter and no matter how much I am willing to tear a path through the entire village to get to her, I can't have her. Worst of all, I want her to suffer like she made me suffer. The terrified and broken teen in me wants to take a hold of Holly and never let go, yet another and more unhinged part of me wants to roar out years of anger, frustration and disgust at how quickly she walked away from me.

Nadine and I head away from the memorial, and it takes every ounce of willpower not to look back over my shoulder at Holly's premises. I knew someone had taken over the old bakery, but I had no idea it was Holly. I glance back once more as I place Nadine's hand securely in mine and walk away from the one woman who I felt at one point gave me a purpose.

Holly isn't there like I hoped. Just like when she had disappeared and no amount of begging her father had helped me find her. My head was such a mess back then, and with everything going on with Sarah, I didn't look hard enough. I was heartbroken, a wreck, and going through the nightmare most people only ever read about. I clear my throat and try to dispel the growing nausea. I promised this lady lunch and I will give it to her.

Several hours later, I drop Nadine at her place and head home to finish the decking. The sun's out and I want to make the most of it. Need to. I crave solitude, need physical exertion to keep my thoughts at bay. Working hard into the evening, sweat pours off my skin, but it won't keep the anger or guilt away. I ponder over how Holly must have felt these years, how justified she must believe she is, and her avoidance after accusing me of sleeping with Sarah when she couldn't be farther from the truth, or how dishonest I'm being with Nadine. But mostly, there is this anger. Anger at Holly for thinking so little of me, for never giving me a chance to explain, for leaving me to deal with the hell that followed that night. Anger at myself for wanting a woman I can't have with a need that is eclipsing everything else. I slug and hammer away, throwing wood about, not caring who I disturb with the noise. I want to hurt something, roar. I feel cheated and a laughingstock all in one, like some sick entity from above is watching me squirm now Holly is back and enjoying the aerial view.

With a heave, I launch a sawed end of wood onto the growing pile, and it *thunks* on the ground and Nadine's voice jolts me out of my spiralling thoughts. "Easy now." She laughs nervously. I look back at her in shock, not expecting anyone to come by. She eyes me cautiously. "Hey." She smiles.

I stand and wipe my brow, drenched in sweat and not liking the sudden scrutiny I'm placed under. "Sorry, I was in my own world."

She knows something is up, but I can't admit what. When she looks at me, I nod her over. She comes like I knew she would, and as soon as she is in reach, I pull her and slant my mouth over her startled lips. As she sighs, I clench my eyes tight, forcing the image of Holly out of my mind. I need to forget her, like I had done before. I need to forget that anything is wrong with me.

Holly flashes through my mind, and I kiss Nadine more aggressively, forcing the image of my ex away. She gasps, and I push her against the fence, lifting her quickly.

My mind is screaming for any memory of Holly to go away. "Fuck." I concentrate on kissing Nadine.

"Cam, it's okay," she murmurs, her soft hand gliding up my arm and to my neck. Her wide eyes are begging for me to open up to her. "Do you want to talk about it?"

I shake my head. "Something happened the other day, and it brought back a lot of bad memories," I admit, pecking at her neck and avoiding her gaze.

"With Holly, you mean?"

Shit, I stop and pull back slowly, lowering her to her feet. What the hell does she know? I look at her in shock.

"Kerry told me you guys had history and that it was pretty bad. I figured something was up and I put two and two together," she whispers, looking awkward and worried.

For herself or me? I don't know.

My shoulders sag. "It's not what you think." It's exactly what she thinks and then some.

"Okay." Her trusting voice sends a blade of guilt through

me. Sighing, I drop down into the chair on the wrap-around, and she takes the other. "I don't know what happened, and you don't have to tell me anything, but I care about you, Cam. A lot," she admits on a soft breath. "I'm not giving up on you," she adds stoically. "I'd heard the stories about you. Some even warned me away, and I knew what I was getting into with you."

Does it surprise me that people are still talking about me after all this time, that they feel I'm still a danger?

No, it doesn't.

"I also know from meeting you and spending time with you that all those stories are utter bullshit." Nadine sighs, taking my hand.

Stories, I bet. I heard a few circling around myself, twisted and fabricated to paint me in the worst possible light. It doesn't matter; they were proven wrong. I was cleared of all charges, but those stories still float around because people are too quick to believe a lie.

"Did you love her?" she pries.

Vomit rushes up to my mouth, and I swallow it back.

"I don't really know her anymore." And it's the truth. I once knew Holly, but that was years ago. We are different people now. On that fact alone, I should let her go, walk away and start fresh with Nadine. Perhaps, I need closure. Maybe I can suggest Holly and I meet up to talk it out, then I can say goodbye to the possibility of us reconnecting for good.

My heart stutters with fear.

I don't want closure. I want her, Holly goddam Matthews.

"It was a long time ago. I didn't expect to ever see her again, and now I have, it's come rushing back. It was a really dark time in my life, and I thought I could put it to rest and then she's suddenly back. I don't know what bothers me more," I say raggedly, shocked that I have opened up as much as I have. Maybe I think I love Holly, the Holly I once knew. I don't know this version of her. They might look the same, or more beautiful, but I could find that by getting to know her that I don't love her. Fuck, maybe I need to confront our past and lay it to rest, because I can't love someone I don't know, or base my future on a woman I used to know and give up something that has been good for me. Nadine has been good for me.

I sound like a pussy.

"Does it matter which?" Nadine says. "Both bother you and maybe you need to have it out with her, say your bit, let her say hers, then walk away, like she did. She left you, Cam, left you to deal with hell. She ran and left you to pick up the pieces, so it makes sense you're so mad." She leaves her chair and straddles me and cups my face. She's a lot more confident around me recently.

I finally had my life on track, then Holly waltzes back in and starts the gossip train back up. Looking all innocent and demure whilst I get painted the lying piece of shit again. A pained sigh leaves me, and when I look up, Nadine is staring at me, her soft hands comforting me, supporting me. Holly had never done that and even with the lies hanging over me, Nadine had still taken a chance on me, was still taking that chance. Risking her own reputation. Was I really about to throw that away for a woman I don't know, a woman who runs?

Absolutely not.

"Come inside, we can talk."

"I don't want to talk. I'm done talking," I admit roughly.

"Then let's go inside and forget everyone else for a bit," Nadine pants, her fingers sliding into my hair. That's what I do, or try to do, because no matter how loud I make her cry out or how sexy she looks squirming beneath me every now and then, a flicker of Holly jolts through me and I'm back in my teens, having the most unexpected and incredible sex ever.

. . .

NADINE IS SNOOZING LIGHTLY beside me, while my thoughts are lost somewhere between now and the past. Did Holly think I had moved on? I twist my head to look at Nadine. The sex has always been good, it's great. She's fun and cute and all my friends like her, and before this week, there was nothing stopping me from taking things further with her.

Now, doubt is plaguing me. A secret part of me wants to rewind the clock and just watch Holly saunter back into my life with her gorgeous little girl. I want to walk up to her and kiss her hard in front of the world and declare she is mine, and that I won her back. I imagine she would slap me on the spot. The thought makes me hard. I head to the bathroom and flick the shower on. My cock is already thick and dripping with precum and I do the one thing I haven't done in years; I jack off to Holly Matthews, beautiful, shy Holly Matthews. I get lost in the past, drunk on the memory of her mouth on my cock, her hot tongue swirling shyly and her small hands trembling on my thighs. Her sweet body knelt before me, eager, trusting. So fucking perfect as she bobs her head, sucking and moaning as I jut my cock to the back of her throat. I come undone with a guttural cry, staggering forward as I paint the tiles. Groaning in satisfaction, I grip my cock and suck in a deep breath, willing my heart to slow. Eventually, I snap the shower off. I drag a hand down my face and curse myself for giving in to her memory. Pulling a towel off the rail, I wrap it around my hips and step out of the ensuite. I find Nadine sleeping soundly, innocent and unaware I was fucking another woman in my mind. I'm a bastard. I drop in the chair and watch her for some time. I can't have Holly. That ship has sailed, collided with a lie and become shipwrecked. I make a mental pact there and then to make a go of things with Nadine. She stirs and I stand, making my way to her. She blinks, sees me and smiles happily. I tug the quilt and drop my towel. Nadine moans and crawls across the mattress towards me, and I smirk.

Holly ruined what we had. She chucked it away and believed what her insecurity wanted her to see. Nadine would never do that. I'd be stupid to fuck this up with her. She deserves so much more than my indecisiveness and past. I've not wanted to make love to a woman in all these years, but I can do that for this woman. She kneels up, and I pick her up so she is perched just shy of my cock. "Hey." I grin at her shy smile.

"Hey, yourself." Her full breasts rub over my chest, and I block all other thoughts out.

When I wake late, I find I'm alone in bed. I pull on some boxers and go downstairs looking for Nadine, who's standing by the kettle waiting for it to boil. The sound drowns my footsteps out so I slip my arms around her stomach, chuckling when she jumps.

"Cam!" she mutters and twists, looking up at me. Her eyes carry that same cautiousness from yesterday, but I don't want her to have those thoughts. I tuck a strand of hair away and lean in, pecking her lips. "Morning." She sighs.

"Morning." Grinning, I cup her face and go back in for another kiss. I sweep my tongue in, deepening it, and press myself into her. "Last night was..." I chuckle at seeing her blush, then pull back and smile. "Thank you for not giving up on me."

Her gaze softens, and she presses her mouth to mine. "Thank you for not giving me up." She clears her throat, keeping her eyes downcast.

I lift her chin. I need her to believe that was never an option. I don't want us to go into this with doubts. I vowed to myself I would give this woman what she deserves, and that's the best version of me, a version that puts her first. "That was never going to happen. It's in the past, and you turning up last night made me realise you're my future." Cupping her face, I lean in and kiss her softly. "I know we've not discussed it, and we agreed to keep things simple, but I don't want that." When I first approached Nadine, it was with the intent of fun. I told her as much and she held up her end of the bargain without complaint.

"You don't?" Panic enters her voice, and I shake my head at her.

"No, I don't want to *just have fun* with you. I mean, we can have plenty of fun, but I like the direction we're going in," I admit, pressing myself into her as the kettle clicks off.

"And what direction is that?"

"Are you going to make me say it?" I laugh.

"Absolutely."

"You, as my girlfriend, us seriously working towards a future together," I murmur.

"I like the sound of that," she whispers, kissing me back when I run my lips over hers.

"Good, how about breakfast in bed?" I ask, knowing she hasn't got work until later. She nods, smiling widely. I breathe a sigh of relief and lean past her to make our drinks.

"Cameron, I do think you need to talk to Holly and put your mind at rest," she says.

"I don't need to. You put my mind at rest." I press a quick kiss to her head, hoping to ease her worry.

"Thanks, I guess." She laughs lightly, her gaze wavering as she licks her lips nervously. "I'd feel happier knowing you've settled it with her and it's nothing to worry about."

"I just asked you to be my girlfriend. Why would you be worried about her?"

"I'm not, but it bothers you, and I can see the tension in you. We live in a small village. Wouldn't it be best to clear the air? I mean, what if we want to go to her shop, can we?" Nadine sighs. "I don't want to walk on eggshells." I can see how unsettled she is by Holly's return. I was losing control, and she could sense that. Plus, Holly is stunning. I've noticed a few men watching her. It's hard not to be attracted to her quiet appeal.

"I'll talk to her," I say, "but after that, it's done, and we move on. Me and you. I don't want to relive my past, Nadine. Whatever you've been told isn't nearly half as bad as it was." She has to know approaching Holly is like ripping a raw wound open after it's knitted.

"I'm sorry for what you went through, but she deserves to know the truth and apologise for the pain she caused."

"She doesn't deserve to know anything. I really don't want to talk about it. I said I'd talk to her," I say firmly, striding towards the stairs with my mug.

"I can see you're upset."

"Nadine, I admitted I want a future with you, and within minutes, you're shoving my past down my throat. It's a no-go area. I will talk to Holly for you."

Her eyes widen and she moves in and pecks my lips.

"Sorry, it's just, you're you, and I keep pinching myself as it is," she admits sheepishly. "And then she came back, and I panicked." Her soft tone is shaky. "Whether you decide to talk with her or not, it's none of my business. The past is done." She pouts, waiting for me to make a move. And I do. I lean in and solidify our decision to move things to a more serious level with a kiss.

Once Nadine has gone, I decide for myself that, if we will all live in the same village, I should set a boundary with Holly. Plus, I look after Grace and she and Beau are becoming friends. It's best we are all civil. Last night at the park had been awkward, and I spent too many years feeling like I wasn't welcome in my hometown after Sarah. I refuse to feel like it once more just because Holly has come back.

Chapter Five
Holly

Marcus left after breakfast. It's nice having an extra pair of hands and support with Beau, but Marcus can be staid at times. Beau's enthusiasm and naivete can be a little too much for him to contend with. Several times I have had to remind him she is only five. Not that her continuous chatting would suggest so.

"Ready for summer club? Grace might be there," I say, plaiting her hair down her back.

Her little shoulders lift in a petite shrug. "I guess."

"Grace will be there to look after you," I assure.

"Can she come to play at my house?" Beau asks. I knew this was coming.

"That would be fine, but we need to check with her mummy first," I tell her. I don't want to spring it on anyone, let alone myself. I'm still trying to smooth myself into the fold of Richmond and find my feet.

"She wants to come!" Beau tells me loudly. "She said so. She likes ponies too!"

"Oh well, she will love your bedroom then." I laugh. "Look

at all the ponies in here. If your bed wasn't in here, anyone would think it was a stable." I squeeze her little hand in mine.

Beau turns and gives me her serious face. "Mummy. Stables are stinky," she mutters at me pointedly.

"Yes, they are. I did see a sign for stables. Maybe we can book you in for horse riding. Would you like that?"

"Yes!" she squeals. "Yes, yes, yes!" Grabbing a stuffed horse, she rams it between her legs and begins gallivanting round the room. "Yee-haw!"

"Right, cowgirl, let's go to summer club." She follows me out and down the stairs. I'd packed her bag over breakfast so we slip our jackets on and lock up.

Beau races to the car, her toy hanging in her hand. "I'm a yee-haw!" she declares proudly.

"Are you all buckled up?" I call back, and she nods in the mirror. "Next stop, summer pony club!"

The club is well into the swing by the time we arrive. Many children are enjoying activities or are out in the garden.

"Morning, Claire. Beau has brought her toy pony along today."

"Oh, she is lovely. Beau, maybe we can find other horses for you to play with and we can groom them?" With little encouragement, Beau takes the other lady's hand. Grace soon appears, so I head to work, feeling better about her being in the club. I know the shop is the best thing for Beau and I, it's our future, but I can't help the mum guilt I'm confronted with when leaving her. I've started to take Beau a little later each session so I could miss any other parents, namely one. Cam wasn't there again, and I'm glad to avoid him. It's a short car journey to the shop. Keeley is popping in at some point today to go over a few bits with me. Until then, I plan to sort out their contracts and print paperwork off.

The new bell above the door dings. I wasn't expecting to hear it soon, at least not until opening. I'm balanced up high, arranging stock. "Sorry, we're not actually open yet," I call breathlessly from the back. Keeley isn't due for a while yet.

"I know." That voice. Deep. Confident. I jolt on the stool and grip the shelves for support. *Cameron.* "Can we talk?" He sounds gruff now, serious.

I tighten my hands on the shelf. "Just a sec." Closing my eyes, I count backwards from ten to collect myself. I smooth down my dress and check my reflection on the blank screen of my phone. Cameron is patiently waiting for me when I step out from behind the back. I keep the counter between us, needing the distance from him. He's wearing gym shorts and a sweat-stained top. Even damp and hot faced, he looks gorgeous. His appearance surprises me, or at least my reaction to him does. I stare at the counter and clear my throat. "What's up?"

My response rankles him, his calm, controlled mask slipping as he scowls at me. "What's up?" He laughs, then shakes his head as though I'm the unwanted punchline to a bad joke. "Honestly, Holly, I never thought I would see you again. I never suspected you'd return home."

Home. It was my home until he tainted it.

His hands slap down on the counter, startling me and pulling my thoughts back to him. He frowns out of the window, and I follow his eye line. I expect to find his wife waiting outside, but the green for once is empty. He gives another humourless laugh, then looks back, and it instantly puts me on edge. The look in his eyes is no longer warm. I still remember the look on his face when he noticed me at the village fete and he'd come over. "For years, I planned what I would say to you." His tan cheeks flare with colour; he's embarrassed by his admission. "I wanted to say so much," he confesses hotly, yet the heat in his eyes no longer shows the desire I was used to as a love-stricken teenager. Now, it's replaced by anger.

At me!

If anyone is to be mad, it's me. For years, I too thought of what I would say to him, yet I'm speechless now.

"And now that you're here, I've realised I no longer have anything to say to you because it's not worth it," he mutters scathingly.

"Excuse me?" I scoff.

His eyes regard me with something like disgust. "I mean, after all these years, surely it's done." He says it in a way that seems like a question, but it isn't voiced as such. So I don't reply. I'm not giving him any ammunition. I want to tell his cheating arse to go to hell, but I don't. "We're both adults now. We've moved on." He shrugs, and my mind goes straight to his wife, his beautiful wife, who is absolutely nothing like me. "We live in a small village, so we are likely to bump into one another. I'd rather us clear the air and be civil."

"For a moment there, it didn't feel very civil to me," I bite through a tight smile, which he reciprocates with one of his own. God, the arrogant prick. He's even more full of himself. How awful for him to have been screwing two girls; it must have caused him some damage. My eyes flash with all the unsaid words, and he sucks in a deep breath. I can see he is ready to say more, but I don't let him. "I'm here for Beau, to give her a decent life and upbringing. I have been nothing but polite. If anything, you just made this more awkward," I snap. Tears burn my eyes, and I narrow my gaze, refusing them access to run free.

"Holly, if awkward came up and slapped you on the back of the head, you wouldn't know it," he grits, and I somehow laugh. Who the hell is this man?

"Cameron, I don't even think you know what you want. One second, you're saying let's brush it under the carpet, and in the next breath, you're condemning me for something that y—" I stop. I'm not getting into this. The time for arguing about his indiscretion is long gone. "—for something from years ago," I say instead, and his jaw locks. "If you have something to say, just say it!" I snap.

His chest inflates and, for a moment, I think he is about to unleash hell on me, but he grips the side and shakes his head. He sags inwardly and deflates before my eyes. The bristling man is gone and in its wake is someone who looks defeated. "You're not worth it," he whispers. I'm glad he isn't looking at me because I physically flinch at his harsh admission.

No, I won't cry. I blink back the hotness in my eyes and lift my chin. "You made that clear enough a decade ago. Thanks for stopping by and being civil," I grate and turn, leaving him standing in the shop alone. It's a few minutes before I hear the doorbell chime again, and only when I know he's gone do I drop down in my office chair and stare at the wall.

How dare he come here to my place of work, my business, and demand we be civil? Nothing about his temperament was civil. What small polite interaction we'd had before now is moot. He stuck a massive spanner in the works!

He cheated!

I don't care how young we were; he was old enough and mature enough to know what he was doing. He deceived and betrayed me. I have half a mind to storm out of the shop and have it out with him and I nearly do. I make it across the floor and have my hand on the door when I see him striding around the far corner and stop. This is best. It's clear that neither of us can be friends. Not after that. Maybe this is easier. We can keep our distance and go about our days, move forward with our lives, without contact. There are other places he can go for coffee. Cameron Stone can take a leap and jump, for all I care. I secretly hope his wife doesn't like my arrival. I hope she gives him shit about it. It's probably why he was so pissed. Maybe she is giving him a hard time and he is taking it out on me. Whatever the hell his problem is, it's not my business. He can forget about me being polite to him! I may have been a quiet and shy teenager, but he has yet to meet this Holly. I stomp to the coffee machine and smack a cup down, wishing this thing poured wine out instead. "The absolute gall, stupid, arrogant prick!" I mutter under the loud spray of the machine.

"Who is a prick?" Keeley asks, dumping her bag on the counter.

I scream and whirl round. "Oh my god, shit, you scared me!"

"Sorry." She winces. "Are you okay? You look mad." She smiles at me cautiously.

"Yes, sorry," I sigh. "Bad morning, coffee?" I say, trying to dispel the anger from my body.

I go through Keeley's contract with her and give her a full tour of the stockroom, upstairs, and the office. I talk about my ideas for the shop and ask her to read up on a few books, giving her a few to take with her. "It just helps to sell if we all know the books, some I haven't read, but what we do know will aid in supporting purchases." I smile, seeing her apprehension.

"What if I don't like the book? Do I lie?" she asks me worriedly.

"There will be something in there you do, so focus on that. Be as honest as you can without giving too much away." I lean over, picking a book off the shelf. It's a thriller, which I loved. "This book kept me on the edge of my seat, so much was happening and yet I still had no idea who the killer was. It was gritty and sad, so well written, thick with detail and intrigue."

"Well, I kind of want to read that one now." She laughs, and I hand it to her.

"Just remember to drop it back in the basket upstairs."

"So is your house like a huge library?" Keeley wonders, following me across the floor.

"Not yet." I have so many plans for the house, but I didn't want to throw Beau out of the loop with too much change, it was hard enough for her moving to Richmond and her grandfather no longer being here, I want to ease the changes in. The kitchen was always big enough for a dining table, so I plan to move that in there and make the dining room a library and snug. I need to find someone who can build me shelves. I don't want or need anything too fancy. "Beau and I are still adjusting to being back and getting into a routine."

"Oh, did you live here before then?" Keeley wonders.

"Yes, my father recently passed and left the house to me. I grew up here but moved away in my teens. It's good to be back."

"I'm sorry to hear that," Keeley murmurs, looking suddenly awkward. My father was a hermit, and given how young Keeley is, it's no surprise she is unaware.

"Thanks, Beau loves being here." I clear my throat and pick at my shirt. "In fact, do you know anyone who can make me some shelves? The company I hired for the shop, although great, was pricey, and I want to find someone a bit cheaper this time."

"Oh yes, Cameron Stone. He is the local handyman he also makes custom-made furniture, decking and fencing. He does a bit of everything, plus he is really hot." She laughs.

"Oh right, is there anyone else?" I ask, moving to neaten a shelf up now that there are fewer books.

"Why would you want anyone else?" She giggles.

"Cameron and I don't see eye to eye, so if you do know someone else, I'd appreciate it if you could let me know."

"Oh." She looks flummoxed. "Sorry, I didn't know. I can ask around."

"Great, so is there anything else you need to know before next week?" I ask quickly and check my watch. "I'm due to collect Beau in about half an hour."

"No, that's it. I think we should be good to go on Monday. It's Emily who starts too, right?"

"Yes, she works at the summer club, but with school starting, she needs to find another job. You'll like her."

"I think I've seen her about."

"She's lovely. Thanks for coming in today, Keeley. I'm looking forward to us working together." I open the door for her and smile as she steps through.

"Me too. Thanks, Holly, see ya!"

As I turn back to go inside, I catch sight of Cameron's wife watching me from across the other side of the green.

Is she bothered by my return?

I never returned for Cameron; I honestly never thought he would be here. He'd had his whole life planned out, university, a job in London where I could visit during my weekends between studies. He'd wanted to be in banking, so how come he is doing joinery work? I peek through the window and see his wife still flicking glances this way. Cameron has been out of my life for so long, I never suspected we'd meet again or that he would be a part of my life. And I don't want him to be. Am I shocked I still find him attractive? Yes, but that's skin deep. I know that below that flawless exterior is someone who can harm, who isn't loyal. Beneath is ugly. Desperate to not be consumed by my thoughts, I check my emails and confirm the baked goods with Danielle for opening. Everything is as it should be and we're ready to open. I could have pulled the date forwards, but I wanted to give myself plenty of time to adjust to having a new schedule and getting everything prepared. I've offered an opening discount for each book purchased to rally some business, and with being such a small community, there are always fetes, events and celebrations to pull more customers through the door.

I arrive at the summer club and find Beau sitting with Grace playing with stables and horses, each girl putting on a voice and speaking for the horse. It's so cute and exactly what I envisioned for my little girl when I returned home. "My mane is the longest in the stables," Grace says, flicking the horse to waft its hair.

"My hooves are the shiniest." Beau giggles, and they begin clip clopping on the carpet, and that's when I feel a presence beside me. I twist, seeing Dan smiling down at both girls.

"Hello," he whispers and drops a look to Grace, who must sense he is here.

"Daddy!" She laughs, scrambling up his front as I make the connection.

"Hey, squirt, this looks fun." Unlike other parents who collect their child and hotfoot it out the door, Dan sits, taking up plenty of space on the carpet. He grabs a pony and makes a poor attempt at neighing. I can't help it. I laugh, and the girls do too, because his impression is terrible.

"Okay, I'm no horse." He holds his hands up, smiling. I'm still coming to grips with the realisation that I had this whole situation wrong.

"Daddy!" Grace sighs dramatically. "That's Beau's horse." She removes it from his hand and passes it back to Beau. "She has riding lessons. Can I go?" Grabbing his face, she squashes his mouth into a pout. "Pleeease!"

"Oh." I feel bad. "I mentioned it to Beau this morning. She's really excited." I grimace.

"Erm, well, I need to check times and see about work."

Grace seems instantly deflated.

"You always work," she moans. "Please, I love horses." She gives him puppy eyes, and Beau joins in for measure.

"Grace, I'm sorry, I can't just swap work." He hugs her close, but she is tearing up.

"Daddy, please!" Her lip is out, and Dan looks close to sweating. "Uncle Cam can take me!"

"No, Grace, Cam already does lots to help me out. He has his own job."

"I could take her." The words slip right out, and I have no way to take them back. "I mean, if you're happy for her to attend?"

"Really?" Dan asks, shocked. I nod, not wanting to get into too much of a conversation with him. For a moment, our eyes lock, and I see the swirl of guilt swimming back at me. Does he wish he had never laughed at me back then, mocked my relationship with Cam?

I swallow roughly and look at Grace. "Grace, I need to check that I can take Beau. My work might be a bit busy too, so let me find out first before we all say yes, okay?" My gaze flits between both girls, ensuring they understand, and they nod excitedly. "I'm happy to take her. Beau will enjoy the company too."

Dan stands and looks from me to the two girls, already concocting plans. "Are you sure this is okay? I'd hate to put you out if you have work?"

"I need to check their sessions, but I should be okay to do it in the afternoon. I may have to collect the girls straight from school and take them to the shop before riding. Would that be okay?" I'm in a muddle. I came to collect Beau, and now I'm making plans with my old nemesis.

"Yes, sure. Here, let me give you my number so you can update me about it all. If it's not feasible, then don't worry yourself," Dan says, pulling out a business card. I take it and turn it over to see his name and CEO in bold silver lettering. I'm not surprised to see he has his own software company.

"Okay, sure, I'll head there now so the girls aren't waiting to find out." I shift uncomfortably.

"Thanks." He sounds gruff and likely feels as awkward as I do.

Regret flashes in his eyes. He holds my stare and I shake my head in warning. I can sense where this is going. "Holly." He swallows loudly and looks to where the girls are sitting to play once more. "I'm sorry. I was young, stupid and arrogant." Cameron should take a leaf out of his friend's book, but I don't want to talk about the past, at least not so soon after Cam blindsided me.

"I know." I give him a brittle smile, and he nods, his face taut and cheeks pinker than they were moments ago. "I'll let you know about riding," I add before he can respond, and he wants to, I can tell. His mouth opens, but I cut him off and ask Beau to collect her bag and toy. By the time she comes back, Dan and Grace have left.

"Will I get to ride a pony?" Beau asks, giving her teddy a kiss on the head. I help her into the car and buckle her up.

"Hopefully, let's go to the stables now."

Chapter Six
Holly

The stables are a short journey on the outskirts of Richmond, and Beau is super excited, pushing up from her seat to look out of the window. "How many horses will be there? Do they have ponies? What if I'm too small?"

I jump in with a response whilst she is sucking in air. "When we get there, we will know. We can have a look around." I laugh at her nose pushed up against the glass. Could she be any cuter?

"I'm going to call my pony Bella."

"Oh, I think these ponies are already named," I say.

"I can't have one, then?" She frowns, trying to clock the stables from her viewpoint.

"Not really. These belong to someone and they let you ride them, hopefully," I add, trying not to get her hopes up.

"Like borrowing?"

"Yes, that's exactly right, borrowing." I smile, happy she understands me.

"Like the cardigan you gave back to the shop?" Beau wonders idly. I go red-faced, recalling needing to get myself a pashmina for a work event, which I returned after wearing it, much to my mother's dismay.

"Erm. . .yes, sort of. Mummy doesn't always do that, it was just once." I grimace. "Here we are!" I sing-song, changing the subject. We head down a small track which veers off to an old gate, which looks worn and is hanging in a way that suggests it will fall off soon. I hope the stables are better-looking than this. A dusty car park opens up and beyond that are well kept stables. Shame about the entryway. I park up and Beau is unclipping herself and pushing free of the car as a huge horse clops by with a rider on.

"That is a giant!" Beau exclaims, looking worried. She scrambles up, and I hold her tight, keeping my laugh at bay.

The rider, a middle-aged woman, waves at Beau. "A gentle giant." She winks and plods off towards a field.

"Don't worry, they will have little ponies for you and Grace," I tell her, walking towards what looks like an office; it's more of a stockroom. Inside, a woman is cleaning her tack and lifts her head at our arrival. "Hello, sorry to just turn up like this."

"That's okay, dear. How can I help?" She walks towards us with her jodhpurs and boots on. Beau looks like she has met her first Olympic rider. The woman gives me a once-over, her gaze narrowing. Does she recognise me? I'm not sure I recall her.

"Do you offer riding lessons? This one is horse mad." I smile.

"And Grace!" Beau chimes in.

"Her friend also."

"Yes, there are different classes. Has she ridden before?" the lady asks.

"Oh no." I laugh, squeezing Beau reassuringly.

"So, a beginner then. My granddaughter has been riding since she was three," she tells me, leaving the storeroom.

"Wow, an early starter. Both girls are beginners. I wanted to see which days you have available as we've just moved back and I start work on Monday," I tell her as we make our way into the main stable yard. Groomers and assistants are all busy cleaning, feeding and grooming the horses. Beau tugs my arm and points their way.

"How old are they? Five, six?" she asks.

"Five." Beau holds up her hand.

"Wednesdays at four," she informs me, then removes her glove. "Sorry, I'm Amanda Jessops, the owner." I take her hand. Jessop? That name is familiar, but I'm not sure I know this woman, but by the guarded expression on her face, she knows who I am. I don't let it deter me and keep my smile in place.

"Holly, this is Beau." I smile down at my girl. Amanda nods politely at me, and I wonder if she is on Team Cam. Everyone else seems to be.

"Well, Beau, do you want to come see the riding school?" We follow Amanda, and Beau is happy to get down and walk, taking it all in. She is bopping around, waving at anyone who acknowledges her. Amanda gives us a full tour, showing us the indoor riding school, fields and paddock. The place is great, and Beau is happy. I collect forms and leave with an overexcited child.

When we arrive home, Beau races inside, yelling about making Grace a riding school card. She will be entertained for ages doing that, so I pull out Dan's card and give him a ring.

"Daniel Ocean," he answers on the third ring. I get a weird cramping sensation in my stomach. This is my life now, buddying up with people who had little care for me. I twist and look at Beau. This isn't about me but her.

"Hi, it's Holly, the riding school has availability on Wednesdays at four. There are some forms to fill in, but I can take the girls," I say in a strained rush of air. Conversing with him, Cameron and anyone else from that group still brings out a level of insecurity I didn't know I had left. I thought I had banished it all. I clear my throat, determined to sound far surer of myself in the next sentence.

"Okay, great, thanks. That's Cam's day, so I just need to square it with him first."

"Sure." I clear my throat and look at the forms. "I can drop the form to you tomorrow."

"Yeah, if you don't mind dropping it off, I'll text you my address."

"Okay, great."

"Holly, erm. . .thanks for this." He clears his throat, and I'm glad I'm not the only one finding this whole situation surreal. "I mean, afte—"

"Of course." I hang up before he can finish his sentence and begin preparing dinner. Beau is scribbling away at the table, so I have ample time to think. Cam's words from earlier are still vivid in my mind. I don't want to dwell on it, but I'm shocked that he had the audacity to be angry with me when I was hurt by his actions years ago. I'm annoyed at myself for allowing this to govern my life, and with Cam's snarky attitude, it's about time I let it go. I no longer want to be dictated by my fears and pain, but be stronger because of them. Yes, I think determined. I will be stronger because of this, Beau too. We eat, and I spend the evening with Beau, making Grace a card for riding school.

"That's your phone," Beau says, colouring in another card.

"Oh. I didn't even hear it." I laugh and get up from the lounge floor. "Hi, Emily, everything okay?" I say, answering her call.

"Hi, I just wondered if tomorrow is a good time to collect the contract, or if I can get it tonight, whatever is easiest?"

"I'm having a day out with Beau tomorrow so I'm not in the shop. I can send you my address?" I propose.

"Sure, I'll head over now and get started with it."

"Fab, see you soon!"

When there's a knock on the door, Beau jumps up. "Can I

get the door?" she asks, already racing towards it. I nod and she hauls it open and takes Emily's hand. "Hi, Emily, look at the card I made."

"Sorry, she'll try to keep you here for eternity now." I laugh, seeing Emily look sheepish.

"I don't mind, she's a little star," Emily compliments.

"Drink?" I offer.

"Sure, whatever you're having." She laughs as Beau pulls her into the lounge and thrusts her card under Emily's nose.

"I'm ready to hit the wine." I smirk, still feeling the sting of Cam's visit earlier.

"Sounds great." I leave Emily with Beau, who is no doubt boring her with horse information, and pour us both a glass of wine.

"Here we go. Shall we sit outside? It's probably a bit cooler." Beau hotfoots it outside, and I chuckle. "She has one speed."

"You mean fast?" Emily comments. We sit in the back garden and watch as my daughter tires herself out on the trampoline.

"I don't think I ever recall having that much energy," I groan. Beau is like a buzzing bee.

"Me neither. I love how inquisitive she is, always eager for more of everything." Emily watches, fascinated, as my little girl pings around inside the trampoline netting.

"She's a sponge," I mutter playfully. "It's cute, and Beau is a dream, but some mornings, the last thing I want is to be asked if frogs have ears at five am," I drawl, and Emily laughs into her glass.

"How was today? Didn't Keeley stop by?" Emily asks.

"It went well. I think once the store is up and running, we will get into the swing of things." I shrug around my glass and Emily rests her head back on the chair.

"One hundred percent. We'll get into a routine, and it'll be as easy as riding a bike."

"Or a horse. I signed Beau up today for lessons."

"Oh, she will love that!" She smiles and turns her face to the last bit of sun. "This is nice. I'm in a flat so the memorial is my garden." She laughs, which turns into a long sigh.

"You mentioned you're new to the village. Is it just you, or did you move with anyone?" Her gaze flashes with an emotion I'm used to—hurt.

"Just me, needed to clear my head and get a fresh start."

"Oh, okay."

"Fleeing a disgruntled ex." She frowns through her admission.

"I know all about them, I returned to one." I scoff.

"Oh no, really!" She sits up. "How's that working out for you?" She pulls a face and waits for me. It's nice to have a set of ears, ears that aren't biased.

"Not so great. He dropped by the shop saying he wanted us to be civil and then told me I wasn't worth it in the same breath." I shake my head in a silent laugh when I see her jaw drop. "Yeah, I looked like that too."

"You're kidding, so he just rocked up and—"

"Yep, he told me the village is small and we're likely to bump into each other."

"True," Emily concludes.

"Said he had so much to say to me, and now I'm back, it's not worth it."

"Ouch."

"Well, I wouldn't mind, but he cheated on me," I exclaim quietly so Beau doesn't overhear.

"No!" Emily's face gapes.

"Oh yes!"

"Men."

I scoff and rest back in my chair. "It was years ago, and I never really wanted to come back, but when my father passed and left us the house, I decided to come home, give Beau the kind of upbringing I had in a village. I didn't think he would be here," I confess. "He had plans. I didn't know he was still in Richmond, and my father never said anything."

"Does it bother you that he is?"

"Yes and no," I admit. "He has moved on and is in a relationship. I have Beau. A lot has changed. It's just awkward. I was so humiliated when he—" I stop myself from divulging all my life to her. "Sorry." I sigh. "I was adjusting to being back and I was shocked to find out he and all his friends never left, but I was coping, you know, moving forward and focusing on Beau and the shop, then he turns up and..." I frown into my glass, swallowing painfully.

"You still have feelings for him," Emily whispers sympathetically. I should hope not after what he did.

"Not this Cameron, no. The old one I held on to, but coming back has taught me a lot. He's not the same person. I'm not."

"Grace's uncle?" Emily pries.

My lips twist, and I sigh. "He's not actually her uncle, but yes."

"He's really hot and her dad," Emily says with an apologetic grimace.

I hum, not wanting to admit I still find Cameron ridiculously attractive. "Anyway, now you're away from your ex, are you dating or...?" I smirk.

"Same as you, just focusing on me. I'm not sure I want to date yet."

"I'll drink to that." I laugh, sipping my wine. "Another, or are you driving?"

"I walked." She holds out her glass for me. When I return, she is watching Beau with intrigue. "This is probably super personal, but—"

"You want to know about Beau's dad?" I say, seeing that same look on her face as I have on others.

"Sorry, it's none of my business." She looks back to Beau with a heap of horses and unicorns on a mat.

"It's fine. No one really dares ask, but Beau knows the truth. I used a sperm donor." I'm open about it; it's not something I go around telling people because Beau knows and understands in her own way that it's just us, and that her dad gifted her to me. I explained he doesn't know about her, but he'd love her if he did.

Emily blinks, surprised. "Oh, I mean, you're stunning. I thought there was some guy floating about, a deadbeat dad, an estranged ex, armed forces." She scoffs. "Sperm donor was not on my list." She chuckles.

"I think after the whole cheating thing, dating was never on my radar, but I wanted a family, and I decided to just do it alone. My parents, although they are separated, have supported me with her and she's amazing." I smile at Beau's scrunched-up face, trying to pull the mini brush through the horse's matted mane.

"She is, you are, I can't believe you have brought her up alone. Wow."

"I'm taking that as a compliment."

"Do it. Hell, I haven't even got my life together and you're a mum of one, own a business and house. You must be so proud of yourself," Emily says with a shine of emotion in her eyes.

"I guess I am." I smile softly. I can succeed with all this, but the thought of dating sends me into a mild panic. Here I am, comparing myself to Cameron's wife, wondering about their relationship, about his life, when I should be wholeheartedly focused on mine. I'm doing well. I'm achieving, and I have an incredible daughter. Emily is frowning into her drink, now looking thoughtful. "We all reach our goals at different times. You're just readjusting your course. You'll get there."

"I know. I had it all, a mortgage, a partner, this luxury lifestyle, and I find out it's all based on a lie, so I left." She shakes her head. I realise at that moment she is as lost as I am. I may seem like I have it together, but I've been floating through life with Beau at the helm for focus. If I can help this girl get back on her feet, then I will.

"What do you mean?" I say softly.

"He had a gambling addiction. Had gambled everything away and plunged us into thousands and thousands of pounds of debt. We hadn't been making payments. Even when he was caught, he lied. That's what I couldn't forgive. I packed some things, cleared what was left in my account and walked away."

Poor girl.

"Well, here's to new things." We clink glasses, and I sigh, happy to have found myself a friend.

"Let's get this form to Grace's daddy, then we can go out for the afternoon."

"Yayy!"

After a five-minute journey, I turn down a street lined with big houses that are modern and beautiful. "Wow!" Beau croons.

Indeed wow. This is something else.

We're directed into a wide drive, leading through big gates. I park up and Beau bursts from the car. "Look how big their house is, Mummy!"

"I know, it's so big." I smile. Dan has done well for himself. A Range Rover and a sleek sports car are parked up. I didn't expect him to be home. We make our way to the door, and Beau knocks lightly, while I press the bell and we wait. I planned on posting the form through the letterbox and waiting to hear from Dan, but I suppose we can iron a few things out now. Just then, tyres crunch and a third car pulls into the driveway.

Cameron's.

. . .

Angry green eyes watch me with a deep frown as he parks up and gets out of his car. His scowl turns to a smile when Beau sees him and waves.

"Hi, Beau," he murmurs.

The door opens and Dan's face is a myriad of emotions, shock, worry, awkwardness.

"Hi, Dan," I breathe, trying to keep my voice even. "I hadn't realised you'd be in," I say.

"So why knock then?" Cam mutters, giving Dan a pointed 'what the fuck look' that he doesn't conceal from me. Asshole!

"I saw the cars," I spit. Then look at Dan, clearing my throat. "I saw your car and thought I would give you this in person." I fish the form out of my bag and hand it over. Cam is standing with his arms crossed, glowering at me.

Grace appears, and Beau hops up and down. "Hi, Grace." She giggles, stepping between both men and slipping out of my reach.

"Oh, Beau, wait, you can't just go in."

"Can I show her my room, Daddy?" Grace asks.

"Quickly. I have a call in a minute."

"God, sorry, we can go. Beau!" I shout as they race off.

"Holly, relax, she can come in. Here." He steps back, silently inviting me in. Cameron fumes and clears his throat. Dan rolls his eyes.

"I can wait here. The forms are pretty simple; like I said, lessons are on Wednesdays. I think we can start the girls as early as this week, providing we get the forms in. I know they go back to school, but at least they will get into a routine quickly," I rush out and flick a look at Cameron, who's turning redder by the second.

"Wednesday is my day," Cameron says slowly, glaring at me with unveiled disgust at Dan.

"Oh, sure. I was just getting information should Grace want to join. Beau is signing up so I can just be a backup." I smile awkwardly at Dan.

"Grace doesn't need a backup because I won't let her down." Cameron enunciates each word.

"Okay." I clear my throat and look to Dan for help.

"You were actually going to let her take Grace on my day?" Cameron laughs scathingly at Dan.

"It's not like that, Cam. Holly was just getting information for me," he mutters.

"I was going anyway," I elaborate, seeing Cam and Dan getting more short-tempered by the second.

"I would have gotten the info. After *everything,* you're rubbing shoulders with her," Cam spits furiously.

"Cameron, mate, fuck off." Dan checks over his shoulder for the girls, but they're nowhere in sight. "Holly was doing me a favour. *Grace* a favour."

"This is bullshit," Cam snaps and storms by me.

"I'm so sorry," I whisper as the girls thunder down the sweeping staircase.

"It's fine. Thanks for this, Holly." He lifts the paperwork.

"Sure."

"Can Beau come and play?" Grace pulls on Dan's top.

"Not today, Gracie. Daddy is working."

"Come on Beau, let's go, say bye." I smile through my confusion at Grace. "Bye, sweetie."

Chapter Seven
Cameron

I wheelspin out of Dan's drive and race off up the street, slamming my fist into the steering wheel, making the horn blare. "Fuck!" Grace is my goddaughter. If Holly thinks she can just sweep back in and start playing little miss innocent again, then she has another thing coming. I'm fucking furious with Dan. He knew how crushed I was, how broken, what that year did. I was in a dark, dark place, and Miss Sunshine just pops back up, playing the victim card, bringing old memories and gossip back to light. I fume silently and indicate at the lights. I head straight for Nadine's, knowing she is home today. She only works a few shifts at her hair salon. My brakes screech as I come to a sudden stop outside her place. My phone chimes and it's Dan. If I answer now, I will lose my mind and he will get the brunt of my anger. Nadine's confused face appears at her front window. I take the call. "You are unbelievable! Her, of all people?" I snap, stepping out of the vehicle.

"Cam, come on. It's for Grace. I didn't plan this to fuck you over."

"I'm feeling pretty arse fucked right now. Of all people, you are the last, *the last person* I thought would buddy up with her,"

I growl, pacing on the path. Nadine opens the door and sees me on the phone. "You're my best mate!"

"Cam, I'm not her mate, but our children are. Grace needs Beau."

"There are plenty of other kids she can be mates with." I laugh at his failed attempt to justify this.

It's Dan's turn to laugh now. "That worked out so well for me last time. Grace is nearly six and even she clicked on quicker than me that half the mums want their kids to buddy up so they can get a chance to drop knickers. Let's face it; Holly is hardly going to want to shack up with me after all that shit and I'm not interested in her!"

He's right, but I'm too angry to see logic. "Shit, that barely happened to her. It was me who suffered, me who was dragged through the mud. I lost everything!" I roar.

"Because of Sarah, not Holly. Her only fault was not giving you a chance to explain."

"Like I want to fucking talk about that night," I hiss, shaking, angrier than I have felt in a long time.

"So she's in the wrong because she never gave you a chance, but you won't tell her either."

"Whose fucking side are you on!"

"Yours! I stood by you. I always have your back. This is about Grace, Cam. It's horse riding. That's all this is, not Holly stealing your day or taking Grace from you, but giving her an opportunity to grow in confidence and enjoy having a friend. I love you, Cam, but I will always choose Grace." He's right. So right. I hate that Holly is back. I wanted her home. I thought having her back in my life would put an end to all this, but it's dredged everything up for me.

"Fuck you." I disconnect the call and look at Nadine's house. I can see her silhouette, and I debate going in. I look to my car, then to her and back to my car, pacing indecisively. I get in and shut the door, dropping my head to the wheel and breathing deeply. Trying to calm myself, I sit there for an age. Still feeling angered and now stupid for my dramatics. Fuck!

A light tap on my car window brings my head up. Nadine looks at me through the glass with a concerned smile. Sighing, I open the door, and she drops to her hunches. "Hey."

"Hey." I blow out a deep breath. "I had a bust up with Dan."

She nods, pulls the door wider, allowing her access to climb in. Straddling my lap, she cups my face. "Give each other some space. You're too close to ever fall out." She is right, but that's not what is needling me. It's Holly fucking Matthews. "Well, I'm glad you came to me," she whispers.

I did, didn't I? And that means something. "Lay one on me," I mutter, staring at her. She grins and leans in, pressing her soft lips to mine. But like every other time I'm intimate with Nadine, Holly's face flashes through my mind and it's her sitting in my lap, lazily stroking my tongue with hers. My cock swells, and I grind her down. Fuck yes, that feels damn good.

"Cam, baby, come inside." Nadine's voice splinters the mental image in half, and I blink at her. Shit. She sits back and tucks her hair behind her ear. This new position pushes her tits forward and pressures my cock.

"Fuck." I rock her hips and her mouths pops in an 'O.' I drop my head back, not giving a flying fuck we're in the street; I need to fuck this girl. When I open my eyes, Holly's car is heading up the street towards us. As she nears, her face snaps my way. Her smile falls. I slam my mouth to Nadine's and grind her down roughly. Fuck Holly Matthews and her gorgeous face.

"Cam, we need to go in," Nadine pants.

I help her out of the car and walk her close to my front to disguise my erection as we head up the path to her front door. As soon as we are inside and shut away from the outside world, I yank at her dress and strip her. Her hands are as rushed as mine, and as soon as we are free of clothes, I lift her, position myself and drive deep, holding her locked between the door and my angry hips.

"Oh god." She blinks, moaning when I slide out, swivel and pump back in. Yes. I need this to clear my fucking head. I scrunch my eyes and plough in, letting her warmth hold me deep. A blonde-haired woman moans in my mind. I open my eyes to relieve myself of the image, but it's still Holly I see. Holly with her slim body and perfect pussy. I hammer away, kissing her like crazy, maddened by my hatred at her for being back and desperate to fuck it all away. Forget it ever happened. I pretend I'm back in my youth, ten years before, and I somehow gained the attention of the most gorgeous girl in Richmond. She was nothing like the superficial girls that circled our group, nothing like the girls I had dated, and everything I didn't know I needed to feel like I was living my best life. I fuck her into the door, groaning loudly and touching her everywhere.

I miss you. I want to shout at her, to demand why she left me.

"Cam, oh god, now, Cam!" Nadine screams, and I stagger back in shock seeing her crumple and whimper through her solitary climax. I lost my mind to a fantasy. I hate to admit it, but I have been fucking Holly in my mind all these years, and I hoped Nadine would be the one to crush the habit. I jolt into action and sink back in.

"Ride me." I twist and take us to the floor and let her work me to climax. Holly springs to my mind, and I shake my head and blink. Anything to interrupt my mind's betrayal.

We lie exhausted on the floor. Nadine hums and rolls, panting across my chest. "Remind me to thank Dan," she whispers.

I laugh and rub her back. "Yeah, I will after I left hook him." I frown and cover my eyes with my arm.

"Is it that bad?"

"We'll work it out. I'm starving, shall we order lunch?" I'm keen to change the subject. I have no doubt I am justified in how I feel about Dan and Holly. He should have been upfront with me. Finding Holly at his place blindsided me, but I know Nadine won't side with me. She will question why I'm bothered and overthink it. There is only so much drama I can deal with and my own is enough. At my angriest, I wanted to shake Holly and demand to know why she had come home. It's useless. She's back. I'm still stuck here, reliving the past and unless one of us moves, we need to accept we are back in each other's lives. Plus, I have Nadine, and Holly has that wormy looking fucker. It's done. I need to work through my emotions because for the first time in a long time, I'm feeling a lot and all at once. I probably need a break. To get away for a few days.

Bollocks, I need to speak with Dan.

THREE DAYS LATER, I turn up at Dan's first thing to collect Grace. I've got some work I need to do, but the rest of the day is ours, and if Dan has got his shit together and sorted the paperwork for riding, we can enjoy that too. I knock on the door and wait, not sure how else to play this. Dan and I hardly ever row. He's my closest friend, my brother. I'm not letting Holly or my emotions jeopardise that. The door swings open, and Dan pulls back. "Why the fuck are you knocking? Just come in." He scoffs. I'm forgiven then.

Grace bounds through to the entryway. "Uncle Cam!"

"Hey, baby cakes." I scoop her up and carry her through to the kitchen on my forearm.

"She's got to finish her breakfast," my friend tells me. I drop Grace back in her chair as Dan comes over and kisses her hair.

"Dan, abou—"

"It's done." He slaps my back, and I let out a deep sigh. "You and I need to chat, though. Cole and Brant are coming over later to watch the game. You up for it?"

"Yeah, I'll grab some bits."

"No need, catch you later. Bye, Grace, love you."

"Bye, Daddy!" I watch my friend walk away and take a seat opposite my favourite girl. I call her that too.

"I thought Nadine was your favourite?" She purses her lips.

"Nope, you first." I wink. "That cereal looks good. I'm gonna grab some." I collect a bowl and some cereal, but I choose yoghurt and not milk. I select a few berries and load my bowl up; I'm two mouthfuls in when Dan calls me.

"Riding at four at Jessops," he tells me.

"You did that on purpose," I accuse.

"You're less likely to have a hissy fit in front of Grace." He laughs down the line. "If it's an issue, Beau's mum can take her," Dan throws at me casually.

"We're not using her name now?"

"Not until you and I get to the bottom of this."

"When did we get married?" I chortle.

"Cam, you're struggling. It killed me last time seeing you like that. We're not letting you get to that again."

"I'm not!"

"Good, Jessops at four." He disconnects the call, leaving me to churn over my thoughts. Like always, Dan has left me a bag for Grace, not that it matters. I have a key, so if we need anything, we usually whip back. For the last three years, Grace and I have developed a routine. She knows I might do some work in the morning, usually with one eye in the back of my head for her and the rest of the day is for her. Every other day, I do a full day, if not longer, but I give Grace the time because she deserves the damn world. She helps me lock up, then we walk to my car. "What's in this bag?" I lift the small gym holdall.

"My riding clothes."

"Okay, let's hit the road." I secure her car seat, and she buckles up.

"Are we going to have a great day?" I always ask her that.

"Yes!" she yells, piercing my eardrums.

"Damn right!" We make the journey back to mine. It's not far and soon we are parked up and Grace is off. It's a second home for her. I bought the old Bilson place when Reverend Bilson passed away, as his wife Mina went into assisted living. The property is nestled by the church grounds and the fields that touch the edge of Richmond. It's damn good real estate. I moved in as soon as I had the keys and began work straightaway.

"Grace, stay where I can see you!" I shout, walking out back to my workshop. The old summer house has been the perfect place to work from. I gutted it, installed my machinery and began trading again. The house I knocked through, re-designed and fitted a wrap-around veranda with decking, but for now, I have a bespoke gothic headboard I've been contracted to do. It needs another coat and then it's ready to be shipped. I position the headboard and myself so I can watch Grace in the garden.

A little bit later, Grace wanders in. "Uncle Cam, I'm hungry." She picks up a wooden bear door stopper and smiles at it. "Can we have some lunch?"

"Yeah, sure, give me two more minutes and I'm done for the day."

"Okay." She puts the bear down and runs back off to play with the few toys she keeps here. I probably need to ask Dan to exchange them for others from home.

Grace and I spend the afternoon out and about. I buy her lunch, then take her to the park, and when we pop to the shops, I treat her to a unicorn DVD, popcorn, and sweets because she will be bored stiff whilst we all watch the game. It's nearing four so we head back to mine, and I pick up her bag. "Grace, come get your riding gear on!" I call out into the back garden.

She wanders in, looking confused. "But I'm going with Beau."

"I'm taking you. You will see Beau there." I smile, pulling her things out.

"I want to go with Beau." Her voice quivers.

"Beau is probably on her way. Let's go meet them," I say diplomatically.

She shakes her head and cries. "I want Beau!" I walk to her quickly because I hate seeing her cry. When I scoop her up, she pushes me away and runs off.

"Grace!" I blurt, panicked. She's never acted like this with me. "Grace!" I catch her just short of the front gate. "You do not run out the gate!" She screams loudly, and I nearly drop her. An elderly lady is walking by with her dog and sticks her nose up at what she considers bad parenting.

Grace is off again, running another way. I chase after her and stop her from trying to climb the back fence overlooking the fields.

"Grace, what are you doing? Do you want to go riding or not?" I say forcefully. My deep voice makes her go still, but then she wails louder and I groan. "Beau is already there. You will miss riding. Your dad told me I was taking you," I say firmly. Her little hiccups make me feel shit, so I pull her into my chest and rub her back.

"I want Beau!"

"Either we go and get your gear on or you're not going!" I tell her in a sharp tone. Her little shoulders sag, her head drops and she nods. Ah, man, I rub my chest, feeling physically in pain for upsetting her. "Let's get ready then." I take her hand, and she follows me inside. Every time I try to spark up a conversation with her, she simply shrugs her shoulders and doesn't talk. Jesus, her future boyfriend will have his work cut out if she has mastered the silent treatment already. We arrive a little later than expected, and when I pull up beside Holly's car and help Grace out, she shrugs me away. "That's enough now. We've had a lovely day and you're being really rude, Grace June Ocean." Hearing her full name brings her head up. I'm about to hug it out with her, but Beau races over, her helmet too big, and the added weight has her stumbling about. She looks like a pissed-up foal. Holly's laughter splinters the air, and my gut and balls clench.

"Oh, Beau, you look so cute!" She laughs with tears in her eyes. Amanda Jessop is laughing too. Holly's in a tiny jumpsuit that shows off her killer legs and full breasts. Fuck me, this isn't fair. My own goddaughter is hating on me, then I have to come see how beautiful Holly looks. Grace and Beau speed off, and Amanda walks to me. She never believed any of the shit being spread about me.

She gives me a big hug. "My, my, you get more handsome every time I see you."

"Like I keep saying, Mrs Jessops, if John wasn't about and you were ten years younger..." I take her hand and wink. She gives a light, tinkling laugh, the cheeky flirt. I catch Holly rolling her eyes. She turns away and goes to join the girls standing at the side of the paddock watching a horse be trained.

"I didn't know you'd be bringing little Grace." She turns back to where Holly is waiting, and we watch as she leans down and gives Grace a hug. I want to go over and rip her off the child. I don't want Grace favouring her.

Amanda says, "How are you, I mean, with Holly being back?"

I'm not doing okay, that's for sure. Amanda, along with the village, were aware of all facets of my life back then, thanks to the local paper. I doubt Holly even remembers the Jessops; they never got involved in Richmond affairs and stuck to themselves, but Amanda came to my aid when my parents suddenly moved away, leaving me stranded in a place that hated me, with nowhere to live. She had let me use the outbuilding to their home as a place to stay until I got on my feet. Dan's father had been just as supportive and gave me a job in the upstairs office of their estate agency. I'd been out of the way, cooped up and in hiding from my own village. After a short while and lots of dark days, I'd managed to get back on my feet and get a flat.

"I'm good, just taking each day as it comes," I say breezily. "I noticed the gate on the way in."

"Oh, I know John reversed into it and it's just old."

"I can make you a new one, you know that, right?"

"I know. I keep meaning to give you a call." She holds her arms out and shrugs.

"I'll drop back tomorrow to get a proper look at it."

"Thank you, Cameron." Amanda sets Grace up with a helmet, but she still looks miserable as sin. We all move into the indoor school where there are other children being assisted on horses.

"Bye bye, Cam," Grace says, grabbing Holly's hand. Whoa, what the hell!

"I'm not leaving, Grace. I'm going to watch," I say and take her other hand, glaring at Holly over my goddaughter's head. She slips her hand free and smiles demurely at Grace.

"But it's girls only!" Grace sniffles.

"Anyone can watch, Grace. There is even a boy on a horse. Stop being rude, otherwise we're going home," I say under my breath. That does it; she has a full-blown tantrum and screams the damn place down. Holly looks at me expectantly. Fucking hell, how am I supposed to deal with this? I try to pick Grace up, but she wails and kicks out, and I honestly want to turn to the blonde beauty and tell her this is all her fault, that even my goddaughter is hating on me.

My phone rings. Relieved, I answer and hear Dan whistle down the phone. "Fuck me, you sound like you're at a zoo." He laughs.

"That zoo just so happens to be your child," I mutter.

"What the fuck? What's going on?" he demands.

"She was pissed that I was taking her, pissed that I'm staying because, apparently, it's girls only, and now she is having a mammoth fit in front of the entire riding school," I hiss, embarrassed.

"You poor bastard." Dan winces. "Look, leave her with Holly. I will grab her later, then we can unwind with a beer."

"No."

"Cam, don't be a baby. Leave her with Holly, go get some work done, and I'll see you later."

"I'm not fucking leaving my god—"

"Cam. She's my daughter and I'm telling you to leave her with Holly. Trust me, she is not going to get out of that tantrum with you around. She's too stubborn." Dan sighs.

"I'm not giving her the satisfaction."

"Who, Holly or Grace? Go home, man." Dan sounds weary. "My appointment is here. I'll text Holly. Catch up later." He's got her number? I feel savage.

I glare at Holly from across the room and drop down beside a crying Grace. "I'm going, Grace. Holly will look after you," I say with a thick ache in my throat. I'm gutted she doesn't want to hang with me. No sooner are those words out does she stop crying, the little shit. She jumps up and runs towards Holly, who gasps, then looks straight at me. I shake my head and stomp off.

"Cam, I—"

"Not interested, Holly." I cut her off and get in my car, leaving all three behind.

Chapter Eight
Holly

Cameron leaves me to fend off multiple accusatory glances. I approach Grace now smiling freely at Beau and not displaying the same level of hysteria from moments ago, cheeky madame. "Grace, I'm looking after you now."

"Okay!" she chirps. Crouching down, I give her a kind smile. "Grace, sometimes we have to do things we don't always want to, but getting upset about it and shouting doesn't make us feel better. And shouting at people isn't a polite way, do you understand?" I say gently. Grace blinks at me, and I can see the guilt swimming in her eyes.

"Your unky will be sad," Beau points out. I wink at my daughter and inwardly smile. She is so cute in the hat. The little girl looks thoughtful.

I don't want to upset Grace, but I felt I needed to say something. "Let's have fun," I say excitedly and rub her little arms. She gives me a small nod and wipes the last of her tears away. "Let me take a picture for your dad." Grace smiles widely, showing a missing tooth, and I snap a few images, then quickly text them to Dan and tell Beau to smile for her photo. The phone gets yanked out of my hands, and I stumble back in shock. "What on earth!" I cry.

Cameron shakes in front of me, my phone in his hand. "Did you just take a picture of Grace?" he snaps aggressively. "You better not have posted them on social media, or so help me god, Holly!" He looks through my phone with an angry groove carved in his forehead.

I snatch the phone back. "How dare you!" I spit, then check over my shoulder to find everyone watching. "I sent it to Dan. I don't even have social media, and if I did, I wouldn't assume to think it was okay for me to share images of someone else's child!" My phone pings, and I see Dan has replied with a thumbs up, thanking me. I twist the phone to show Cameron and he clears his throat. Shaking my head, I pull in a deep breath. "I can't keep doing this, Cam. Please stay away from me." My voice croaks. Everyone is staring at us, and I can feel the heat burn through my face. "Come on, girls, you're up next," I whisper, trying to keep my voice in check.

"Mummy, your hand is shaking," Beau worries.

"Forgot my coat." I nearly crack. "I'm cold."

"But it's warm," Grace adds, skipping along next to me.

"Oh, look at the ponies!" I try to draw their attention away, but a hand lands on my shoulder, and I jump.

"Holly." Cam sounds resigned. I slap a smile on my face, even though my vision is blurring and look over my shoulder.

He holds up a car seat and grits his jaw when he sees my unshed tears. "I came to give you this."

"My car is open," I say quickly and walk away with both girls. When we reach the other students, I see a pristine-looking woman with blonde hair and high heels looking me up and down. Mandy. She watches me with a look of disdain. Oh, great, another member of Team Cam. I smile, but she sticks her nose up, turning away. "Arabella, sit straight. No, you're still slouching, straight... No, straight, chin up, smile!" she instructs loudly. Jeez, poor kid.

The girls are bouncing off the walls when they finish their lesson. I took a few more photos for Dan and myself. Beau looks ready to burst. They both did so well. We hand the helmets back to an assistant, and I walk behind as both girls chat animatedly about the horses.

"Can Grace come to play at our house?" Beau asks as we all get in the car.

"Yes, I think her daddy will collect her later. Let's go home and get some ice cream. You girls were fantastic!" I exclaim. Grace and Beau disappear outside as soon as we arrive, with a box of plastic horses clattering between them. I find them a few minutes later with little fences balanced in the grass, stables and lots of horses littering the garden. Both girls are acting out their play, galloping around and talking in different voices.

"Look at our stables!" Grace shouts, pointing to the array of buildings. "We are making a riding school." She smiles, showing me that missing tooth again.

"Wow, it looks brilliant. Here we go, ice cream for the best riders in Richmond." They giggle and take their ice creams.

"Can Grace sleepover?" Beau asks, and Grace gasps, looking at me hopefully. Oh bugger.

"Well, not tonight. I can ask her daddy," I tell them. I leave them to it and make myself an ice cream and take it on the decking. Sending Dan the other photos, I ask if Grace can sleep over one night, but he never replies. I check my phone every now and then, but he hasn't even read my message. He's probably driving. The girls are occupied and playing happily. It's nice for Beau to have a friend, I think, watching them from the kitchen as I prepare for dinner. I even whip up a batch of cakes for them to decorate.

An hour and a half later, there is a knock at the door. I suspect it's Dan and swing it open with a smile, but it drops like a lead balloon. "Dan is stuck in traffic. I need to collect Grace," Cam says stiffly. My phone pings so I pull it out my pocket and see a text from Dan himself.

> Stuck in traffic. Cam on his way.

I LIFT MY PHONE AWKWARDLY, letting him know I got the memo. "They are out back. I will go get her," I tell him, and when I see him move to come in, I close the door quickly. He's not welcome in here, and if I'm being honest with myself, I don't even want him at my door.

"Grace, your uncle is here to get you. You can stay another night, okay?" I say quickly when I see her face fall. "It is very short notice and maybe your daddy has plans."

"His friends are coming round," she murmurs, reluctant to leave.

"That sounds fun. You will have a great time!" I try to keep upbeat, but she scrunches her nose up.

"I don't like football."

"Oh, you can definitely sleep over another night. Let's get your things." I had packed her bag so I pick it up and hook it over her shoulders, opening the door to find Cam looking as awkward as me.

"Thank you." Grace smiles.

"You're welcome, but next week, Cam will take you riding. Remember what we spoke about earlier. You will still see Beau at school and at riding." Grace nods and goes into Cam's arms. She yawns, and he smiles lovingly at her.

"When will my daddy be home?" she asks, flattening her palms to his stubbled jaw.

"He's stuck in traffic. I have that DVD and treats for a movie night. I'll watch some with you before the game starts."

"Are you sleeping at my house?" Grace asks. She rubs her palms over his face, smirking when his beard tickles her.

"I think me and your dad are too big to share a bed together." He laughs. "Say bye," Cam tells Grace, lowering her to her feet and taking her hand in his large one.

"Bye, Holly! Bye, Beau!" Grace waves.

"Here's her seat." I lean down and hold it out to him. Cam stares at me, and our eyes lock, and for a moment, neither of us moves. My breath catches and he looks at me with sadness in his eyes. It's too poignant to be about the stables. I feel the weak structure of my heart cracking. His vibrant green eyes are still my undoing, with his dirty blonde hair and tanned skin, his eyes are so bright, I suck in a deep breath and will him to look away because I can't break the connection. Cam opens his mouth to say something, but I panic.

Clearing my throat, I smile brightly at Grace as Cam takes the seat. "Bye, see you soon!" Beau is waving frantically. I scoop her up, needing the closeness of her to support my racing heart. I close the door, but Beau wants to wave until the car goes, and I can feel Cam eyeing me through the window. I'm still suckerpunched by that look. As soon as he stands tall and moves to get into the driver's side, I walk away and watch Beau from a distance.

Later that evening, I'm sitting in the bathroom as Beau takes a bath. Cam's panic at me sharing Grace's image plays on my mind. "Does Grace talk about her mummy with you?" I casually ask, folding the laundry.

"She doesn't have a mummy like I don't have a daddy. She went away," Beau says, walking her horses along the bath edge.

"Oh, that's sad. Why did she go away?" I wonder quietly.

Beau shrugs her little shoulder. "Grace wants you to be her mummy," she replies. God, Cam would go nuts if he heard

Grace voice that. It's clear he doesn't want me to have any interaction with her.

"Well, I can be her friend, and maybe her daddy has a girlfriend."

"No, he has dates," Beau tells me.

"Will I ever get a daddy?" she suddenly asks, and I feel my chest give way. Oh god, I knew this was coming, but I just never suspected it would be this soon. Cameron flashes through my mind, making me feel sicker by the second.

"One day, we just need to find someone who loves us both," I tell Beau, smiling at her. I haven't given dating any thought, let alone putting it into action, but I can see Beau is becoming impressionable and will want male interaction. She will compare herself to others around her and wonder why they have a daddy and not her. Although she knows she is my gift, she doesn't understand the true depth of what her conception means.

"Like how Unky Cam loves Grace? He was sad," she whispers, pressing her chin on the bath edge and watching me. Her hair is in wet strands and her big blue eyes stare softly at me.

"Yes, he was, but it's all okay now." I assure her, finishing the pile of clothes and placing it aside. I move over to her and help wash her hair.

After all the excitement of today, Beau crashes early, so I carry her up to bed and tuck her in, kissing her hair. I switch on her nightlight and pull her door too.

Dan seems laidback, so my gut instinct tells me something bad happened for him to refuse the use of images of Grace online. I've never been one to share Beau on a social platform. I deleted mine when I left Richmond and then licked my wounds in tearful silence. It takes that one thought for my mind to wonder back to my college days.

. . .

I was in the school library during my free period, when green eyes latch onto mine from between the bookshelves. Blushing, I look down and try to work, but I can't help notice that the warmth in my stomach is spreading until it is blooming in my chest. I spend my entire school life being invisible. But not from this person, though. No. They keep on watching until I have to pack up my things and leave.

It wasn't until the week leading to the summer holidays I finally met the boy with the green eyes. I'd been rushing down the corridor when I slam into someone's chest. I yelp out in surprise, and find myself up against Richmond's finest. I knew of each kid. They were rich, arrogant and loud. The girls flock to them, the boys want to be them. Me, I want to be left alone.

"Sorry," I mumble, securing my bag on my shoulder.

"Are you okay, Holly?" How the hell does he know my name? My head snaps back in surprise as I come face-to-face with Cameron Stone. School heartthrob. My eyes widen in shock, and he gives me a lopsided grin. "Everything okay?" he asks again. Someone shoves him, mimicking him, and I simply nod and rush away. My heart is erratic, my mind abuzz with confusion. Cameron Stone is the person watching me.

For the first time in my life, I was aware of myself not as a person but as a young woman. I purposely went to the library to see if I could see him again. Each time we were in the same place, we watched one another from a distance. Him observing me with a slight smile. Me assessing him with interest and some scepticism. He was one of the popular kids; why would he be interested in me? I couldn't work it out, him out, but it hadn't mattered what I thought because almost a month after I had realised it was him, he approached me.

"Hi, Holly."

"Hi." I dart my gaze everywhere but at him. He was stupidly handsome, especially for someone his age.

"What are you reading?" He plucks the book from my hand and smiles down at me when I gape at him.

"Nothing, I need a new book," I croak. Is this a dare? I frown at him, annoyed that he might play with me. "Why do you keep looking at me?" I ask, shocking myself.

"I could ask you the same thing." He grins.

"If this is some joke you and your mates are playing—" I start, but he shakes his head.

"Not a game. I like you," he says softly, and gone is the cocky attitude. He's looking at me with desire in his eyes.

"Cameron," I stutter, not sure what to say or do, but he doesn't let me fret over it long. Hands cup my face, full lips press to mine and then he is kissing me softly, slowly.

We never looked back. Cameron dragged me from my social darkness and gave me a level of confidence in myself I hadn't known I was missing. Girls couldn't understand his interest in me, boys suddenly took notice of me, but none of it mattered. We were in a bubble. We were in love. We'd been a couple for a year and a half when I caught him in bed with Sarah Daniels.

I'M NOT sure why I let myself get caught up in the past. Cameron is no longer my future, so anything that happened before now it's irrelevant. Telling myself this doesn't stop me from going up to my room and pulling out an old box hidden in the back of my wardrobe. Lifting the lid, I rummage through the contents. Slowly, I pull out a book '*Joinery for Beginners*' and sigh. Cameron had kissed me that day in the library, pulled back with a happy sigh and slid a book free from the shelf.

"Here you go. Doesn't matter what you loan, you won't read it."

"Won't I?"

"No, you'll be thinking of me." He'd been right that whole weekend I had been consumed by the thought of him. This book had gotten stuffed down the back of my bed and forgotten. It was months after my breakup with Cameron that my father arrived in London with my belongings. All our keepsakes had somehow travelled back and I couldn't part with it. It's only now as I stare at the worn pages, I realise Cameron has his own joinery business. Does he remember giving me this? I never read the book, but tonight I take it downstairs with me. I fill up a glass of wine and sit out on the decking, looking at the book index and flicking through to read up about joinery and carpentry. At least I will know what I'm talking about when I contact someone to make the shelves in the dining room. Perhaps whoever does the shelves can fix the decking. There is the odd plank that needs refreshing and new nails banging in. Then I can use the book to throw at Cameron for his constant distaste and aggression towards me.

Chapter Nine
Cameron

I leave Holly's house feeling wound tighter than a damn coil. I crick my neck and sigh loudly. I want to punch something, but I can't. Grace is humming in the back seat, so I grip the wheel tight enough to choke the car itself. The last thing I want to do tonight is knock back a few beers and hang with the guys. Gritting my teeth, I tap the wheel to keep my mind from drifting down a closed path. What I think I want, I can't have. I wish I didn't want her, nor do I want anyone else to have her. Self-disgust reminds me of how I felt after that night. One night, mere minutes, a spec in time, and my life had come crashing down around me. My personality had suffered. I became angry, my life was falling apart and I added to the downfall. I'd annihilated my parents' house in a rage, ripping furniture from the walls, punching holes in any surface. It resembled a dump. One fucking night and I lost everything, my future, Holly and my family. They couldn't wait to get away from me. The residents of Richmond had withdrawn from me, and all I had back then were my friends, the ones who mattered anyway. I still had them, despite the anger they had faced. Their families' anger at sticking by me, my anger at feeling so out of control. That same anger is breathing its way out my chest.

"Why are you not Holly's friend?" Grace suddenly asks.

"I am her friend," I snap, then realise what I have done. "We're friends," I say, softer than before.

"No, you're not." Jeez, what's with her attitude today?

"Grace, some adult things are hard to understand. We can't always explain it to children."

"Holly explains things to me," Grace answers. There is a note of smugness in her young voice I don't much care for.

"Different things. Look, it's not for your ears. Me and Holly are friends," I state tiredly. Fucking hell, I can't be doing with having a kid pulling me up about shit too. I still feel like an ass for upsetting Holly, seeing her hurt. Hearing her ask me to leave her alone made my gut plunge with guilt. I was knowingly being a prick to her. It was the easiest way to define where we stood with one another. The less we get along, the easier it will be for us. The irony is, I can't seem to stay away from her, and I don't want to get close to her either. I'm being choked by a mix of emotions, all too much for me to handle, and Holly was getting the brunt of my anger. With any luck, I have scared her off for good. She's not someone I could ever be friends with. Not after what we shared. I don't care how young we were.

When I reach Dan's, Cole and Brant have already parked up. Brant is leaning on the bonnet and Cole is sitting in the driver's seat. I park beside them and help Grace out as Dan pulls in. "My daddy is here!" Grace jumps down from the car and hops about, waiting for Dan to get out.

"Hey, baby." He scoops her up. "Did you have a great time at riding?"

"Yes, and Uncle Cam shouted at Beau's mummy," she declares loudly.

"Thanks, Grace." I tut when my friends glare at me. "It wasn't like that."

"He did. She was shaking and said she was cold, but it's sunny out," Grace imparts, making me feel like the biggest piece of shit in Richmond. Dan frowns at me, and I give a light shake of my head.

Fuck.

"Okay, well, I will have words with him," Dan tells Grace, who turns and gives me a smirk. She's such a little fucker. Groaning, I hang my head when Cole gives me a pointed stare.

"I need a beer," I mutter in the hope it will distract them all, and we follow Dan in. Grace is going ten to the dozen about riding and how she and Beau are best friends.

"That's great. So you had a good time, then?" Dan asks, handing us all a beer. I twist the cap and guzzle half of it down. This day needs to take a running jump.

"Yup, and we need to be nice to Holly." Grace swings a glare at me. Cole coughs, Brant sniggers, and Dan smirks. "Yup, because I want her to be my mummy," she tells us all proudly. The way she says it sounds as if she has done Dan a favour.

I spray my drink everywhere, coughing and spluttering. I gasp for air and wide hands slap my back. "Fucking hell, not again!" someone says.

"Swear jar, swear jar!" Grace shouts. "You swore!" I watch her through my watery eyes as she stomps over and points a finger at Brant.

Dan and Holly. The visual makes my gut shrivel and my head explode. It was hard enough coming to terms with Holly and the wet fish guy, but Dan and Holly, over my dead body. I finally catch my breath and look right at my friend. I glare at him, and he holds his hands up. "Nothing is happening." He sighs, evidently tired of me throwing yet again another hissy fit.

"It better not be," I growl, not caring how much of a psycho I sound. Holly is mine, they all know it.

Dan walks over to Grace and drops in front of her. "Gracie, I know you want a mummy, and I know Holly is lots of fun, but Daddy doesn't like Holly that way."

Holly is stunning, kind, sweet, gorgeous, fun. Fuck. Fuck. Fuck. "Oh," Grace murmurs, "So she can't be my mummy?"

"Just friends," Dan tells her softly. "You want her to be your friend, don't you?"

Grace nods and gives Dan a hug as she holds on to him. "She could be my mummy and you can be Beau's daddy."

"Beau has a daddy, sweetheart, you can't just—"

"No, she doesn't," Grace whines. "You can be her daddy, please?" she begs, her big eyes making Dan go pale.

"Grace, Beau has a daddy," Dan says more sternly. I silently plead with him to dig further. Where has Grace got this idea from?

"No, she needs one. She was a gift," Grace huffs, wriggling free and running off. I hear the tail end of her crying and Dan stands up, looking baffled.

"I can't even cope with this day anymore," he murmurs, staring ahead like he has been given an unsolvable equation.

"What's all this gift malarky?" Cole says, leaning on the countertop.

"Fuck knows," Brant huffs. "Game's starting soon. Did you get crisps? Kerry is starving me, says I'm putting weight on," he mutters, moving to open a cupboard.

"Yeah, snacks are in there. Cole, grab the dips. I need to put some dinner in for Grace," Dan replies and goes to the freezer.

"You couldn't have pressed a little further?" I mutter, annoyed.

"Why? You're with Nadine, it's none of our business," Dan says, pulling open drawers and grabbing a pizza. He slams the drawer shut and looks with a glint in his eye.

"I'm gonna go check on Grace," I grumble, eager to discover what she meant. Beau doesn't have a father? What the hell does that mean?

"Do not grill my daughter. She's not your informant, Cameron."

Dammit.

"I wasn't going to. I already told her I would watch a bit of her movie with her." I stomp through the kitchen and ignore both Cole and Brant watching me with loose smiles. I snatch up my beer and give them the finger over my shoulder when I hear them laughing at my expense. Grace is sitting in her playroom, watching some pony shit.

"Hey, kiddo."

"Hmm."

"Oh, come on, don't be like that. Your daddy will meet someone soon," I tell her softly, picking her up. I move to the sofa and sit her down with me. "Are you going to watch your film?" I ask.

Shrugging, she toys with her hair, then twists to look at me. "Does Mummy love me?" she voices quietly. I open my mouth, then swallow all the anger I feel whenever her mother is mentioned. A shadow moves to my left, and I see Dan standing in the doorway.

"Your mummy loves you," I tell her emotionally. "She just loves you in a different way than how your daddy does," I say slowly, thinking over the words as I release them. I don't want to hurt her, but I can't lie to her either. "Your mummy is unwell, and she needs to get better. She couldn't love you how you deserved. That's why you live with Daddy."

"So, my mummy will come back?" Grace asks hopefully.

"She might, but she isn't very healthy, Grace," I remind her gently.

"She could get better."

"That's right, but she doesn't want to be better. That's why we all help Daddy out, because we all love you lots."

"Holly can love me too, like Beau does. She's my best friend." She looks at me with that same hope in her eyes.

Swallowing, I chance a look towards Dan standing gutted by the door. "She can love you, but as a friend," I suggest. *That's all you get, kid. The woman is mine.*

"But not as a mummy."

"That's right. You sound like you had a great time at Beau's. What did you do?"

"We had ice cream and played ponies, we built a riding school and we decorated some cakes," Grace blurts quickly, trying to list it all off so she doesn't forget. She gasps, jumps up and nearly head-butts me. "My cakes!" she shouts, panicked. "They're in my bag. I made cakes with Holly." Grace runs off and grabs her dad's hand on the way out. "My cakes, Daddy!" I hear her telling him excitedly about her unicorn cakes.

It took everything in me not to question her about Beau's dad. I'm eager to know what the hell is going on. Now that I think about it, I've not seen the wet fish for a few days. So he isn't her dad, but that doesn't mean he isn't Holly's partner? Nausea ripples through me. I can't bear the thought of him touching her.

"Dude, you coming to watch the game, or is *My Little Pony* too interesting for you?" I snap around to see Cole leaning against the door frame. My little what?

"It worries me you knew what that was." I laugh, walking past him.

"You good?" he asks, clapping a hand on my shoulder. I rub my forehead, muttering about being fine. He frowns at my tired expression. "Cam, I have no idea how you're feeling, but you've come so far to let Holly send you back to that place. I'd hate to see you like that again, man."

"I'm good. Grace is making it seem more than it was." I waft him off and drink the rest of my beer, side-eyeing him. The arsehole even shakes his head disparagingly at me.

"So what was it?" he questions casually. "Holly's home and it bothers you, admit it."

"It was nothing, and I don't care about her. I'm happy," I lie. "This one-to-one has been cute and all but," I mutter, "I want to watch the game."

"Are you sure you're really happy?"

"Of course I'm sure. Have you seen my missus?" I laugh, but it doesn't quite reach my eyes. I turn away and carry on walking down the hall.

"You're going to snap at some point, man, and we'll be here when you do." Cole sighs and follows me into the main living room. Everyone is already seated, and the frown Cole mentioned I have is firmly fixed in place.

"Dude, we could balance a crisp on your forehead." Brant laughs and throws one at me. I knock it away before it hits me.

"Fuck off, we could balance a beer crate on your gut."

"Swear jar!" Grace shouts from behind the sofa, making Cole and I jump.

"Jesus!" Cole laughs. "Grace, hun, I think I have grey hairs now." He laughs.

"You already have grey hairs," she tells him, her shrewd eyes meeting mine. "Jar, Uncle Cam!" She points out the door, and I get up on a sigh. Cole gets up and goes to the mirror, checking his hair.

It's late by the time the game finishes, and both Cole and Brant are happy to watch the highlights. "Cam, can you have Grace overnight on Friday?" Dan asks.

"Yeah, sure, got a date?" I query, opening another beer.

"Sure do." He grins.

Brant and Cole leave shortly after, and I kick my feet up on the sofa. I've drunk too much to drive, so I will probably crash here unless I call Nadine and ask her to pick me up. "So who's the chick?" I ask Dan.

"Rebecca. She works at the coffee house across from the office."

"She is new then?"

"Yeah, seems nice enough."

"To fuck." I tilt my head to look at him. He shrugs and takes a long sip to avoid answering me. Since Melanie, Grace's mother, he has kept women at an arm's length. I don't blame him and, honestly, whoever he settles down with will have me on their case. I love Grace like my own, and her mother doesn't deserve her. "Still keeping it casual?" I ask, standing to pick up the empty bottles everywhere.

"Still pretending you don't want Holly?" He throws in my face.

"Gee thanks, man." Arsehole.

"Cam, what's going on? It's me and you. What happened with Holly today?"

"Nothing," I mutter, taking the bottles out and shoving them in the recycling, when I turn around, Dan is standing with his arms crossed giving me the stink eye. "What are we, married?" I scoff, and he laughs.

"You couldn't handle me." He chuckles.

"I'm gonna be sick."

"Cam, come on, why did you shout at Holly?" He grabs my shoulder, stopping me from passing him.

"She took photos of Grace. I was worried she would put them on social media," I admit quietly.

"Cam, for years, we looked for Holly online. She doesn't have Facebook or anything else."

"Yeah, I know, I panicked. I didn't want Mel knowing you've come back." I sigh and rub the back of my neck. "I lost it." I shake my head, remembering how hurt and embarrassed Holly looked. After Melanie tried to hurt Grace and herself, Dan moved away for a year, but he's been back for a while now, and we're all on edge about Melanie returning.

"Cam, this is Holly, she is always thinking of everyone else. She's that person. The woman disappeared from our lives for years, and now that she's returned home with her family; she isn't here to cause trouble. She's here to settle down."

"Don't say that," I grunt, hating hearing the words. "Anyway, Grace said Beau hasn't got a dad," I remind him.

"Ah, man, don't tell me you asked Grace?"

"No!" I elbow him out of the way.

"Cam, you're tittering on the edge. Holly being home has sent you back." He slaps my chest.

"Why does everyone keep saying that?" I accuse, throwing myself down on the sofa. They need to get off my fucking back.

"Because you flinch when anyone says her name, you're constantly trying to get information on her, and since she returned, you're on edge. Focus on you and Nadine. Holly has a family. You have a good thing going. Don't fuck it up," Dan responds carefully. "I'm going to hit the sack." He sighs. "Spare room is yours."

I'm too wound up to sleep, so I let myself out of Dan's house and go to my car, looking for my gym kit. My feet pound the ground, and my heart begins to pump like a piston. I lap the village and keep going. I run until I'm struggling for air, grabbing my knees and panting loudly. I should have brought a drink with me. Standing to my full height, I put my hands on my waist to dispel the stitch I have. As I drag in a deep breath of air through my nose, I look around. I'm outside Holly's. My heart seizes momentarily, but instead of shirking it away, I let it twist me up. I always felt like that around her. How I hadn't noticed her for all that time in college still baffles me now. I'd caught sight of her going into the library. Her blonde hair shining under the light, gentle eyes and pursed lips. She was hidden behind a stack of books and in her own world, oblivious to the racket going on around her. My feet had moved of their own accord, following her through shelves of books until I could watch her. She was so eager to learn and chewed her lips as she worked with a creaseless frown. My feet had taken me to her, much like now. I'd had no intention of coming here and yet here I am. I slip through the gate and circle the house so I'm in the safety of the back garden. Stopping dead, I find Holly curled up under a blanket with a book and a glass of wine out on the decking. She has headphones in and her lips twist upwards as she reads what's in front of her. I smile. It's nothing like the smiles she has given me since she returned; this is unreserved, full and free.

She shifts, her back going straight as her eyes sweep the garden. Fuck. I stand still knowing I have the coverage of the trees and bushes, but then she moves inside hurriedly. The door slams shut and locks loudly. She knew someone was there. I scared her.

Great, I've become a fucking stalker.

Chapter Ten
Holly

Today is the big day. I'm both nervous and excited. I've been up since five am, fretting that I've missed something. I have showered, dressed and my makeup looks seamless. As I check my reflection for the fourth time, I stroke my summer dress, looking for creases. I pinned my hair up into a large bun, and I'm messing with tendrils when Beau excitedly patters through to me. I'd hung up her school uniform, ready for her first day at big school, only her cardigan is inside out and she has her shoes on the wrong feet. "Big school!" She smiles, flapping her hands because the sleeves are too long.

"Oh, boo." I laugh. "Here, let me help you." I get her straightened up, then give her a big kiss. She looks grown up and yet so small and innocent at the same time. "You're such a big girl."

"I am big." She's proud as punch. "Can I have plaits?" she asks, pushing her hair out of her face.

"Sure, let's brush our teeth, get breakfast and then I'll plait your hair."

"Pancakes?"

"I'm out of eggs, but I did get some of that unicorn cereal you like," I offer, spritzing myself.

"Yay!"

I LEAVE an excited Beau at school. Dan gives me a polite smile as we cross paths on our way out of the classrooms. I catch sight of Cam standing further away as he, too, watches Grace start her first day at school. Both men look emotional, but neither truly shows it. Cam rubs the back of his neck, waving to Grace, and Dan is beaming a mile wide. I'm glad to have the distraction of the shop. School is Beau's world now. She and Grace clutch hands, then they are off.

"Bye, Mummy!" Beau calls through the window, and Cam's head snaps round, searching the playground. I wave brightly, avoiding looking to my right, to where I can feel dark green eyes sending a prickle of awareness down my cheek, along my neck, then across my body.

"Bye, boo!" I call back, my eyes heating with happy tears. I bite my lip so she doesn't see me getting choked up.

"Good luck on your opening today, Holly!" A parent beams. "We'll be in later for a brownie!" One of the parents smiles as she passes, a few others murmuring similar congratulations, and I blush, smiling in thanks at their interest. I had put flyers up around the village over the weekend and dropped them into the shops and summer club during Beau's last session. We even drove into Barton the next town over and posted the flyers to garner as much interest as possible. I also handed a stack into the church to be passed around at Sunday service.

"Thank you, see you later, hopefully," I say to another parent as he tips his head towards me. Tucking a strand of hair behind my ear, I lift my head and find Cameron is staring across the playground at me. We talked about dropping our first child at school together, enjoying their first day, and how we would celebrate with them in the evening. The reality is so far from the dream we spoke about that I feel my chest concave. It detracts from the joy I felt only seconds ago for Beau. I don't want his presence to ruin my happiness. With a deep sigh, I get in my car, and my phone rings. "Hi, Mum," I answer.

"How did she go in?" My mother's cultured voice eases down the line. She is pristine and a self-proclaimed socialite, while my father was a college professor. He was happier surrounded by paper and knowledge. They say opposites attract, and for a while, they did. They had me, and when I was six, they divorced. My mother's world was nothing I wanted so I stayed with my father.

"Great, she gave me a hug, then she was gone." I laugh. "She's made a new friend and they are excited to be at school together."

"How wonderful. I remember your first day," she tells me with a nostalgic lilt in her tone.

"You do?"

"Of course," she mutters. "Marcus loved being with you. He mentioned inviting you both back here?" I blink at her sudden change in topic.

"Oh well, the shop opens today, and I'm going to be so busy. I really need to focus on that and Beau, so maybe in a few weeks."

"He's a good man." Oh god, not this again.

"Mother, Marcus is a friend and nothing more." I recite like I have done the last two times she has brought this up. I thought it was a ploy to keep me in London, but she won't let it go. Ever since I've been back in Richmond, each phone call or text we have shared has alluded to Marcus and I being more than friends.

"Friends develop feelings. He has plenty of time for Beau and lord knows it's hard to find someone willing to take on someone else's child," she protests.

"My feelings are very platonic. I don't want to date, Mother. I really have to go now. I need to get to the shop."

"Very well, good luck. We'll see you soon."

By "we," she means her and Marcus.

"You will. I need to concentrate on the business, then we will visit."

"Just before I go, Marcus mentioned Cameron is still there." I suck in a breath and close my eyes.

"Yes, Dan, Cole and Brant too," I reveal, swallowing dryly.

"And you're okay with that?" She sniffs. She had to single-handedly deal with my misery. I turned up out of the blue, red eyed and heartbroken.

"I'm okay with Beau being happy. I don't want to get into it. It's an adjustment, but I want to learn to laugh in the place that made me cry. It'll take time, but it will happen," I say, sounding more determined. I'm still working through my thoughts and feelings, but having her question me only serves as a reminder of the pain I'm letting go of.

"That's one way to look at it, I suppose." My mother doesn't seem satisfied. She rarely is; she's only happy when she is the one making the choices.

"I really have to go, Mum, thanks for calling," I say breezily.

"Bye, dear."

I don't dwell. I head straight for the shop, and as soon as I pull up in the back, Danielle from the bakery arrives. She has my first order of baked goods. "Morning!" she calls when I get out of my car.

"Hi, Danielle, thanks so much."

"I'm determined to be your first customer." She laughs, opening her boot to reveal several boxes.

"Let me open up and I'll help you bring it in." I smile over my shoulder and almost jog to the door. I'm quick to silence the alarm and dump my bag on the side. Danielle is already bringing the first load, so I head to her car to get the next lot. It's heavier than expected. "Christ, Danielle, when you said rocks cakes, I didn't think you actually put rocks in it!" I pant, struggling to the door as she comes out laughing.

"Baker's arms." She grins, giving me a little flex.

I get a waft and smile. "Oh, wow, that smells amazing." Licking my lips, I pick up the cloth on another tray and see a fluffy blueberry muffin. "Just sampling if they're good enough," I wink, knowing full well Danielle would offer nothing less than perfect.

A light tap at the door brings both our heads around. Emily is waving through the door at us, so I rush over and unlock the door. "Morning!"

"Starting without me?" Emily asks, smiling at Danielle. "Hi, I'm Emily."

"Danielle, you're new in Richmond, right?"

Emily nods. "Yes, oh, what's that smell?" she says, looking around.

"That would be Danielle's baked goods," I tell her, as Danielle lifts the cloth and reveals a tray of muffins, brownies and cakes.

"Have one," Danielle says. "I baked a few extra," she reassures.

"Thanks, I didn't have breakfast."

By the time Keeley arrives, Danielle has gone and Emily and I are stocking the counter with muffins, cake, biscuits and other calorific goods. The place smells amazing, a perfect combination of books, coffee and cake. All my favourite things. I stand back and allow myself a moment to take it all in. This is mine, I did this. Pride fills me. Gripping the side, I allow the emotion in.

"There're a few people headed this way." Emily nods out

across the green. She's right, and what's more is a line is forming to get in. I throw an amazed smile at both girls and check my watch.

My day goes by in a chaotic happy rush, the place so busy that I worry about leaving to go and collect Beau. I even gave up my lunch, eating it in the car on my way to get Beau from school. From the moment we opened, we have had a steady stream of customers, some opting to eat in and others choosing takeout. The weather is good enough that the tables and chairs outside and being used. My book sales have been fantastic, but I try to keep a rational head on me. It's a novelty and things will ease off into a steady turnover. I leave Emily and Keeley to handle the shop, as it's quieter with people needing to collect their children from school, but I can imagine we will fill up as quick when they head back this way. Stuffing the last of my sandwich in my mouth, I sip my now cold coffee and make my way down into the school grounds to wait for Beau. It's only as I'm walking down I realise I still have my apron on. I untie it, fold it up and pop it in my handbag. I recognise a few parents from being in the shop earlier. The door opens and Beau comes pelting at me, her plait hanging together by mere threads, big bags are under her eyes and her cardigan is buttoned up wrong. I bite my lip to stop from laughing and drop down to catch her when she throws herself at me.

"I had the best day!" She grins. "I had cake, and we had stories. I told my teacher, Miss Badger, that you love stories too!"

"I do," I say, smoothing her hair. "I missed you," I admit with a soft smile.

She hugs me tight and squeezes. "I missed you this much!" She strains, making me laugh.

"Wow, you missed me a lot." I peck her head and lower her onto her feet. "Shall we get back to the shop? I saved you a brownie."

"Yay!" Beau takes my hand, and we head back to the car and straight back to work. I'm glad it's only a short journey, else I think she would have fallen asleep. As soon as we get in, I see people heading our way.

"Beau, it will get a bit busy, so you need to be super good for Mummy and stay in the office. Do you want a milkshake with your brownie?"

"Yes." She pulls out a chair in the back office, climbing on with her book bag. She rummages through and takes out her book. "This is my new book. I read the words." I doubt she will always be this compliant and sitting in the back will lose its charm after a few days.

"That's so great, Beau, you're so clever. Let me go get your brownie, okay?"

"And my milkshake?"

"And your milkshake." I laugh, leaving her with her head bent over her book. I serve a few customers, so Emily takes the brownie to my girl.

"She's fine."

"Thanks." We all work in tandem, serving, cleaning down tables, taking orders from the customers and keeping the countertop stocked. Most of Danielle's stock has dwindled. I regret not ordering more, so when I see her enter through the back door with another tray, I want to cry. "Are you a mind reader?" I laugh.

"I could see how many people were coming in and out and thought I would check if you needed more stock. Figured you would."

"Yes please, can I add this to my next invoice?" I ask.

"Sure, whatever you don't sell, just refrigerate and get it sold tomorrow. I've got to head off. I've left Carol, and we had a big birthday order for today." I take a minute to check in on Beau and find her doing the hopscotch in the small office. I lean against the frame as Danielle pokes her head back in. "Place looks great. Congrats, Holly!"

"Thank you." Danielle was a few years below me in school. I'm sure she remembers me, but neither of us talk about it. When I approached her about the possibility of stocking Beau's Books & Bakes, she was hesitant at first, worrying she would lose customers, but after negotiating a few things and ensuring her that people were more likely to buy a cake, she slowly relented.

Beau looks up and sees me. "Watch me, Mummy!"

"I am. I used to play that at school too. Maybe we can make one at home on the driveway," I tell her excitedly. She reciprocates with an open-mouthed smile. God, she is adorable. I collect her up and check for empty tables, then place her on one. "Stay in your seat, okay?" I instruct. She pouts and begins to grumble. I pick up the crayons and roll them onto the tabletop for her, and she trudges to climb up.

"I'm tired."

"I know, boo, we're nearly done."

Huffing, she frowns at the crayons. "I don't want to!"

"I know, sweetie," I soothe, but it only brings on her tears.

Emily rushes over with half of a biscuit, and Beau grins and picks it up, her other hand reaching for a crayon.

"Good girl." I beam, wiping her cheeks and smirking at Emily as we get back to work. The rest of my shift goes quickly. Every now and then I have to attend to Beau, but for the most part, she is enjoying being in a new environment and getting attention from all the customers.

As soon as the last customer leaves, I place any leftover cakes in the fridge and wipe the tables down and Emily appears with the vacuum cleaner. "I figured if I hoover and Keeley mops, we'll all be out of here sooner rather than leaving you to do it."

"Oh, Em, thank you, and you Keeley, yes please. Beau looks

ready to drop." I wince. Whilst Emily begins to vacuum, Keeley helps Beau pack her book bag up and moves her to the back office again. We're done quickly and Beau is eager to get home. When we pull up, I see a bouquet on the doorstep. Beau trudges to the door, and I want to laugh because she looks like she escaped an apocalyptic event. "Dinner, bath and bed," I say, picking up the flowers and sniffing them. The fact that she doesn't argue with me tells me she is running on empty fumes. I check the flowers for a card but can't see anything, so I find a vase and fill it with water to pop them in. I prepped a pasta bake this morning, so I cook it and we sit at the dining table. Seeing her so worn out, I'm not sure how she will cope with horse riding on Wednesday. School seems to have knocked her sideways.

With an evening completely to myself, I get on top of a few jobs before I sort the dishes and arrange the white roses. I double check out the front for a card, but there is nothing. I'm assuming Marcus sent them, so I send a quick text asking about his day and telling him how well Beau and the shop did. I wait for Marcus's response with a glass of wine. Firing up Spotify, I play my chilled acoustics playlist, then I remember I have a stash of Jaffa cakes in the cupboard, so I grab a box and pig out on them whilst sipping on my wine. Today has been a good day. It can only improve from here.

I get out and pull on my bath towel, making my way downstairs, where there's a small white envelope on the doormat I'd expect to see attached to my flowers. Frowning, I peer out of the window, but it's too dark and I can't see anyone. I slip the small card out, which has a single white rose on it. Turning it over, I read the note.

CONGRATULATIONS ON YOUR OPENING. *C x*

. . .

THE INITIAL CAN ONLY BE one person.

Cameron.

I have no idea why he would send me flowers. It's obvious he hates that I have returned to Richmond. I place it on the side and forget about Cameron Stone.

Chapter Eleven
Holly

"That's £6.68." I smile at Mrs Ludlow, who's a regular now.

"Thank you, dear." I hand over her coffee and cake.

The morning so far has been steady but quiet, both Emily and Keeley taking their first break so it's just me manning the shop. The bell goes, and I turn, smiling to find Cameron's wife eyeing me. Her friend is smirking, and they both laugh. Call it a woman's intuition, but everything about their mood is off. Until now, I haven't had to deal with either Cameron or his wife coming in, which only confirmed my suspicions that she has an issue with me.

I hold my smile and turn away when someone comes up to the counter ordering a refill. "I'll just be a second," I inform, taking their cup for a fresh one and moving to the machine. My eyes flit to the wall clock, but both girls aren't due back for another five minutes. Great! I hand the refill over and brace for impact.

"Chai Latte, regular," Cameron's wife says, coming up to the counter.

"Hi." I smile purposely, highlighting that she left her manners outside my shop. "Will that be all?"

My over friendly demeanour catches her off guard. "Just the latte."

"Sure thing." Turning away, I begin making her order.

"Did Cam say where he was taking you to dinner?" the other girl asks.

His wife gives a self-indulgent laugh. "No, he always treats me like that," she muses. "The other night, he gave me the best surprise ever." Her voice drops, but I can hear her loud and clear. They are doing this on purpose, oversharing to make me uncomfortable.

"With what, jewellery, flowers?" her friend asks excitedly.

His wife's voice trails off as the machine hisses, but I hear the tail end and wish I hadn't. "Up against the front door, he was like a madman," she breathes.

Biting the inside of my cheek, I turn with her drink in my hand. "Here you go." I smile brightly. "That's £4.45, please." I hold her cold smile with a kind but false one of my own. She pays by card and soon her friend is taking her place. "Hi, what can I get you?"

"Same."

"That will be £4.45 then, please."

Cameron's wife's friend pays, and I make quick work of her drink. No sooner have I placed it down, she snatches it off the side and walks away without thanking me. Urgh, immature bitch! They take a seat not too far from the counter and continue to talk about Cameron. Oh, for the love of god.

Emily and Keeley come back soon after, and Emily widens her eyes when she clocks them. I give a subtle shake of my head and try my utmost to ignore their antics. "Want me to pour coffee over them?" Emily whispers, making me giggle.

"God, don't tempt me."

"She feels threatened by you," she says under her breath.

I shake my head in answer. I'd never steal someone's man or try to make someone feel uncomfortable.

Sighing, Emily moves close by and whispers, "Honestly, Holly, if I was with a man, no matter who, and you showed up, I'd become insecure," she tells me.

"What?"

"Come on, Holly, you're like the complete package; Hugh Heffner would snap you up in a second." She chuckles, grabbing a brownie and sticking some change in the till. "Sorry ass."

Snorting, I lean against the coffee machine, avoiding looking at the women haggling for my attention. "Hugh, no thanks." I gag. "And hey, are you saying I look fake?" I pout.

"Not at all, that's why he'd go ga-ga for you. You're naturally stunning. Your body is smoking, and you have this whole innocent vibe which I think sends men loopy," Emily tells me, picking at her brownie with more decorum. "Your tits are real, aren't they?"

"Yes!" I splutter.

"Lucky bitch." Her shoulders droop, and she shoves another chunk of brownie into her mouth. "Oh god, incoming." She draws my head round to the counter where Cameron's wife is standing impatiently.

"Sorry," I apologise. "Another latte?" I ask, reaching for a clean cup.

"Actually, no, this one tastes off."

Emily groans, and I try my hardest not to laugh. This woman has got it in for me. Keeley glances up from re-stacking the shelves and frowns.

"Oh, I am sorry, let me get you a refill," I offer.

"Check it first. I don't want another shit latte." She smiles sweetly. I turn to find Emily glaring at the woman.

Emily tugs the mostly finished cup out of my hand and sniffs it. "Oh, you're right," she says. "It smells like..." She contemplates her words, then looks into the cup. "That's it. It smells like insecurity."

"Emily!" I gasp, turning to look back at Cam's wife, but she is on the phone.

"Relax, she didn't hear. I wish she had, the stuck-up cow." I smother a laugh and make a fresh latte, taking it to the table. She's still on a call and when she sees me, she smiles.

"Okay, baby, can't wait to see you later."

"Here you go. Sorry about that. Is yours okay?" I twist to her friend still drinking hers happily. Jeez, they could at least fake it together. She flushes and nods, drawing a sigh from Cam's wife. "How bizarre. Enjoy."

"Tweedledee and Tweedledum happy now?" Emily mutters, pulling a snort of laughter from me.

"They got a latte time on their hands," I deadpan, and Emily barks out a laugh. Outside on the green, residents begin setting up for the outdoor theatre, taking place this weekend. "I can't wait for tomorrow. I've never seen The Greatest Showman," I confess, popping my cloth in the wash basket and getting a clean one out as Keeley slips behind the counter.

"Oh, I love it!" Keeley says, "I love musicals."

"I've not seen it either. Who are you going with?" Em asks her.

"I have a date!" she squeaks.

"Wow, what a fab first date." I smile. She looks so happy, nervous but happy.

"What would your perfect first date be?" Keeley asks me wistfully. Emily leans her elbow on the counter and grins at me.

I tap my teeth and hum. "Best first date," I murmur, thinking. "Prosecco picnic, meadow, bit of music and lots of stars." I list them off on my finger, mentally fighting with picturing it with anyone but Cameron.

"Lame," someone mutters. Emily glares over my shoulder, and I know it's the Cam brigade.

"What about you?" I ask Emily, refusing to react to Cameron's wife.

"Well, if you hadn't already noticed from my fat arse, I like food." She laughs. "I'd want to go to a swanky restaurant and then a late-night walk after or some other kind of exercise." She winks with a grin. She means sex.

"Your ass is not fat. I'd die for your curves." I admit. "Favourite food?"

"At the minute, brownies. Damn you, Danielle!" she fake cries. "But it's probably Italian."

"We should all go for a meal," I suggest to the girls. They agree, and with that settled, we get back to work.

***

"Come on, Beau, our seats are up here." I point ahead, showing her where we are going. The village green has been transformed into a big open theatre, an enormous white screen is positioned against the far side and in front of it, rows and rows of coloured deck chairs fill the crisp grass. Much like a cinema, the rows are lettered and the chairs are numbered. Beau takes my hand, and we all make our way over. "Here we go, Em, we'll sit on the end, in case Beau needs to use the toilet."

"Okay, here, pass that cool box and I'll pour our drinks."

I heave it up and hand it to her before turning back to help Beau into her deck chair. It swallows her whole and her pigtails go askew. "Ahh, Mummy, help!" She giggles, grappling to get up, but she can't. I laugh loudly and Emily looks over, bursting into laughter.

"Oh, boo!" I try to help her sit upright. Her eyes are big and wide. I can't stop myself. I pull out my phone and take a photo of her. "Right, sorry, Mummy will help."

"I'm stuck!" she grunts, trying to shift, but she's all arms and legs and nothing else.

"Please stop moving," I say.

"Mummy!" Beau whines.

"Holly?" a male voice says, pulling all our heads round to find a tall and angular man looking down at me. "Holly Matthews?"

"Yes?"

I look at Emily quizzically, but she gives her head a slight shake.

"It's me. Jeremey Laughton."

My eyes pop wide.

"Jeremy, wow, I didn't recognise you!" I apologise, stand and give him a hug. "How are you?" I smile. The last time I saw Jeremy was on that night. He was my ride from hurt to help. Unlike the others who had laughed at me and mocked my pain when I caught Cameron with Sarah, he'd taken pity. He'd followed me out of the house where the party was held and offered to drive me home. When I asked him to take me to my mother, who lived in London and not my father's house, he had done so without complaint. I'd begged him not to tell anyone where I was, and I believe to this day he had stuck to his word. My cheeks flush with the awkwardness of our meeting now. I was a sobbing, scrawny teen then.

"I'm great, thank you. Are you visiting your father?" he asks, looking down and seeing Beau for the first time. He smiles brightly and drops down to be at her level. "Hello, what's your name?"

"Beau, and I'm stuck." Her arms and legs are wedged uncomfortably over the chair seat.

I laugh and quickly lean down and help her upright.

"Hello, Beau and I'm stuck, I'm Jeremey." His eyes twinkle, and he holds his hand out to her.

"No, silly!" She giggles. "I was stuck in the chair."

"I know, I was just messing. Guess what?"

"What?" Beau wriggles back, placing herself deep in the chair.

"I used to go to school with your mummy."

"Like I go to school with Grace?" Beau asks him. He frowns, and I mouth, "*Dan's daughter.*"

"Yes, exactly like that! Are you excited for the show?"

"We have lots of sweets and Mummy has lots of wine," Beau states, pointing to Emily pouring us glasses.

"I'm not an alcoholic, I swear."

"I am on Fridays and Saturdays." He laughs heartily. "So how's your dad?"

"Oh." I look down at Beau, who is already glued to the big screen playing a music video. "He passed away recently. We moved back."

"Holly, I'm so sorry." He rubs my arm and sighs. "It's hard. My mother passed away two years ago." He gives me a sad smile.

"Sorry to hear that," I reply, checking again that Beau isn't looking. "Beau, strangely, has adapted well."

"Mummy, it's going to start!" Beau calls, dragging us from our conversation.

"I'm in Barton now. I'd love to catch up," Jeremy says.

"Yes, that would be great. I've just opened the shop over there." I point to *Beau's Books & Bakes*. "Drop by and we can sort something out."

"Great, I'll see you th—"

"Jeremy," Cameron's dark voice snaps. I blink in shock and find him bristling behind Jeremy, who on inspection is a few inches taller than Cameron, however his height doesn't seem to factor because Cameron's frame is wider, and he carries himself in a way that suggests he is bigger than the other man. A confidence about him highlights him as *more* than a simple man, more than Marcus or Jeremy. Both seem very ordinary compared to Cameron Stone.

"Hello, Cameron." He sighs wearily.

"What brings you back to Richmond?"

Jeremy stares down his nose at him, yet I feel like Cameron is looking down on him. "Holly, I'll catch up with you soon." He leans to give me a hug.

"Sure." I kiss his cheek and Cameron's eyes bug. Jeremy walks away, and I turn back to Cameron. "Do you always have to be so rude?" I spit.

"To him, always," he grunts and drops to Beau. "Hey, squirt." He grins, ruffling her hair. "I like your glittery shoes!"

She giggles and takes his hand, pointing to the screen. "It's coming on, look, Unky Cam!" It's my turn to bug my eyes now. Unky Cam. Hell no!

"Beau, sweetie, he's not your uncle," I say quietly and move to take my seat. Emily passes my prosecco, and Cam stares right at me, Beau's little hand in his larger one.

"How was your first day at big school?" Cameron asks.

Beau wipes at her hair, and Cameron tucks it away, his other hand looking far too big in her tiny lap. "My teacher likes to read!" she replies. "I played with Grace."

"She showed me the picture she painted." Cameron's eyes flick between my little girl's and mine, as I sit ramrod straight in my deck chair.

"And I painted too," Beaus chirps.

"Wow. I'd love to see it!"

"Oh god, in coming," Emily whines quietly. I look up to see his wife storming over.

"Please leave before your wife gives me more attitude." I use my glass to indicate she is coming. He doesn't even flinch.

"Enjoy the film, Beau." He removes his hand and slowly stands, holding my gaze. "Nadine's not my wife." He sighs before turning and walking the short distance to where she is.

He takes her hand and steers her away. I watch them go for a minute, then look to find Jeremy. I see the back of his head over the top of a seat a few chairs in front. It's ridiculously self-absorbed of me to think I'm the cause of his and Cameron's fall-out, but I wonder if that's why they share a common distaste for one another.

"Well, that was something," Emily comments, sipping her glass.

"What was?"

"He wants you."

"What?"

"Don't 'what' me." She laughs. "Cameron isn't over you, Holly." I gawp at her. *Cameron!*

"Give up. Cameron can't stand me and—"

"Because he can't have you."

"He's in a relationship," I whisper. "It's old news. I'm old news. You're reading into it all wrong," I tell her and grab the prosecco and fill my own glass up.

"Okay." She smirks.

"You are," I protest.

"Uh huh. Oh, look at the film starting. No more talking," she tells me, and Beau shushes me when I open my mouth to argue more. I roll my eyes and drop back in my chair, annoyed.

We don't speak any more of Cameron. Halfway through the film, Beau scrambles into my lap, and I wrap us up in my blanket. "Can I have a cake?" she asks me tiredly. I nod and hand her a fairy cake. When I look around, I find Cameron watching me briefly.

I stare at the big screen, not seeing the movie.

"I'm going to whip home to the loo." Emily grimaces. "I don't want to break the seal, but I'm desperate." Her legs are crossed tight, and she shifts uncomfortably.

Laughing, I find my shop keys. "Go in the shop, it's nearer," I offer and hand the keys over.

"Thanks!" she winces and scuttles off quickly. The film is ending, and Emily isn't yet back, so I start packing her things away when I see her walking across the green with Grace in her arms. The little girl is snuggled into her chest and Emily is smiling happily.

I lift her handbag, showing her that I'm putting her things away when Dan charges over and rips Grace from her arms. "Get the fuck off of her!" he bellows, shoving Emily hard. She stumbles and trips over a tree root, screaming out in pain. Oh my god!

"Mummy!" Beau cries at Dan's loud boom. Swinging her up in my arms, I run over.

"What on earth, Dan!" I snap, rushing to Emily whimpering on the floor, tears pooling in her eyes.

"I thought..." Dan stammers. "I didn't know." He looks around, dragging a hand through his hair as he holds Grace tightly to his chest.

Cam runs over. "Dan, it's okay."

"What do you mean, '*Dan, it's okay.*' It is not!" I shout. "He pushed her over!" I lower Beau and give Emily a hug, who's crying.

"I was just taking her back to them." She stumbles over the words, shaking.

"You did nothing wrong," I say and glare at both men watching close by. "What the hell is wrong with you? She was bringing Grace to you!"

"I'm sorry. I didn't know it was you." Dan clears his throat. Grace and Beau are tearful, and I can't even rationalise what happened. Jeremy appears and Cam snorts in distaste.

"Oh, shut up!" I snap at him, and his eyes widen. "You two have fucking anger problems!" I growl.

"Swear jar," Grace whispers softly.

"Sorry," I mutter and scoop Beau back up.

"My car is just up the road. Go get your things and we can get her to the hospital," Jeremy suggests.

"I don't think it is that bad." Cameron tries to placate us all. Nadine steps up, curling her hand around his arm.

"You probably just twisted it," she offers and pecks Cam's cheek.

"I didn't twist anything. I was pushed!" Emily snaps. "Jeremy, hospital would be good."

"Emily, I'm sorry I thought... I didn't mean to hurt you," Dan admits, rubbing Grace's back protectively.

"Well, you did," I huff. "Em, I'm going to get our things. Are you okay?" She nods, but tears are running down her cheeks.

"Drama queen," Nadine mutters, and we all snap to her. Her cheeks redden and Dan tells her to be quiet. I'm ready to slap this woman.

"We've got it, thanks," I grind out as Dan leans to help, and I glare hotly at Cam. I wait for them all to step away and sag when they begin to make their way back to their own seats.

"I won't be a sec. Beau, sit here with Emily. Give her a big hug for me." I smile at my friend and rush back to our seats, shoving everything into any bag. Jeremy is already helping her up when I get back. "Beau, carry this, please." I hand her a blanket and quickly make my way over to Jeremy's car.

"It's open," he calls from behind me. I flip the boot and shove everything in before I help Beau, then Emily in.

Once we are all seated, Emily looks over her shoulder at me. "What the hell just happened?" she whispers tearfully.

Chapter Twelve
Cameron

"I'm going to the hospital," Dan announces, grabbing Grace's belongings up off of the grass. His daughter is gripping around his neck for dear life. She's as spooked by his meltdown as half of Richmond. Hell, I'm shaking. If Mel got her hands on Grace, we'd never see her again, and god knows what kind of life she would be subjected to. Mel had been a one-night stand and Dan had tried to do the right thing. Their relationship progressed due to the pregnancy, but over the course, Dan had become concerned about Mel and her drinking. She would disappear for days on end and show up still drunk. He'd tracked her parents down and discovered that Mel had a history of substance abuse and mental health problems. When he tried to break things off after she had left Grace unattended all day, she tried to drive her car in the lake, with Grace inside.

So whilst everyone is eyeballing Dan, he and I are suffering with the same rush of fear at losing Grace to her psycho mother. He mentioned that Emily was similar in build and stature to Mel, and it was weird for him. It was for me too when he brought it to my attention, and I can imagine in the dark it would be hard to differentiate both women.

"She will be fine." Nadine rolls her eyes and Dan gives me a pointed look. Great. Tension is running thick, and by the look of my best mate's veins, he's ready to burst a vessel.

"Nadine, cut it out," I murmur and rub her back to soften the blow.

"What?" she snaps round, affronted. "She will be fine, though," she affirms, looking at us both. "Even if she has broken it, it will heal, and she *will* be fine."

"Broken? You think I broke it?" Dan swings to her. "Cam, I thought…" He goes ashen. He drops a couple of bits, then stumbles to pick them back up.

"I know, it's okay. Here, let me take Grace." I pull her, but she clings to her dad and screams. "Or not." I hold my hands up.

"Can you help me?" Dan asks, trying to shove a blanket in a bag. "I can't even think straight." He chokes, gripping onto Grace tightly.

"Sure, do you want me to come with you?" I ask, taking Grace's things off him and loading it in the bag. My gut aches for him. I don't want Emily to be hurt, but it's far better than the alternative.

"You've got to be fucking kidding me." Nadine laughs bitterly.

"Back off, Nadine!" Dan snaps. "And quit swearing in front of Grace." He storms past her. "Grow up. Not everything is about you."

"I don't care that she's there!" she calls after him defensively.

He swings around and laughs. "So why mention her then?" He shakes his head, and I hook his bag over my shoulder.

"He's hardly going to bed her in the waiting room," Dan spits and Nadine snaps back, hurt, and I groan.

"What have you said to him?" she questions, her eyes narrowed. Jesus Christ. This is supposed to be about Emily and Grace, making sure they are okay. How is it about her again?

"Nothing. Our relationship isn't anyone's business. All evening, you were making digs, babe. It wasn't fun," I admit softly.

"But you went over to them." She frowns, still hurt I'm acknowledging Holly and Beau.

"I went over to Beau," I repeat. "She hasn't done anything wrong."

Biting her lip, she looks to where Dan is retreating over the green. "You're going to the hospital, aren't you?" she mutters.

I sigh. "Yes, even if it's to calm Grace and bring her home."

"She's not your kid." Her mouth twists in annoyance and my face shutters. Did she just go there? I feel myself starting to lose my patience with her. Where the hell has this side of her come from?

When she lifts her miserable face to mine, she blinks in shock at the level of anger I'm holding back. "Cam." She sighs, taking my hand.

I pull my hand away. "You're right, she's not, but she is my goddaughter, and they are my family. Remember that," I snap and walk off. Fucking hell.

Dan is putting Grace in her seat when I reach his car. "Sorry, I shouldn't have said that to her." He rubs his hand down his face.

"It's fine. Here." I dump the bag in the back and wink at Grace, who is looking confused and upset.

"Are you okay, monkey?" I ask, ruffling her hair.

"I hurt Emily," she wails, her sharp voice ringing through our eardrums.

"No, baby girl, Daddy did, but we're going to go check on her, okay?" He strokes her hair and gives her a kiss. Murmuring words, he holds her whilst she sniffles all over his shirt.

"And Cam?" Grace sniffles.

"I could do with the backup." Dan sighs, knowing full well not only will my presence not be received, but it will cause an issue with Nadine too.

"Sure."

WE ARRIVE at the hospital and make our way up to A&E, but I can't see Emily or Holly anywhere. "Where are they?" Dan asks. He hoists Grace up and she grips his neck.

"Beau!" Grace calls, sounding herself for the first time in a while. We move past a family as Holly comes out of the toilet with her daughter. Beau giggles and runs over, but Holly is glaring at us both.

"I don't think I've ever seen Holly so angry," Dan comments.

"I have." I sigh wearily, and he laughs lightly.

Beau is already running over, and she tugs at Grace's foot. "Come down."

Grace shakes her head, and Beau frowns, clearly confused. Her gaze moves and she lifts her arms up for me to pick her up. I don't even look at Holly as I scoop Beau up and she smiles at me. "Hi."

"Hey, squirt." Her hands are clutching my collar, and my heart beats unnaturally.

She could have been mine.

She was supposed to be mine.

When we began dating all those years ago, there was never any doubt in my mind that I wouldn't marry Holly and have a family with her. With a shuddering breath, I look to Holly, who is ready to explode. Does she wonder what our life could have been like if Sarah Daniels had never happened? Does she hear an old song and think of the nights we hung out together, or our first kiss, our first night together?

I can see how vulnerable Holly feels with me holding her

daughter and it reminds me of that night, how vulnerable and beautiful she was.

"She's in triage," she says and holds her arms out for Beau.

"No," Beau whines. "I want to be next to Grace." She takes her friend's little hand.

"It's fine," I assure Holly, but the withering glare she gives me tells me it is not fine that I am holding her daughter. "I could hardly say no."

"Where's Jeremy?" Dan asks, looking around. I'm hoping the stuck-up twat has gone.

"He is with Emily," Holly says flippantly.

"Holly, it really was an accident, I can't go into details because, well"—he points to Grace—"ears. I thought she was someone else, someone not trustworthy. I was genuinely concerned."

Holly frowns and chews her lip. "She can't put any weight on it," she says and looks back across the room. "We're sitting over here." I follow her, and Beau giggles when I jiggle her about.

"Did you like the film?" I ask her softly.

"I like the moosick," she tells me, and I laugh. This kid is adorable.

"Yeah, I liked the moosick too." I sit her down with me. Holly is watching me like a hawk. Her eyes are tight, her face drawn. She isn't happy about me holding Beau. "Do you want to get down?" I offer, but she shakes her head.

"Grace is sad."

"A little, but she is happy you are here."

"Her daddy shouted," she whispers, her hands grasping my collar. I smile at her beautiful little face, and for a minute allow myself to believe the impossible. That she is mine. Our daughter. I look over to Holly, but she snaps her head away.

Dan finally takes a seat next to me, and Grace smiles at Beau. "You okay?" I ask her, and she nods, holding on to her dad. "Do you want to come home with me?" I ask, but she shakes her little head and turns, shoving her nose into Dan's neck once more.

"Why did he shout?" Beau asks me, cupping my face and pulling it round to her. Her hair is a mess, and she has frosting in the corner of her mouth.

"He got scared. Sometimes, when we get scared, we shout," I offer quietly.

"Like you shout at Mummy?" Beau frowns. Guilt plagues me.

"I didn't mean to do that, I'm sorry," I whisper and sigh deeply when Beau yawns into my neck.

"It smells funny," Beau says loudly, and a few people look around. Holly goes red and groans into her hand, making Dan and I chuckle. The hospital is clean and shiny, the A&E department was recently done up and has new chairs and equipment. The place smells naturally of a hospital.

"That's because they need the place to be super clean because sick people come here."

"And babies are borned!" Beau chimes in. Opportunity flashes before my eyes. I glance at Holly, but she's looking over her shoulder for Emily.

"Yes, that's right, your mummy and daddy will have been in the hospital with you," I say gruffly, rubbing her back when she snuggles into my body. My chest aches and I know it's because I love this little girl already, just how I love Grace. She's sweet and innocent and bloody adorable. No matter the distance between Holly and I, there is no shortage of love for Beau. I realise I want to be in this child's life.

"I don't have a daddy; I was a special gift." What is it with this gift thing? I frown and find Holly watching me closely. I've lost my window to delve deeper. Fuck! I give her a small smile, and she scoffs.

She stands and moves over to take Beau from me. "Beau,

come here." She holds her hands out, and Beau moves into her mum's arms.

"I'm a gift." Beau smiles at me. "From the dough hur."

Holly glares at me with venom in her eyes.

"What have you been asking her?" she demands.

"Nothing, she said babies are born here, and I said that her mummy and daddy will have had her in the hospital," I mumble.

"Jesus, Cam," Dan huffs, nearly giving me away. I eye him, silently telling him to shut the fuck up.

"What the hell is a dough hur?" I say, annoyed that she is pissed off with me.

"Donor," Dan says quietly, apparently far more in tune with child talk than me. My eyes bulge. She used a fucking donor!

"Is that true?" I demand loudly. All these fucking years, I thought of nothing else but her and the life we could have, the children. And she uses a donor.

Dan groans, and Holly laughs scathingly. "It's none of your business," she spits and grabs her bags up. Beau looks befuddled. *Me too, kid!*

She grabs her mum's face. "You was ready to love again." Beau nods, and Holly hugs her close, kissing her hair.

"I don't understand," I stammer.

Holly hooks her bag over her shoulder, her hands shaking.

"Excuse us." She moves away quickly and finds a chair away from us.

"What the hell!" I look at Dan.

My friend eyes me hopelessly.

"Can you believe she used a *fucking* donor?"

"Yes," Dan says shortly.

What? He can? This is bullshit. "Seriously?" I scoff, outraged by Holly's decisions and my so-called mate's understanding.

"Yes, Cam, she's all or nothing."

"I know that."

"But a donor, I don't get it." I'm confused, angry. Hurt. Can I be hurt? Yes, I'm fucking hurt that my chance to give Holly everything she ever wanted was handed over to her by an unknown. Beau is incredible and no one would ever wish to change her for the world, but how could Holly give her a life without a father.

"How is it I'm more in tune with your ex than you?" Dan mutters, looking around for Emily, but she hasn't returned.

"Go deep throat yourself," I grunt.

"Beau said she was ready to love again," Dan reminds me. "Holly is all or nothing. She gave it all to you. So she isn't ever going to give it to another man again, not after she thought you did wrong by her. She gave it all to her daughter," he explains in a tone that suggests I'm stupid. "That's one fifty for the therapy session."

My eyes widen with realisation. Was she ever with anyone else after me? What if she never was able to move on and meet anyone at all? That's bullshit, that dweeb Marcus is always lingering about. The guy is like a stale fart. Holly is now at the main desk and looks concerned.

"I'll go find out." I stand, but Dan grabs my arm.

"Leave her alone, Cam."

She begins collecting all her things up again, struggling with Beau and the bags. Ignoring Dan, I walk over and pick her bag up.

"What are you doing?" she snaps.

"Helping. Give me the bags." I yank them from her and smirk when she glares at me. Holly always relents. She was always easy to break down. It used to be our thing. She'd be stubborn, I'd wear her down and then I'd fuck her slowly to thank her for giving in to me. Beau said she had her because she was ready to love again. I do the calculations quickly. Beau is five. Knowing what I know about Holly, she wouldn't have dated in the time before Beau if she wasn't ready and if she chose love with a child, then she never met anyone else. I was her last. I was also her first. Fuck. Marcus is a friend. But he wants more; he's in this for the long game. Stupidity tells me I have a chance again.

"Emily has gone for an X-ray, suspected break."

"Ah, hell, Dan is going to feel shit."

"Well, good," she huffs and begins walking down towards the doors. I see a group of guys in their early twenties eyeing her up and I want to run over and beat the shit out of them with Beau's bag. I step in their way and one of them sniggers.

"Dan," I call, and he gets up quickly, Grace now fast asleep in his arms.

"What's going on?" he asks.

I don't want him feeling bad so I answer before Holly. "She's gone for an X-ray just to cover all possibilities," I say quickly, and Holly frowns, her mouth opening to correct me.

"Shush, gorgeous," I say naturally, and she snaps her mouth closed, her cheeks crimson.

"Shit." He sighs. "I feel sick. I'd never hurt a woman. I can't believe I pushed her."

"You thought it was Mel. I get why you reacted the way you did, but Grace is safe," I reassure him. He nods, unconvinced.

"She could press charges, Cam. Even if I explain that I thought Grace's safety was at risk, she can still press charges."

"She won't," Holly says quietly, looking to Grace in worry. "You really thought she was in danger?"

"Her mum isn't stable," Dan admits. "I have full custody, and she's tried before. To hurt her. Holly, I swear it was a genuine mistake."

"Why don't you wait here, and I will go check on Emily?" she suggests.

"Why is Jeremy with her?" I ask suddenly.

"Beau needed the loo, and she got called in. They only just

met. I can imagine it's a bit awkward in there," Holly says, distracted. She pulls at her bags, but I step out of her reach. I'm keeping these damn things so she has to come and get them.

"We'll wait out here," I tell her.

"I want to stay with Grace," Beau grumbles.

"We're just going to check on Emily," Holly says.

"I can hold her," I say, and Dan rolls his eyes. I kick his shin and smile at Beau, taking her off Holly before she can argue. "See you in a minute." I grin and the little blonde in my arms giggles.

"See you in a minute," Beau repeats and grabs hold of my collar again. Holly hesitates, but Dan nods her off, and she kisses Beau's hair. I get a waft of perfume and the insane urge to grip Holly's hair and drag her mouth to mine thumps through me.

"Be good for Mummy," she whispers.

"I will." I laugh.

"Shut up." Holly chuckles, then walks away.

I smirk at Dan, happy I made Holly laugh.

"You have a girlfriend," he reminds me coldly.

"Given that you got your end away last night, you're in a right mood." I scoff and walk away, taking a seat. Beau is sleepy as hell and soon nods off, her legs hanging on either side like two ropes, one hand caught up in my collar and the other in her hair. I sit and watch her as she seeks comfort against my chest.

"You're playing with fire." Dan shakes his head and leans to check Grace is still asleep. My phone buzzes and I shift to pull it out of my back pocket. It's from Nadine.

> I'm sorry about tonight. I miss you x

I don't open the message but read it from the home screen. I shove my phone away and find Dan watching me. "Is that Nadine?"

"Yeah."

"She's feeling insecure."

"She has no reason to be."

"No?" Dan's eyes drop to the little blonde girl in my lap. "You've been different since Holly has been back, we can all see it. Nadine can see it."

"Whatever," I spit quietly, rolling my eyes.

"Not a break, just badly sprained. She has a support on, though." Holly appears, telling us quickly. She looks to Dan sheepishly. "I mentioned that things are a bit fragile with Grace and that you were acting on genuine fear. She said she appreciates that, but she'd rather not see you," she recites on Emily's behalf.

"Understandable," Dan mumbles, rubbing his face. "Do you need a lift back?" he asks her. Say yes!

"Jeremy is giving us a lift, but thanks." She looks to me and says, "Thanks for watching Beau."

"She's a great kid." I pass her to Holly.

"Yeah, she is." Holly stares at her daughter. "Thanks again." She smiles awkwardly and takes the seat I was sat in.

"Thanks for the update. Night, Holly," Dan says.

"Night, Dan."

"Night," I say quietly, hoping for her to look up, but she keeps her face on Beau when she says goodbye.

Chapter Thirteen
Holly

Jeremy escorts Emily into my house. He is bundled up like a donkey with all our belongings. "These tablets will make you sleepy," he informs her, reading the prescription.

"Good," she grumbles, shifting on the sofa. I thought it would be better for her to stay with me as her apartment is up a flight of stairs. Emily has been quiet on the journey back. I think she's in shock. Jeremy and I share a concerned look.

"Do you want a drink?" I whisper over Beau's sleeping form. She could do with a sugar kick.

"I'll do it. You get Beau to bed," Jeremy tells me. He gives me a stern look when I try to argue. "Holly, you can't be everywhere. I can manage a kettle. Go." He nods me away, and I sigh.

"Thanks. Cups are in the third cupboard on the right," I tell him, walking away with Beau. She barely flinches when I undress her and get her into bed. I tuck her and her unicorn teddy in and pull the door. I pop into my own room and pull back in horror when I see the smudges of mascara under my eyes. "Bloody hell!" I use a wipe and remove most of my makeup. Once I find pyjamas for Emily, I grab the wipes up for her too. Jeremy is busy in the kitchen when I return downstairs so I go to Emily. She is frowning at the TV. She doesn't blink, not even once. "Hey, Em, how are you feeling?"

Jolting, she turns and shakes herself off, but I can see unshed tears in her eyes again. "Sorry." She waves her hand, trying to dismiss her emotions.

"It's fine. You're in shock. In pain." I smile, rubbing her arm.

Sniffling, she tries to smile, but it turns into a quiet sob. "God, I'm such a mess." She laughs, making me frown. There's more to this. What's she not telling me?

"You can talk to me, you know." I keep my tone quiet and check for Jeremy, but he is still tackling the drinks.

"I know. Sorry," she says on a shaky exhale. "It brought back some not so nice memories."

"Oh, Em." I lean in and give her a big hug. My support unlocks something in her because she breaks down and sobs into my neck. Jeremy comes round the corner with the drinks and shrinks back in horror. I give a little shake of my head and he takes two steps backwards and stalks off quickly. If Emily wasn't crying, I'd find his reaction comical. Em would, too. "You're safe now. Us women stick together," I say, giving her a tight squeeze.

"God, this is so silly. Dan's not my ex. Sorry. Thanks." She blows out a long stream of air and sits back. She doesn't meet my eyes, so I know she is embarrassed by her admission.

"Our minds sometimes have rules of their own." I smile. "Don't apologise. Are you in pain?"

"Yes. It's throbbing." She rubs her forehead and sits back, trying to get more comfortable.

"I'll get your meds; Jeremy probably has our drinks." I leave her and find Jeremy checking his phone in the kitchen.

"All okay?" he asks.

"It's tear free now." I smirk.

"Okay. Ha ha, I ran." He rolls his eyes and holds my drink out for me. "How is she?"

"In pain. Where did you put the painkillers?"

"Here, I'll get her some water too." I take her coffee and pills and leave him to sort the water. Jeremy joins us shortly after and we all settle into the living room. So much for a relaxing evening on the village green.

EMILY, Beau, and I are all bundled up on the sofa the following morning. We decided on a pyjama day after yesterday's antics, and we are glued to the screen watching some god-awful unicorn programme.

Someone knocks on the door.

"I bet that's Jeremy." I'm starving. He phoned first thing to check in on us and offered to bring breakfast over. After a chaotic evening and eventful night with Beau waking up repeatedly, I'm exhausted. I wasn't about to pass up a free brekkie.

"Surprise!" my mother's voice reverberates through the house. I snap at Emily, confused. Shit, was she coming? Did I forget?

"Hi!" Marcus's voice follows.

"Oh, wow. Hi." I smile, unsure of the sudden visit. I tighten my robe and Beau whips past me. When we last spoke, I reiterated how busy I would be this first week with the shop.

"Mamar!" she cries, throwing herself at her immaculate form. Marcus appears and frowns at my attire.

"Oh heavens, Holly, you do look a mess. Go and get cleaned up." Margaret, my mother, gestures to the stairs.

"Hello, Mum, how are you?" I mutter and find Emily pressing her lips together.

"Very good, thank you. Yes, hello, my little button." She hums at Beau, dropping down to hug her. "We thought we would surprise you both and go out." She turns with a practised smile, the smile that leaves no room for argument.

"We're having a jama day!" Beau announces. "Emily has a poorly leg." She grasps their hands and swings in the air, making them both jolt forward.

"No human swings, dear!" She gives Beau a polite pat on the head. "Come on, Holly, go get some clothes on." She looks at me expectantly, her lips pursed.

"I'm sorry, we've not eaten yet and I'm looking after Emily. We had an eventful day yesterday," I tell them both. They peer past me to see Emily on the sofa, her leg propped up and in a support.

"Good grief, what on earth happened?" Margaret presses her hand to her chest.

"Dan shouted and," Beau gives Marcus a big push, "he did that to Emily."

"What!" My mother's shriek makes Marcus's eyes twitch.

"It was a misunderstanding," I assure, and Emily scoffs. "Maybe we can spend the day here instead?" I suggest, throwing Em an apologetic smile.

"Hi," Emily waves in greeting.

"Oh god, sorry. This is Emily. She works with me at the shop," I explain. "Emily, this is my mother and Marcus." My mother gives her a pinched smile and I want to crawl up the stairs and hide. Marcus nods politely.

"Mamar, come look at my new riding shoes." Beau says as Marcus closes the door.

"Can I get you both a drink?" I offer, hoping to break the ice.

"Perhaps go put some clothes on first?" She suggests coolly. I snap back, affronted. It's barely nine in the morning, a Sunday morning at that. We're all shattered, and it's my house! "Oh, don't look at me like that, child. You have guests, go clean up," she tells me quickly.

"But our jamas?" Beau whines. The door knocks again, and

I sigh in relief but groan, knowing my mother will complain about our attire even more now that Jeremy is here.

I tug the door wide and Jeremy holds up a few bags that smell of thick syrup and pancakes. "Breakfast has arrived!" he announces and lowers the bags when he finds my mother's sharp glare pinning him to the front step.

"Morning, Jeremy, thank you. Come in."

"I would have gotten more if..." He looks to her and Marcus, waiting for another introduction.

"No, it's okay. I didn't know they were coming," I explain quickly, and he looks confused.

"Oh, I do apologise. Should I book an appointment next time?" my mother drawls.

"I didn't mean it like that, I was just explaining to Jeremy," I placate gently. My hackles are up. Moments ago, I was relaxed, in a stupor on my sofa, and now, I'm riled.

Jeremy senses my mental overload and steps forward. "Jeremy." He shakes my mother's hand. Marcus steps towards me and puts his hand on my lower back. My eyes widen, and I twist to Emily, who pulls her blanket up, covering her face. Traitor.

"Marcus."

"Pleasure." Jeremy steps back, giving me a quizzical look. I move out of Marcus's hold to take the bags. "I will take these," Jeremy says, pulling them away. "Go, relax on the sofa. I'll sort it all out."

"Oh, you don't need to do that, Jeremy." I say, cheeks bright red.

"I know. Holly, you look beat. Relax, let me sort this out. You've got your hands full so go sit down." He tugs the bags out of my hands and smiles cheekily at me. Was that a dig at my mother? If so, I need to high five this man. I bite my lip from smiling and relax a little.

Half an hour later, we are squashed into my living room; Beau is doodling on her water mat while Marcus is staring at

Jeremy with open dislike. "So, Jeremy, how long have you known Holly?" he asks over his cup. My mum is sitting beside him and twists, giving him a supportive smile.

"We went to school, actually. We recently reconnected, and after yesterday, I offered to bring breakfast." He winks at me, and I smile. He's as kind as he was when we were teenagers.

"And what exactly happened yesterday?" my mother queries.

"Oh, a simple misunderstanding," Emily chimes in this time. "I was accidentally knocked over. Jeremy drove me to the hospital," she explains and then lifts her cup to cut off any further questioning.

"Beau alluded to it being more than that," she quips.

"Beau is also five," I say. "It was an accident. We got in late. Beau was up during the night, so we are tired and decided after a hectic week to have a quiet day." I keep my tone light, but my mother senses the irritation in me.

"Okay, dear. No need to get so prickly." She tuts at Marcus, who looks less than pleased with me too. Jesus, what is this?

My shoulder sag, and Emily rubs my back in support. I love my mother with every fibre. I do, but it takes a lot to deal with her. She is insufferable and demanding.

"I can go home," Emily suggests quietly. I shake my head.

"I'm going to go get dressed," I say, desperate to get away and gather my thoughts.

Leaving everyone downstairs, I rush into my room and rub my eyes. The last thing I needed today was to be controlled at every possible turn. I filter through my wardrobe and find jeans and a plain tee. Shrugging my dressing gown off, I choose some underwear as Marcus comes into my room. I grab the nearest decorative pillow to cover myself with. "Marcus, what are you doing? I'll be down in a minute."

"Why are you hiding? You didn't seem to mind being in your sleepwear in front of Jeremy." He frowns and moves into my room further. He looks at the plain décor and scrunches his nose.

"I was in a robe. Get out!" I snap.

"What's going on with you?" He comes over to me and rubs my arms. I sigh deeply and lift my head with what little patience I have left.

"I am standing in my underwear. *Please leav*e," I grate.

Blinking, he seems to come to his senses, and with a muddled nod, he walks out. "I'll wait here." The door shuts, and I sag into the chair. I know my mother has been filling his head with ideas of him and I being more than friends.

I dress quickly and scoop my hair up into a big bun. Marcus is where he said he would be, outside the door. "Marcus, I appreciate we are friends, but I'd prefer you not to let yourself into my bedroom." His cheeks taint a light pink, and I congratulate myself on laying out boundaries with him. I will have to if he is trying to place himself more securely in my life.

"Of course, sorry." Cam wouldn't do that. He'd tell me if he wanted to come into my room, he damn well would. I have no idea where the thought comes from, but it knocks me off guard. Marcus is so formal. He is a good friend and kind, but being back in Richmond has worked as a reminder of how lifeless my life was before now. Marcus and my mother are narrow-minded and snooty. They pick fault where they deem it. They patronise and belittle.

"Look, I feel I need to address something. My mother has made a few comments and I just want to smooth things out, clear the air," I begin.

"Address away." He smiles and straightens my hair. I tug away and his hand drops to his front.

"She has suggested that you and I are more than friends."

"Aren't we? We've been through so much together; we love one another as closely as family. I'm here for Beau," Marcus says, and I shrink inwardly. He thinks this is more than friendship? God, does he assume we are dating?

I hum awkwardly. "Well, I just class that as a friend. A friend of the family," I tell him gently. "I never really viewed our friendship as anything more. I'm sorry if I led you to believe otherwise." I give him a sympathetic smile.

"Is this because of Jeremy?" he mutters, looking pissed off. He shoves his hands into his trouser pockets and stares at his feet.

"This has nothing to do with anyone. I value your friendship, but I have no intention of dating you or anyone else," I admit quietly. Beau and I aren't yet settled here, then and only then will I consider dating someone. Someone I like and not who my mother considers is suitable.

"You can't stay single forever." He tuts. "Besides, I've put years into us and Beau."

"We have never even kissed or discussed our friendship progressing. You can't just assume you're dating me, Marcus," I say, confused. I'm somewhat appalled the situation has got this far without me realising.

"I know that, but I at least thought after all we have shared, it would progress," he mutters indignantly. "We have so much potential, Holly."

"We're friends. That's all I wanted," I declare firmly, hoping he will understand this isn't going any further.

"What about what I want?" He scoffs, seeming more like my mother by the second.

"You never voiced what you wanted. Even now, it was me who brought it up because my mum kept making remarks," I remind him. "I didn't choose to discuss this to argue. I wanted to clear the air and move forward."

"I'm not sure I can," he admits, shaking his head in disgust at me. "I put so much time into you, Beau. You're being so selfish, Holly. Your mother can see this is a good fit. Why can't you?"

"It's evident you discuss this far more with her than you ever felt was necessary with me," I reply. "You seem to have a closer and more open relationship with her, so perhaps she would fit you better." His face drops in shock. I head down, finding my mother washing up and tutting about the mess on the kitchen table.

This is her doing. "Leave it," I snap, and she swings to look at me through narrowed eyes. Marcus comes barrelling down the stairs and out the door, slamming it as he goes. Beau yelps and runs at me, crying.

"Hey, whoa, it's okay," I shush her. "It's just the door." She's still shaken up from last night.

"What on earth!" Margaret calls. "What did you do?" She marches towards the door, giving me a heated stare.

"Of course it was my fault." I sigh, rubbing Beau's back.

"Well, I don't see you leaving in a haste."

"That's because it's *my* house."

My mother rears back at my remark. Rarely do I ever argue back with her.

"Holly, you are being unpleasantly rude."

"As opposed to being pleasantly rude, which you have been since you arrived?" I toss a brow up. "Marcus thinks we're dating because you filled his head with nonsense. That's not okay. I know you miss us, but manipulating his feelings to suit you isn't okay. It's not what I want for myself or Beau," I tell her calmly. "We had a good friendship. Now, all of a sudden, he thinks we're set for marriage."

"Oh, don't be ridiculous," she spits. "Well, I'd like to say this was a nice visit, but unless you check yourself, we won't be coming again." She picks her bag up from the side table.

"Beau and I will be sad if you don't visit. But this 'We' business of you and Marcus concocting stops now. Date him yourself if he's such a catch," I huff as she storms out. The door slams, and Beau flinches. I blow out a breath and stare at the door for a few minutes. Silence rings through the house. My eyes prick, and I twist into Beau's hair, calming myself.

"Are you okay?" Jeremy's voice breaks the quiet. A quiet that feels too loud. This is so embarrassing. I nod and smile over Beau's head at him.

"Sorry. As you can see, life is still a whirlwind," I joke.

"Rather that than tumbleweeds." He winks. "She's an unforgettable woman," he comments. He watches out the window as the car reverses out of the drive.

"I'm amazed you and Emily didn't sneak out the window," I quip, trying to lighten the mood.

"We tried, but her leg support was too big."

We all laugh, and Beau jerks her head up. Her big eyes are tinted with worry. "Can we have hot chocolate?" she asks, twiddling with my bun.

"We can. Are you staying?" I ask Jeremy.

"For hot chocolate, always." He gives Beau a thumbs up.

"So, your mum seems nice." Emily smirks at me later that evening. Beau is fast asleep and we are in the living room watching a rerun of *FRIENDS*.

"Oh, a real dime, that one." I scoff. "She practically set me up with Marcus without me knowing," I groan.

"What happened? You were upstairs for a while." Em crunches on a few crisps.

"I was in my underwear, and he just walked in. Like honey I'm home, and by the way, we're dating." I wave my arm around dramatically.

"What, really!" She snickers.

"I'm being over the top, but yes, when I mentioned that my mum had suggested we were more, he seemed to think as much." I shake my head and pick up my wine. "I've known him for years, and I do love him as a friend, but I never once thought we'd ever be more."

"No offence, he's a bit of a wimp."

A wimp! I cough and choke, spraying wine out my nose.

Emily roars with laughter, and I do too. My nose is burning, and my eyes are watering. "You looked like a dragon," she cries. "Wine was just," she points to her nose, "oh my god. I'm gonna wee!" she howls.

"God, that really burnt," I complain a few minutes later, twitching my nose.

"I'm not surprised it looked like an exorcism was taking place in your living room." She chuckles. Well, I seemed to exorcise my mother and Marcus from my life. I will give it a few days and contact her.

"How are you feeling?"

"Sore, but it's not throbbing as much. Elevating really helps." Emily winces.

"Do you want more ice before I go to bed?"

"No, I'm okay. Are you sure you're going to be okay in the shop on Tuesday? I mean, can Jeremy even work a till?" she mutters. He offered to take the day off and help me in the shop, as Emily is still resting. The doctor suggested a week's leg rest. She is flapping and I've taken it on the chin. We will be busy and overworked. I have no idea how I will manage the shop or with collecting Beau, but I'll somehow make it work.

"Probably not, but even if he cleans up, it will help," I muse.

"Dan has a lot to answer for!" she mutters sullenly.

"Maybe you can ask him to kiss it better," I joke.

"I did think he was seriously hot until he knocked me over."

"Really?" I sit up, intrigued.

"Not anymore, though. I hope he gets a flat tyre on the way to work, and he ejaculates too early with his next date." She huffs and we burst into laughter.

Chapter Fourteen
Holly

Four Weeks Later...

WE'RE HAVING the best evening. Em, Jer, and I have become a trio, and I'm enjoying my new life back in Richmond. The shop is doing great. I've patched things up with my mother. Beau is happy. I'm happy. I'm flipping great!

"Let's go in here," Emily calls us back when we pass a brightly lit bar called The Lounge. It's a cosy setting with low sofas, hanging lights and industrial tables. It looks nice. Lively.

"Sure." I hook arms with Jeremy, and we all make our way inside.

"Oh, I love this song!" Emily whoops and shakes her way to the bar, not a wince in sight. Her leg has healed nicely, and she carries on sashaying her way through the place, mouthing the lyrics.

"She's so pissed." Jeremy chuckles. I grin at him, and he takes my hand, spinning me round like a ballerina. I look more like a drunken waif as I stagger away, and he tucks me back in. Giggling, I hold on to him for support as we reach the bar. I'm drunk too. I haven't consumed this much alcohol since before Beau. Or actually ever! I'm drunk and happily so!

"G and T please!" I sing when I stand beside Emily. I slap my hands on the bar and frown when my fingers stick to the surface. "Gross."

"I already ordered. Jer, did you know you have a ketchup stain on your top?" Em informs him with a slur.

He moans. "For fuck's sake. This is new!" He scrapes the stain, but I shoo his hand away. "I look like I had a nosebleed," he mutters, squinting at the speck on his chest. We ate dinner in Barton before having drinks and getting a taxi back to Richmond.

"I'll get it out," I tell him and lean into his bicep as we wait for our drinks. "I think I'm seeing double," I comment dryly and twist to Em, grinning deviously.

"That will be the double shots." She pulls a mischievous face and smacks a kiss on my cheek. "I needed this night out. I am so sloshed I could make some hefty mistakes tonight." She laughs freely and looks round the bar.

"Not on my watch!" Jeremy sniggers.

"Uh oh. The she-devil and her obsessive, confused BF are here," Em mutters. "Oh, and the village bully too."

Jeremy and I both turn and see Cameron and his friends across the room. They look to be playing pool. I've not had to see any of them over the last few weeks. At horse riding, both Cam and I stick to opposite ends of the yard. It's perfect. Emily hasn't forgotten her grudge even after Dan sent her an enormous bouquet, but when I catch her watching him coquettishly, I wonder if he will be one of her many mistakes.

"Let's hang by the bar," I suggest.

"Who is the obsessive, confused BF?" Jer murmurs, craning his neck to find out. "BF? What's that stand for, *butt fuck*?"

Em and I cry out with laughter. I grip his arm and shake my head as tears fall. Butt fuck. Oh my. That's just brilliant.

Jer gives me a goofy grin. "What? Well, what does it mean?"

"Best friend, boyfriend," I titter, wiping my eyes. "I can't believe you thought it was butt fuck. You're such a guy."

"Thank god." Wrapping his arm around my neck, he pulls me in and chuckles. "I assume you're talking about wham-bam-thank-you-Cam?" he muses, looking at Em and me.

"Wham bam what?" Em cries in shock. She grips the bar for support and crosses her legs. "Oh fuck, I'm going to wee! I can't pee here!"

Player.

That's what that means, right? Not wham-bam-thank-you-mam, but Cam. They thank him for fucking them? I feel sick.

"That's what they call him. He's a dick and ditch," Jeremy informs us, shooting a disgruntled look their way.

"Dick and ditch!" Em wafts her hands near her face as tears stream down her cheeks. "My bladder is going to burst. Jer, no more talking. Not until my bladder is empty!" she shouts and stagger-runs to the toilet.

I feel as though I've had icy water poured over my head. "Is that really what they call him?" Why am I surprised? Before me, Cameron had many girlfriends, so why would he change that after me? He has that presence. That *thing* only a handful of men are gifted with. I don't know what that thing is or how some men can master it so well, but he has it in spades. Always did. I flick a look across the bar and Cameron is bent down, cue in his hand and ready to take his shot, but his eyes aren't on the ball.

They are on me. I drop my gaze and turn away.

"Shit, sorry, Hol, I wasn't thinking. He has a bit of a reputation," Jeremy apologises, then leans past me to get our drinks. "Especially after that night." The night he cheated on me.

"Nothing to do with me," I cut in and smile, picking up my drink and taking a big sip.

"Yeah, I guess it was a lifetime ago. I never regret taking you to London," he admits, rubbing my back. "I realised that night there we weren't good friends."

"I don't want to talk about it." I give him a strained smile, and Jeremy leans forward, his arm running up my back and into my hair.

"You were always too good for him, Holly. Smart, beautiful. He didn't deserve you." He sighs, dropping his eyes to my lips. He's going to try to kiss me! I blink, unsure of what to do. Clearing my throat, I twist an inch or two away so I'm facing the bar.

"I really don't want to get into it, Jeremy," I repeat and chug down half of my gin.

"Sorry. I'm going to hit the men's. Why don't you find us a table?" He walks away, but I'm not sure I want to stay. I didn't know he would make a pass at me. I frown into my empty glass and sigh.

A loud crack beside me makes me jump. Cameron is glaring at me with an empty glass clenched tightly in his fist. "So, you and Jeremy then, huh?" he sneers at the closed door to the men's bathroom.

"Excuse me?"

"What happened to the worm guy?" He sniggers on a mocking shake of his head. Worm guy?

"You're drunk." I scoff, signalling the bartender over to give me something else to do.

"And you're getting around." He wobbles slightly, so I know he is drunk. Drunk enough to indirectly call me a slut.

"If you're insinuating what I think you are, Cameron bloody Stone," I hiss, turning to glare at him, "then you've got another thing coming, you arrogant, fat-headed di—"

He grins lazily and sighs. "God, you're fucking stunning."

My mouth drops open in shock.

"I've never been attracted to another woman as I have you." I rear back at his confession. "You're stunning, Hol."

"I'm going to go," I say, moving away. Cameron wraps his hand around my wrist, tugging me back to face him.

"Are you and Jeremy together or not?"

"Get off, it's none of your business!'" I yank free and storm off. I'm two steps from the door when someone hauls me round and lips crash to mine. Whistles explode around the room; I'm locked in by two large hands and soft, groaning lips. My eyes spring open to find deep green balls of moss burning back at me. I gasp. He sweeps in his tongue, enticing a flush of heat from me. My god. It's like all those years before. Electric. Charged and all-consuming. Cam walks me back until I hit a hard surface, his body crushing me as his mouth moves passionately over mine. His hands are in my hair, his erection pushing into my stomach. He groans loudly, and I slam my hands into his chest, causing him to stumble backwards. My hand is moving of its own accord until it connects with his face. The sound is loud and sharp. The whistles stop and the bar quietens.

"Holly," he breathes. Desperately. *No!*

"You bastard!" a woman's voice cries hopelessly. Wine splashes over Cameron's face, spraying me in the process.

"Shit!" Lurching away, I blink to see Nadine crying openly. "I didn't. I'd never," I whisper.

"Nadine!" he panics, guilt stricken. Nothing has changed, it seems. Once a cheat, always a cheat.

"Fuck you! Both of you," Nadine sobs. "I've never been so humiliated," she croaks and rushes out of the bar.

"What did you do!" I accuse. How could he do that to her? I stumble from the bar and rush home. I can't believe he kissed me.

In front of his girlfriend.

Publicly.

But he did, and my stomach swoops with a level of emotion that rattles me to the core.

I need to get home. My legs move quicker. My heart beats to the fast click of my heels. I begin to jog, then run until I'm panting my way up the drive and crashing through the front door.

Keeley screams, yanking a cushion up to hide herself. "Fucking hell!" she yelps, wide-eyed and pale. I hear the low wail and scream from the TV. She's watching a horror movie.

"Sorry," I gasp.

"What's wrong?"

"I... Something happened." Shaking my head, I kick off my heels and go into the kitchen in a daze. Keeley joins me and takes a seat at the table. She bites her lip, and I frown at her. "What?"

"Your lipstick is all over your face."

"What!" I exclaim and rush to the mirror by the front door. "Oh my god." Grabbing a scarf off of the side, I start rubbing the red stain off my face. Keeley is laughing quietly.

"So you pulled, then?" she teases.

"No," I mutter, returning to the kitchen and making a hot drink. "Tea?"

"You kiss yourself?" she presses further. "I'd love a tea." She wiggles her brows.

"Whatever gossip you hear tomorrow, it's not true," I warn her. "How was Beau?"

"She was great. I love her. She's such a great kid." I smile over my shoulder at her and say thanks. "So this gossip then?"

"Cam kissed me," I say quickly.

"Really. You lucky bitch!" she gawps at me. "Wait, isn't he dating Nadine?" she asks, puzzled.

"Yes, and she was there!"

"No!"

"Yes!" I drop down into the chair and stare helplessly over the table at her. Keeley gets up, carrying on with my abandoned job.

"What are you going to do?"

"Well, I slapped him. She threw a drink at him and told us to fuck off," I groan.

"But he kissed you?" Oh hell, Keeley is lapping this up. She's almost salivating. "Didn't you two used to date?" she murmurs.

"Years ago."

"So he still has feelings?" Keeley states, filling our cups with hot water.

"What! No!" Her brow lifts, and I slump in my chair.

"You still have feelings for him too?" Her voice softens. She brings our drinks over and takes a seat opposite me. Groaning once more, I drop my head in my hands and hide my face on the table. This is a disaster.

"I don't want to," I admit. I'm drunk. I need to stop talking. Like right this minute. "He wasn't supposed to be here when I moved back." I sigh. "Why did he have to be here? Why is he so hot?" I complain.

"He really is ridiculously gorgeous. Dan, too. Those two are like the only threesome I'd ever want to have."

"Keeley! God, you kinky bugger."

She giggles and lifts her cup up for me to clink.

"What a mess," I muse.

"Hot mess. Cameron Stone has got the hots for you still." She grins over the table at me.

"He cheated on me," I admit in a shameful whisper. Her mouth drops open, and I shrug. "It was a long time ago, but I don't think he's trustworthy. In fact, his actions tonight back up how unfaithful he is."

"Yeah, that is a dick move."

"Dick and ditch," I mutter. How many women has he gone through to earn that title?

"Yeah, I heard that too." She eyes me cautiously.

"Wham bam—"

"Thank you, Cam," we say in unison.

"I don't even know him anymore." I shake my head in despair. I can't believe he kissed me in front of half of Richmond. In front of his girlfriend. How disrespectful. How cruel.

"He has a bad rep, if I'm honest with you. Lots of rumours too, but it doesn't stop women from fawning over him," Keeley imparts quietly. Oh, I bet. With nicknames like that, who wouldn't be shrouded in rumours and reputation. He's a walking slut. I can't get over that he suggested I was. I haven't even slept with anyone since him!

"Good job I got away then," I muse. "I'm going to go to bed," I tell her, standing wearily. I should have seen this coming. Cameron and I have too much left unsaid for it not to detonate. "Feel free to grab the spare room."

"Are you sure?"

"Yeah, it's all made up. Help yourself. Thanks, Keeley."

Chapter Fifteen
Holly

We're having breakfast when Emily rings my phone. "Hey, Em, I'm sorry for just skanking you last night." I didn't even message to say I arrived home safely.

"I slept with Dan!" she blurts, horrified.

She what! Holy hell. "Really?"

"No, I made it up," she drawls. "Yes, really." She sighs. "I looked after his daughter. He pushed me over. I evidently have no self-respect! I'm never drinking again." I hear cupboards slam and the kettle boil. "Plus, I feel like death warmed up."

"Yeah, me too." I glance at Keeley and Beau, but they are busy going through a unicorn sticker book. The entire house is so full of unicorn stuff it seems as if at any minute the place will explode into a thousand glittery pieces. She groans down the line. "That bad?" I murmur, referring to her hangover.

"No, he was great. Hot, so hot. He is very dominating and I can't walk properly. It hurts to sit down."

"I meant your hangover. I don't think I will be able to look at him again now," I admit.

"You can't, what about my poor lady garden!"

"Okay!" I say, shutting her up. "TMI!"

Emily laughs, embarrassed. "It was hell after you left. Cameron punched a wall. Someone had a go at him for disrespecting Nadine." I nod. Good for them. "Dan had to calm him down and then Cameron left in a rage."

"Nadine was so upset. I might get her some flowers," I hum, feeling terrible.

"Oh, fuck her, she's been giving him crap anyway, Dan says."

"She has?" I begin clearing the plates away. Keeley looks up in question and I mouth to her that it's Em. She nods and turns away when Beau asks her where a unicorn horn goes.

"I told you that Cam liked you still." She laughs smugly. "Have you seen Dan's house? It's enormous. His bed is massive." She sighs. "No one has ever made me feel like he did last night. Shit, Holly. I really like him," she admits feebly.

"Are you sure it's not just lust?"

"No, I pretty much was smitten as soon as I arrived in Richmond. That's one of the reasons I was so upset when he knocked me over."

"I guess he had a justified reason to panic, even if it was wrong," I murmur. Dan took her out for coffee to apologise and explained the situation with Grace's mum recently.

"He's been sending me flowers since," she admits, and my brows quirk.

"Does he like you?" I ask, filling the bowl with soapy water and tucking the phone between my shoulders to wash up.

"He likes what he does to me, apparently." Her tone is tight and cynical.

"He said that?"

"Well, I said it too. It's just lust, a lot of it, and mainly on his side. He is killer in bed." Her sigh lingers. "I'm taking what I can, whilst I can." She swallows, and I feel sorry for her.

"Oh, Em."

"We need a proper catch up. How are you? Last night was crazy?" She changes the subject, so I don't press further.

"Yeah, it was. I'm okay. Confused."

"Dan says Cameron has been a mess since you got back," Emily informs me gently.

"You and Dan seem close. He's said a lot?" I query, scrubbing the dishes harder than necessary, picturing Cameron's unfaithful face.

"He was drunk. I left before he woke up. Anyway, I need to grab a shower. I'll pop over later?"

"Sure. See you later."

AN HOUR LATER, I'm at the shop. Keeley had promised Beau she would take her to the park before she went home. After last night, I'm happy for the break to gather my thoughts and make a plan about what I will say to the local lothario about last night's activities. I've got my paperwork splayed out on a table. There are a few statements I want to check over whilst I have the opportunity. Beau is busy, and it's rare I'm given a window like this to work uninterrupted.

Ding!

I groan and swing round, expecting Keeley and Beau, but Cameron walks through the door. His eyes are big, nervous saucers of pain. Sweat stains his shirt and forehead. He ran here. Of course, a man like him, who was drunk last night, can hop out of bed and run his worries away. It's sickening that he has so much fucking energy, sickening and hot.

"NO!" I snap.

"Holly, hear me out, please." His palms press at his chest and despite the harsh glare I'm throwing his way, he continues inside. "I can't regret last night, and I won't," he begins.

"You need to leave."

The door clunks shut and Cameron levels me with a hard

stare. I've seen that look before. It may have been years ago, but I remember it well. Instinctively, I stiffen, bracing myself for his retort. He straightens, and my eyes widen. "Actually, you'll hear me out. You owe me that much."

Owe him. I owe him. He is deluded!

Anger sweeps through me, faster than any wildfire. I've had enough of this man. I grab the nearest thing—a blueberry muffin—and I launch it across the room at him. "Dammit, Cameron. Just get out!" It knocks his shoulder and falls to the floor.

"You stubborn fucker. Always were." He laughs; a nostalgic look in his eye. "It never fails to surprise me. I never expected it with your shyness, but it's still there." He shakes his head. I don't want to see that look in his eyes or hear the intimate way he just spoke.

"I don't want a history lesson, and I'm not ready to talk to you. I haven't even decided what I need to say to you!" I spit furiously. Someone walks by the window and looks in. It's Nadine. Her face cripples with hurt, and I open my mouth to apologise, but I haven't done anything wrong. Oh hell, this is bad. She storms inside, the little ding of the bell that I love, hitting like a bullet.

"Are you fucking kidding me? You ignore every one of my calls, but you can come here?" she screams in Cameron's face. He looks unfazed, and I feel for her, I really do. How can he be so callous?

"Not that you will believe me, but I was on my way to yo—"

She holds his attention with a sarcastic glare of her own. "Oh, sure!"

"I was on my way to see you, when I noticed Holly in here, and I decided to quickly pop in and clear the air." He is so calm. Too calm. Something is wrong. I frown at his back, conscious not to meet Nadine's stare. I don't want to be caught in the middle of this. I mean, I already am, but not by my doing. Oh no, it's all down to him. This man standing right here. Unfazed. Cool as cucumber. I hate how blaśe he is.

Crossing her arms, she twists to me, her head tilted just so. She is livid, and rightly so. "And did you clear the air?" Her smile is insincere. "Did you swap old love stories?"

"I threw a muffin at him. I'm not sure that counts," I mumble, scratching my neck awkwardly.

Nadine pulls a face and swings back to Cam. "You are, without a doubt, *the* most atrocious man I have ever met. I stood by you. Ignored all the gossip, the rumours." Cam's eyes flash, and his jaw ticks as Nadine stabs at his chest with her polished nail.

"Don't throw that shit in my face. I hurt you last night, and I'm sorry," Cam cuts in abruptly, sounding sincere. Nadine scoffs, but shuts up when he steps up and looks down at her. "What? I was good enough to fuck, but now I've hurt you, you're going to throw past accusations in my face!" he snaps.

"Yes!" she screeches. "I stood by you. She didn't. She left, remember? Left you to deal with all that shit alone, shit she caused." She slaps her chest. "I fought off all those remarks, stares. I was here."

"Nadine, you weren't here. You don't even know the whole story. You know the rumours and they aren't true. We've been dating for a few months. You don't get to take credit for something you know nothing about." Cam drags his hand through his hair, and I frown at their conversation.

What rumours?

"I deserve more than last night."

Cam pulls her in for a hug.

"I know and I'm sorry."

Nadine shrugs him off. "I can't believe that after everything she did to you, you're in here." Tears cascade down. When Cameron tries to comfort her again, she steps away. She looks at me, all daggers and hate. "You ruined his life. Even now, people talk. I couldn't even have a decent relationship with him because people were always talking."

"Nadine," Cameron warns.

She snaps to look at him. I'm confused. What rumours, lies? He throws me a worried glance, and I shake my head with uncertainty. I don't know what's going on. "Fuck you, Cameron. She accused you of rape, then left you to fend off a ton of hate!" Nadine snarls. "How can you even be around her. She makes me sick!"

"What?" I cry, outraged. Rape. "Cam," I croak. He turns red-faced. "I never... I'd ..." Rape? I slouch down into a nearby chair. Is this what people are saying, talking about? I shake my head. Tears spring to my eyes, and through my water clogged vision, I see Cameron move.

"Oh sure, go to her!" Nadine sneers.

"Nadine, shut up. Holly never accused me of rape. Where the fuck did you even hear that?" His voice bellows, making me jump and, thankfully, Nadine goes quiet.

Rape. Rape. Rape. That word pounds around my head. I feel sick. Dizzy.

"Holly?" I blink up at Cam.

"Kerry said you and Holly dated years ago, that you were accused of rape and that she left." I stare at Cameron wordlessly, asking him if this is true, was he accused of rape? What the hell have I missed all these years?

"I suggest you come to the main source when digging for information," he growls at her.

"Like I'm going to ask you about your rape trial?" Nadine snaps.

Trial? I gasp and pull away from him, but he takes my face in his hands. "I never cheated on you, Holly. I'd never do that to you."

"But you'll cheat on me." Nadine scoffs.

"*Shut up!*" Cameron and I snap.

"Rape, Cam?"

"Baby, it was hell, I can't even..." Shaking his head, he swallows and gives me a sad smile. "I never raped anyone. Sarah raped me that night. I'd never cheat on you. *Never.*"

Raped him? Gasping, I cover my mouth and search his eyes. It's there, the pain. The shame. "Cam, I... I don't know what to say."

"I'm so fucking angry with you." His voice cracks. Tears fill his gaze, and I drop my head. I left him. Believed the worst. Rejected our love in the blink of an eye and removed myself from his life, leaving him to single-handedly deal with a hell that is still clear in his eyes.

Nadine's dejected voice disrupts our moment. "You're still in love with her." I blink at her over Cameron's shoulder.

"I don't know how not to be," Cam says, shocking me. My eyes flick briefly to him. After all this time, I silently question, but his attention returns to a tearful Nadine. Standing on a sigh, he walks to her and leans in, pecking her cheek. "I'm truly sorry. Take care of yourself, Nadine. I need to get out of here." He swallows thickly, his fists now clenching rhythmically.

Cameron steps out of the shop, leaving a confused and shocked me, and a sniffling Nadine in his wake. "Nadine." I stand, hoping to draw a line under this and move forward with some understanding.

"Don't." Her whisper guts me. I know how much pain she is in. "Not yet. I can't." I offer her a compassionate smile, but she doesn't return it. She leaves in a rush, and I stare after both retreating backs, wondering where in the hell that leaves me.

Full of regret.

That's where. Shame and self-disgust chips away at me for having such a profound effect on so many lives when I could have stayed and dealt with life instead of running towards a safety Cameron was never granted. Rape. I drop my head in my hands and sob quietly in the shop.

Chapter Sixteen
Cameron

"I don't know what the fuck is wrong with me." I catch Dan's concerned stare. "Some sick part of me wanted to tell her the truth and enjoy her guilt, but I feel even more ashamed now than I did back then," I whisper, and stare at a speck of fluff on the floor to stop myself from giving in to my emotions. For the first time in a long damn while, I want to cry. I want to roar and throw my fists. Shaking my head, I pinch the bridge of my nose and suck in a deep breath.

I'm not going to fucking cry.

She didn't care back then, so why the hell should I give a fuck how she feels now?

I don't.

Dan slaps my back. "Let it out, mate."

"Kerry needs to keep her fucking mouth shut," I hiss, shrugging him off.

"Don't do that. She was probably trying to placate Nadine, who, by the sounds of it, came to her own conclusions," Dan mutters, watching me with irritating intensity. He's expecting me to lose it. I'm unravelling. I can feel it. That horrible sensation of being unhinged is dangling at the periphery of my mind, urging me to accept it and snap. I'm not giving in. Shrugging, I dismiss both women's feelings and move away from my friend. I know Dan is being supportive, but his hand being on my back makes me want to break down. I hate this feeling. I'm fighting it with everything I have. Every cell is under attack to an anger I have no control over, to a hatred that's bleak and traumatic. I don't want to be that person again. I hated that person. He disgusts me.

"What did Holly say?" he asks in a cautious tone, goes to the fridge and pulls two beers out.

"Nothing, I left. I didn't want her to look at me in pity," I reply. Who cares what she says or even thinks? She bloody left me, and her actions fuelled others' suspicions. Why would someone helplessly in love with me run a mile if what I was accused of hadn't happened? Sarah's lawyer's snide remark comes back, and I crick my neck.

"Understandable. Why don't you give Dr Peterson a call?" Dan proposes and hands me a beer. I glare at him.

"I don't need a therapist," I mutter and take a long pull of my beer. I did back then, but fuck going through that again. Being cross-examined and having my feelings dissected was bad enough the first time, but pulling the infected bandage off again to relive that night, a moment that cost me my life, my manhood, is the last thing I ever want to do.

"It helped last time," he replies calmly and takes a seat on my sofa. He's right, but I refuse to let him know that. It helped me to accept the nasty turn my life had taken, to accept the confusion and heartache. Slowly, but surely, I came to terms with the ordeal of being dragged through the mud publicly.

Am I over the rape and losing Holly? Never.

"I don't want to talk about it."

"You said that last time, and back then, Holly was gone. She's here now and you're feeling new things. Mate, I can't help you. I haven't got a clue what to say. Ring Peterson," he pleads. I grunt in response and close my eyes. Holly's distraught face slams through my mind. Fuck!

"And for fuck's sake, get rid of this wank sofa," he groans. I side-eye him and smirk at his appalled expression. It is fucking hideous.

"It's on order. Kitchen and bathrooms are coming soon too," I say, happy for the distraction. Another week and my house will be a home. Everything I have been working towards over the past few years is finally coming to fruition, and it feels so good. At Least that part of my life is good. I grip onto it with single-handed determination.

"Holly is going to want to talk to you."

"I'm not interested," I mutter.

"Oh, pull the other one. You need to hash all this shit out. At least talk to her if you're not going to speak to Peterson."

I laugh. "And what is sweet little Holly going to be able to help me with that a practised and experienced therapist can't?"

"You're in love with her. Sometimes, what breaks you needs to fix you," Dan imparts philosophically. I pull a concerned glance at him and stand, weirded out. "What?"

"You and all this la-di-da textbook shit." I shudder.

"Tell me it's a lie." He raises his brow, and I shake my head, trying not to laugh. He's a fucking woman in man's clothing. I swear it.

I don't answer for a few moments, mulling it all over in my chaotic mind. "Dan, I don't want to talk to Holly."

"No?" He smirks knowingly at me, though his eyes are focused on something behind me.

"No. I want to fuck her. End of," I growl. Dan shakes his head in warning at me. "What the hell are you shaking your head for? If I want to fuck her, I will."

"*Nice.*" Holly's disappointed voice shocks me. With gritted teeth, I turn to where she is standing awkwardly in the back doorway. Clearing her throat, she gives me a sympathetic smile. "I think we need to talk."

"No, we don't." I neck the rest of my beer, keeping my eyes on her. She's wearing a pair of tight jeans and a fitted top, showcasing all of her curves. "Like I said to Dan, I want to fuck you, so if you're game, feel free to stay, otherwise go away."

"Cam!" Dan snaps, grabbing my shoulder. "Cut it out."

"What?" I laugh, unfazed by how stung Holly looks at my harsh words.

"You're sabotaging again. Stop it," Dan hisses. "Holly, give him a few days." So, he's planning my life now too? Good to know!

"Yeah, what's a few more days after ten years. How does it feel to know you're in the wrong and not me?"

"I didn't know," Holly whispers.

"YOU DIDN'T WANT TO KNOW!" I roar, standing and throwing my beer to the ground and it smashes. Dan steps in front of me as I charge at Holly to scream all my hurt and anger in her face. She backs up and blinks back tears. "You don't get to cry!" I tell her. "What did you lose?" I snigger. "My fucking parents disowned me." I punch my chest. I suck in short breaths and blink as my eyes burn. Dan pushes me back as I press into him. With a growl, I throw a punch, landing it to his jaw. "Fuck off!" I bellow at him.

"Holly, leave!" Dan snaps.

"Oh god, Dan," she whispers, distressed.

"Holly, it's okay, please go. I can handle it."

I laugh, then launch my fist into the door, leaving a huge hole in it. I want to scare her off. Send her away, out of Richmond. Out of my life. And to think I was even remotely happy she was back that first day. I can't express the level of anger I'm dealing with now that I've confessed what happened. The trauma I had shut down in my mind has sprung wide open and is ready to destroy anything in its path. Destroy me.

The door slams shut, and I stare at the thick wood, panting uncontrollably. "Nice going, hulk," Dan moans, working his jaw. "Next time, aim for my arm."

"FUCK!"

"W ATCH ME, WATCH ME!" Grace giggles excitedly. Dan and I twist from our position on the decking to where she is swinging on a tyre at Dan's holiday home in Cornwall. As soon as Grace finished school on Friday, we bundled into his car, and he drove us straight to the coast and far, far away from Richmond.

Finally, I can breathe. My chest isn't tight with anxiety. My head isn't aching with tension. I'm relaxed. "Go higher!" I shout.

Grace grins. "Daddy, look!"

"I'm watching, Gracie," Dan replies. "Well done, baby," he mutters, rubbing his face tiredly.

I frown at him and notice for the first time how forlorn he looks. His mouth is turned down and he keeps staring off into the distance. "What's going on?" I ask suddenly.

Throwing me an irritated glance, he looks away. "Nothing."

"Bullshit. You've got a case of the feels. Who's the poor lady?" I joke, trying to get him to open up about what's going on.

"I'm fine," he mutters. "Brant messaged, by the way, says Kerry feels really bad about what Nadine said."

I shrug, not letting it bother me. I'm here, miles away from all the drama, and I will keep it that way. "So, you hear from Rebecca again?"

"Not going to work out." He clears his throat and gets up. "Another beer?" He hotfoots it inside. Something's off. I get up and follow him inside. He's checking his phone. With a deep grumble, he slams it down on the side, muttering about women.

"So...there is someone!" I grin, making him jump.

"No. Fuck off!" he spits defensively. His phone dings and we both race for it. He's millimetres away when I shoulder barge him and grasp the phone. I do a backwards roll over him, laughing as he grunts in pain, and I run off reading the message on the home screen.

My eyes widen, and I catch sight of Dan rushing towards me with a scowl on his face. I laugh and read it out loudly. "The other night was a mistake, but thank you for the hot sex and multiple orgasms." I'm giggling like a fucking kid. "Who is this?" I question, diving out of his way, then jumping to the left when he tries to get his phone.

"None of your business."

"So you won't mind if I ring her then, or maybe it's a guy?" I wiggle my brows.

"Quit messing about, Cam." He dives at my legs, knocking me sideways. I grip the phone and the unmistakable sound of the line ringing renders us both speechless. Dan's eyes widen, and I copy him. "Cam, no. She'll think I'm a right letch!"

"They have a vagina. Check." I hold a finger up. "Do I know this woman?" I question, wiggling another finger to check off as Dan tries to grab the phone, but I lift my hand out of his reach.

"She's not answering. Give me the phone." Oh, poor baby, this is priceless. I wonder who's got him by the balls?

"Hi, you've reached Emily's voicemail. I can't get to the phone right now because—" I gape at Dan, and he punches me in the ribs.

"Fuck," I groan.

"Because she is busy with me," a male voice murmurs down the phone. Dan snaps back, affronted.

"What the fuck?" Dan growls loudly.

"Wes, stop it. I can't keep that now." She giggles and screams happily before the line goes quiet and an automated voice tells us to leave a voicemail after the beat.

"Who the fuck is Wes, huh?" I shout.

"Cameron, you prick, give me the phone." Dan argues and snatches at it, but I disconnect before he can delete the recording. "You're walking home."

"Emily, huh? Look at you with your pants in a twist." I grin.

"Fuck off."

He stalks away, lifting his phone. "It was a mistake."

I give him a few moments outside to cool off because he is pissed that Emily isn't interested. Grabbing us both a beer, I wander out to find Grace curled up in his lap, drawing circles in his palm. I place his drink on the side and take my seat. "Don't look." She whines at him, then draws a heart shape. "What shape is that?"

"Love heart," Dan whispers, eyes closed.

"This one." She squiggles another, but I can't see as she leans in the way.

"Star."

"Can we go in the sea again?" Grace yawns.

"Maybe in the morning, let's order takeaway and then we can chill with a movie and popcorn."

"Not Uni-Cornelius," I beg. Whichever douche made a film based in a university, about a unicorn called Cornelius needs putting to fucking sleep.

"But he's my favourite!" Grace defends. She knows I hate it. What's worse is it's not animated; it's some pillock dressed as a unicorn clip clopping his sad arse around the university grounds talking about shit too advanced for kids her age.

"What about Beauty and the Beast?" Dan mentions, and Grace's eyes spark up. Thank fuck for that.

"Not off the hook," I mutter.

An hour later, we are all splayed out in the living room, watching the movie. Grace is whispering along to the songs, and I smile. I wonder if Beau likes this movie. She's sensitive, so I bet the beast scares her. I frown and shake my thoughts away. Nothing to do with me what she does and doesn't like. Holly made sure it was nothing to do with anyone when she got herself a donor and became an incubator for a child who has no father. I'm being pig-headed. I'm blind with jealousy.

The father was supposed to be me.

I barely recognise the person she was, but knowing she raised her daughter alone, braved motherhood single-handedly, reminds me of how selfless and strong she is. Grace wriggles free and walks to the centre of the living room with a blanket draped around her shoulders as she watches the TV and dances to the songs.

"Want to talk about it?" I say to Dan.

"Night of stupidity."

"Why are you so bothered, then?"

Dan glares at the screen and I give him the time to work through his thoughts before he twists sharply and hisses under his breath so Grace can't hear, "Because I wanted another night and then maybe another."

"So you like her then?" This is good news. I like Emily, plus she worked at the summer club. She's good with children and Grace likes her. Win-win.

"I wouldn't go that far; she's fiery and fun."

"You like her," I tell him simply. "Welcome to my world." Ha! For once, I'm not alone in all this.

"Your world is shit. I don't want to be in your world."

"Thanks, pal, don't hold back or anything. Say what you really mean." I scoff.

"I didn't mean it like that."

"You did." I smile despite how it needles my gut, knowing what he thinks.

"What are we, married now?" Dan smirks. We always say that when things are getting a little too personal, and it makes me chuckle. He sighs and looks at me earnestly. "You don't want help, won't accept help, but you need it, Cam." My friend shrugs unapologetically. "You absolutely need to talk to Holly and finally move on, with or without her."

Grace pads back over and climbs in his lap.

"I know." I stare blankly at the TV. "I will when we get home. I just need these few days to think about things."

THE FOLLOWING MORNING, I wake up and head out the back. The beach is quiet, and with the tide out, I run along the shore. I stand tall and drag in the cleansing sea air. Being here is like a ritual. Once we've arrived, we mentally detox and return home better men. I hit the sand at a fast pace and a woman jogging towards me gives me a flirtatious smile, but I drop my head and power on, hitting the sand harder and faster. I run until I'm sweating furiously and my heart is begging for escape. Exercise became my vice during the trial, and I kept it up because for a few hours each day, I was able to forget. I run for a few miles, then turn round and run back to the beachfront cottage.

It's still dark inside, so I catch my breath out on the decking and stare at the property. Each time I come here, I always speculate what I could have achieved had my life not taken a huge nosedive. I'm so proud of Dan and everything he has. He worked hard to build his business up, and the cottage he bought a few years back is a getaway for him and Grace. I have money, but I have nothing to spend it on other than doing up the house back in Richmond. Maybe I can look into investing some of it into a coastal property?

"Morning," Dan yawns when I walk in.

"Hey, man. Is Grace still asleep?"

"Sea air." He grins.

"I know you know this, but thanks," I mutter, not meeting

his eye. He's done a lot for me, keeps doing a lot for me and he puts up with all my shit.

"No worries. But this is it now. We're getting to the bottom of it all. You're letting go of the past, Cam. This is your chance." He sighs sternly. "Don't you miss the old you?" He holds my stare.

He doesn't mean rekindling things with Holly, but laying my hurt to rest. She is here, and I can finally voice my hurt and draw a line under it all. Then I can start to live again, as me.

Cameron Stone. Not this angry, chaotic mess of a man, ready to snap at any second. "I know. Yeah." This is it. When I return to Richmond, I'm heading straight for Holly's. "Let me grab a shower and I'll sort breakfast."

"Full English!" Dan demands, making me chuckle.

Chapter Seventeen
Holly

I leave Cameron's in a tearful blur. I don't recall pulling up at home or seeing Emily out when she agreed to watch Beau after Cameron dropped his bombshell in the shop. I still feel that pull. I wish he hadn't kissed me. It's on a running loop in my mind. Electric and bright, nothing like the dark and foreboding man I just left in a rage. He's no longer the man I fell in love with. It's all my fault. I didn't believe him. I ran. I can't even begin to comprehend how distraught he must have felt, how heartbroken and traumatised he must have been all those years ago. Cameron, for all his good looks and cockiness, was a proud person when we were younger. He was respectful and only a gentleman with me, unless I begged for more. My cheeks flame, and my eyes spill over with tears I have no right to shed.

He's right. I only lost what I chose to give up, but he lost it all. Everything.

How could his parents disown him, and where the hell is that vile creature, Sarah Daniels?

If I want to win back even a shred of his trust, I need to give him time. Space. I owe it to him to make it up to him. If that means fixing what was growing between him and Nadine, then so bit it.

Beau is lying upside down on the sofa watching a programme. "Comfy?" I ask quietly.

"It's all upsy daisy down." She giggles.

"Just be careful," I say and race upstairs to get my laptop. The last thing I want to do is ask around and add fuel to the fire; it'd turn from underfoot embers to a roaring wildfire that sweeps through Richmond with Cameron at the centre again.

I'm so bloody naive sometimes it's infuriating. Clutching my stomach, I stop and breathe in deeply, quelling my nausea. Had I stayed, none of this would ever have happened.

I fire up my laptop and wait impatiently as it loads, and as soon as I have access to the internet, I google Cameron's name, my fingers hovering over the letters R.A.P and…I feel sick. I can't type it. Instead, I type trial, the year, and hit enter. Link upon link, images assault my eyes. My horrified gaze dances over headlines and articles, but it's one picture in particular that grabs my attention. My hands shake when I click to open the photo. I bite my lip to stop myself from wailing loudly and scaring Beau. He's sickly thin. Gaunt. And his eyes are like two orbs of hopelessness. Clothes that once clung to him hang off, his hair dishevelled and uncut. I sob at the image of the boy who I left. The man I helped create.

My fingers move quickly over the keys as I read over articles, seeing mention of a possible prison sentence and court dates. I see a snap of Sarah looking like the snotty stuck-up bitch she was. "Vile human!" I growl. I hate her. How could she? I want to track her down and shake the hell out of her. I realise I'm breathing heavily, and my fingers are clenched tight into a fist. Slamming my eyes shut, I picture that night.

I'd arrived late to the party. I wanted to finish a paper that was due the following week. I can't even recall what it was now.

. . .

Every year, Cole Peters held an end of schoolhouse party. His parents would be off, glitzing it up somewhere, and he'd go wild. The party was in full swing by the time I arrived, and it was clear on entry I was the only person sober. There was an odd atmosphere, a niggling thrum about the place, the people. Some were more than just drunk, and I immediately felt on edge. I searched for Cameron everywhere, but I couldn't see him. The floor and sides were littered with bottles and pizza trays, cups and shot glasses. The pungent smell of smoke was everywhere, but it wasn't just cigarette smoke, but something else. I noticed people I didn't recognise from school, older people. Someone grabbed me and asked for a kiss, and I tugged away, rushing to find Cameron, but instead I found Dan and Cole instead.

"Where's Cam?" They never accepted me. Cam had said they were threatened by my presence in his life, but I never knew if that was really the cause. Seeing their eyes, I could tell they had taken something. "I can't find Cam," I said again. "Have you seen him?"

Shrugging, Cole twisted his neck to look at me and sniggered. "Maybe."

"Cole, come on." I sighed as Brant appeared, staggering. His pupils were wide.

"He may or may not be with Sarah." Cole's older brother ginned wickedly.

"Excuse me?"

"Excuse me," Cole mimicked, earning laughs from all the intoxicated guys. "You're such a prude, Cam needs to sack you off." Cole's older brother scoffs.

"So he's with Sarah, where?" I tried my hardest not to let my thoughts run away, but something deep inside told me something was wrong.

"Spare room," Dan stated bluntly, and I gripped my stomach. My eyes stung, but I blinked my hurt back and gave them an insincere smile. They were drunk and probably high if their eyeballs were anything to go by. Maybe they were messing with me? I took the stairs two at a time. A few jeers started and my heart slammed like a piston in my chest. I gripped the handle. Held my breath and my heart came to a painful stop.

"No!" I choked. Sarah was writhing on top of Cameron, and he was grunting, his hand swiping across her breasts, then pressing at her shoulder, and his face twisted to mine in agonised pleasure.

"No!" I cried, stumbling back. A ruckus of laughter broke out, and I twisted, nearly falling over the bannister. Shakily, I ran down the stairs. My legs threatened to give way, my stomach curdling, and all the while everyone around me was laughing.

"Mummy?" Startled, I slam the laptop shut and smile at Beau, but my face is sodden with tears. "Mummy, why are you sad?" Her lip wobbles, and I pull her to me, holding tight.

"It's okay. Mummy is okay, I just need a hug." I shudder.

"Mummy needs pizza and ice cream?" She twiddles with my hair and kisses my shoulder. Her voice wavers, and I know it's because I'm sad and she doesn't like it.

"I definitely do. Shall we order some?" I whisper, quickly wiping my tears away on my sleeve. She nods into my neck, and I spend the evening making it all about her. I don't want her to see me upset or feel she must comfort me. That's my job.

"This is where the horsey prince lives. His name is Marbullous Marvin." Beau giggles, moving her horse along the floor. I swallow my laugh at her attempt at saying marvellous and grin with feigned excitement.

"So where does my horse live?" I ask her, going to a stable.

"Not that one, the nasty frog man lives there." Beau frowns at me. "He is slimy and eats their food. The prince fights him."

"Sounds very scary," I murmur and follow her finger when she points to another stable we made out of old cardboard and Sellotape.

"Marvin will win. YoYo can sleep here."

My phone pings, and I check to see if it's Dan. I messaged

after I left to see if Cameron was okay. I had to know if he had calmed down.

> Hi, I'm sorry about what happened. I want us to be friends. Marcus x

GROANING, I turn my phone over and continue playing with Beau and her toys. He can wait until I'm ready. I'm still not happy with him. It took two weeks to win my mother over and the only thing that made her change her tune was hearing Beau ask why she was being unkind. I hadn't expected her to come out with it. When my mother questioned me, I begrudgingly admitted that I found her to be mean, and I usually agreed to save myself the argument with her. She's never been an easy person to approach, and her ideals aren't like my own. I'm hoping that she finally accepts what I want.

"Mummy, YoYo needs to go in her stable." Beau sighs, clearly annoyed with me for not paying attention.

"And so does Beau!" I laugh, tickling her side.

I HAVEN'T SEEN Cameron or Dan for a few days, and when I mention it to Emily, she refers to a voicemail she received over the weekend. I haven't confessed to her or anyone else about the conversation that happened between Cameron, Nadine, and I.

"It's really awkward," she confesses on a hush, checking over her shoulder to make sure no one is at the counter, then adds, "Dan has been hitting up my phone, calls, texts." He could have replied to me, the cheeky bugger!

"He's into you." It's obvious.

"I can't give him more," she murmurs and starts wiping the side. This is a touchy subject for her. She has feelings for him, I see that now, and she is scared he will only hurt her like her ex.

"Maybe you should tell him that. He'll appreciate your honesty."

"Well, I did." She laughs nervously. "Then my phone starts ringing. It's Dan," she tells me, panicked, "and I didn't dare pick it up. It went to voicemail, and I forgot to change it. Wes and I are on it."

"Ah."

"No shit." She laughs again. "I get this voicemail and it's Cam ranting about who Wes is, then Dan is yelling at him and that's it." She shrugs.

"Wait, no more texts or calls?" I wonder.

"Nope." Shaking her head, Emily grabs a brownie and eats it. "Not a thing," she mumbles, annoyed.

"So you wanted him to contact you?"

"Well, duh, yeah, he is like..." She stares at me, wide-eyed. "Come on, Dan is *fucking* hot."

"But you told him you're not interested?"

"I don't want to be. Wes and I never had that kind of chemistry, and I want more of that, but I'm scared to dip my toe in the dating pool. Scared because I like him." Her confession is uttered with a deep blush rolling over her cheeks.

"Why don't you have fun and see where it goes?"

"I'm not sure I'm the fun type." She wrinkles her nose. "I get too caught up."

"I think after the other night, Dan thinks you're the fun type," I tell her, and she drops her head in her hands, groaning loudly.

"Enough about me. Have you spoken to Cameron since he

kissed you?" Em asks, following me into the back office. I shake my head but don't turn to look at her. She will know if I'm lying. I've never been good at hiding my emotions. "I heard he and Nadine broke up."

I hum and keep my head down.

"It's okay to be happy about that. You're still in love with him, Holly. I knew it the second I saw you both together. There is this sway about you both. I think you came back because you were finally ready to forgive him." I flinch because although I kept telling myself he wouldn't be here, inside, in a tiny dark and depraved part of me, I wanted him to be here. Wanted him to fix all the hurt I had suffered with. At my own cost, apparently. If anyone needs forgiving, it's me.

"What will be, will be." Her face falls, and I move past her, desperate to get away from the conversation.

After Beau had gone to bed the other night, I researched extensively on his court case and trial. It ran for a year. A year! All that time of being picked and pulled at, having people build up a sick assumption of you whilst others allow it to be exploited for personal gain. I've not been able to look at the people of Richmond the same way. Why didn't they help him?

Someone eventually had, because Sarah suddenly dropped all charges and recanted her statement. Another person had come forward for spiking Cameron's drink and several witnesses stated he had gone in the room alone and seen her follow. As quickly as Cameron's parents had cut ties with him, she had disappeared too. I'm ashamed to admit I searched online for her too, but she is using an alias or hasn't embarked on social media life. I hope karma does her dirty when it finally catches up with her.

"Do you really mean that?" Emily says from beside me as I approach a customer at the counter.

"Yes."

. . .

It's closing time and Beau is scribbling away at a table with some glitter pens. Emily and I are cleaning, and Keeley left early to go on a date. I'm busy with the hoover so I don't hear the door ping, but I do catch sight of Dan striding through the shop to a gawking Emily. I kick the hoover, switching it off as he strolls over to her.

When he heads straight for her, she lifts the dripping mop she is holding, wielding it like a weapon. He knocks it out his way and it clatters to the floor. "You're ignoring my calls," he drawls, eyes dragging down her body. I watch, open-mouthed, as he grips her hair and kisses her.

Jesus Christ, I've never seen Dan so formidable before.

"What are you doing? You kissed me." She splutters.

Biting my lip, I try not to laugh at how tongue-tied she is. Her hand rests on her lips.

"It was not a mistake, and we will be doing it again...*very soon.*" Emily rears back in shock. He means sex! "A lot," he adds. When she doesn't respond, he cups her jaw, and he pecks her cheek. "I'll call you later," he murmurs, then whispers something in her ear.

Wow!

What is it with the people of this village and having all their intimate moments in my bloody shop! Dan smiles at me politely over her shoulder, and I raise my brow. "Is he okay?" I ask.

"He will be. Expect a visit," he warns. A visit? Is that a good or a bad thing? He leaves and both Emily and I are dumbfounded. I hate these damn cryptic men!

"So, that just happened!" Emily chokes out.

"Bloody hell, I can't believe he didn't care I was here!"

"I told you he was dominating," she squeaks.

"What did he whisper to you?" I say without thinking, but she goes even redder. I hold up my hand. "On second thoughts, I don't want to know."

She giggles, then leans to grab the mop, and I start to laugh. "I think I got dirty water on his suit." She cackles.

"You looked like you were wielding a sword."

"I'm so embarrassed," she whines and stomps off dramatically with the mop and bucket.

"Wait, don't go, someone else is coming. I need your ninja mop skills again!" I shout after her.

"This mop will be going where the sun doesn't shine if you carry on!"

"A cave!" Beau pipes in from her spot where she's colouring a book. "Suns don't shine in caves." We burst out laughing.

Emily sticks her tongue out from the back office, then grabs her belongings. "Right, I'm off home. See you tomorrow!" she calls back to us both.

Beau helps me lock up, and we head home after a busy day. She had PE today, so I know she will be out like a light tonight.

"Yeah, Unky Cam!" Beau squeals excitedly. My eyes flash to the house, and there he is, sitting on the front bench. I throw a bright smile into the back at Beau to dispel my unease.

The second I turn the engine off, she is unbuckling herself and pushing the door open. She runs up the driveway where Cam walks to meet her. "Hey, boo!" He smiles, picking her up, and Beau throws her head back on a laugh and grips at his collar.

"Emily hit Grace's daddy with the mop," she announces loudly. Cam looks at me in confusion.

"Don't ask." When Dan said to expect a visit, I thought he meant in the next few days, not tonight. Now. Right this minute.

"Can I come in?" Cam asks, holding Beau with one arm. I have no idea if it's hormones or just him, but seeing him carry Beau is just the sexiest thing. That and him calling her boo.

"Yeah!" she squeals.

"Sure," I croak.

"Relax, Holly."

"Yeah, Mummy, relax. Ice cream and pizza." She grins.

"Maybe another night," I tell her and unlock the door. Cam doesn't let Beau down and she is happy to stay in his arms, she even rests her head on his chest and yawns. "She's super tired."

"It's not a problem," he replies, "is it?" He looks at my little girl snuggled into him.

"Nope!" She smiles adoringly at him.

"Make yourself comfortable. We haven't had dinner, and I've got something in the slow cooker," I say nervously. "Do you want some?"

"Sure."

I rush about setting the table and serving dinner. My girl is adamant to sit next to Cameron. It's odd seeing him sitting at the table with us, quietly chatting to Beau about her day. We keep it neutral and after a few minutes of me trying to negotiate with Beau, I finally relent and let Cameron put her to bed when we finish our meal.

"Let me sort your jammies out and you can brush your teeth, then Cameron can read you a story," I suggest.

"Okay." She nods. "We're reading *The Princess and the Pea*," she tells Cam pointedly.

"Good, I like that one." His chest inflates, and I see him swallow his emotions. He's finding this hard too. We share a moment of understanding, silent pain pulsing below the surface. I hold his stare and beg him to forgive me with my eyes alone. I never meant to hurt him, and I hate myself for my part in all of this.

"Go on then." He nods for us to go.

I twist away and help Beau up the stairs, getting her ready. As soon as she is changed, she stands at the top of the stairs.

"Unky Cameron, come read my story!" I keep quiet as his soft but clear footsteps ascend the stairs. His face slowly comes into view, and I bite the inside of my mouth. Beau grabs his hand and pulls him towards her room, where she runs in and bounces on the bed excitedly. "This my unicorn room!" she informs him, delighted by all the pink, fluffy glitter.

"Wow, I wish my room was like this."

"Mummy, you sit there!" Beau points at the old leather office chair that was my father's.

"Okay." I slip into the chair. Is it me, or are we both taking direction from a small child to save ourselves the stress of making our own decisions?

"You have to lie on the bed like Mummy does," Beau tells him with a shake of her head.

"I'm a bit bigger than your mummy." Cameron smiles. "I can sit here on the floor." He begins reading, and his deep voice floats through the room in a rich lull. Beau grips onto his forearm and smiles, enchanted by him. I cover my mouth because she is desperate for the love of a father. Repeatedly, I want to flee from the room, but some sixth sense tells me this is the only time it's going to happen, so I stay rooted, lapping up the view until my daughter drifts off to sleep.

Chapter Eighteen
Cameron

I can think of a thousand excuses why I shouldn't read to this little girl, but only one has me sitting beside her bed. I love her little blonde head. She's fast asleep now, oblivious to the turmoil running between her mother and me. And there is enough turmoil to fill a dam. I've allowed myself this one memory. We can't have any more. I spent the entire weekend and drive home rallying my brain into what needed to be done. I love this woman and I was telling Nadine the truth when I said I don't know how not to love her. I've loved Holly for so long the alternative is impossible, but I love the Holly from before, and the man I am today isn't ready to get to the know the woman who looks like her. I suspect on some level she feels the same. We are both different people and too much has happened for us to ever get back to hash it out. And for me, that means cutting off the past. Holly and I have been over for a decade, but today, I finally get to say goodbye.

"Can I make you a drink?" Her soft voice grabs my attention from Beau. I will miss this little girl.

"Got any beer?"

"I can check." We leave Beau's room, and I follow Holly

downstairs. She begins closing the curtains and turning on the odd lamp as she makes her way to the kitchen and into the pantry. She turns with her nose scrunched. "I have this. It's cold but not fridge cold." Shrugging, I take it from her, twisting off the cap. "Just going to make myself a drink." She swallows and yanks down a wineglass and fills it to the rim. I want to laugh, but I'm experiencing the same sense of doom too and it's not funny.

"Where do you want to sit?" I ask.

"Through there." She points to the lounge. I'm nearest, so I move that way and take a spot on the sofa. Holly chooses the armchair.

Clearing my throat, I tilt my head and say, "Before we start, what happened between Emily and Dan today?"

"He...well, he was." Holly blushes and frowns down at her hands. "Sex. He wanted sex." I burst out laughing. "Em tried to shoo him with the mop." She laughs. "It was so funny."

"I bet. He likes her."

"I know. She's being cautious," Holly tells me.

"Wes?" I ask, and she nods. God, this is strange. Our conversation is so jilted and full of feigned politeness. She gives me a strained smile, and I can see like me, there is so much she wants to say, but not everything is worth saying anymore. Not after this amount of time. I don't know whether defeat has claimed me, but I feel a ton lighter and I know once I walk out of this door, my life will begin again. I'm resolute in that.

Holly stares at me with wariness. Twice, she opens her mouth to say something, but each time she sucks in a nervous breath and grits her jaw. "I hated you for years," I admit in a pained croak. Her eyes snap to mine. Hurt. "I hated that I still loved you too. That night, Cole's cousin had come to Richmond with his mates and they spiked our drinks. A toxicology report proved that we were all under the influence of a substance. None of us had agreed to take it."

Holly's hand cups her throat, and she holds my gaze keenly. But there is a world of sadness there too.

"I went upstairs to lie down. I didn't feel good, and I was worried that if you saw me in that state, you'd leave me."' She gives me a sad smile because we both know it's the truth. This is the part I hate with every fibre of my being. It's as if any thought or mention of it chips a small part of the already broken me away. "I woke up to Sarah undressing me and..." I swallow a groan of shame. It's like her hands are on me all over again. I feel tainted. Vulnerable. "My body reacted even though my mind was repulsed. I was semi coherent but had little to no control over my body," I force out through gritted teeth. "That is the only thing I will ever be sorry for, but the rest was never on me. I fought her off as much as I could. Tried to call for help. Holly, when you walked through that door, all I could think was, *finally*, someone is here to help me."

Holly flies from her chair and her dainty arms envelope me. "I'm sorry." I cripple in her hold, shuddering out a long breath. When I cry, she stiffens and sobs louder. Our tears tangle like our hearts have been all these years. So much pain. No one can come back from that.

"I was trying to push her off, but my limbs felt like weak poles," I whisper, fisting her hair and keeping my face hidden. I don't want her to see me like this.

Gripping my shirt, she buries her head in my chest and shakes it sadly. "I know."

What! And she never came back for me? I snap back, disgusted.

Panicked hands grip my thighs. "No!" she cries, realising her mistake. "Listen, I know that *now*. I...I couldn't think about that night, but I made myself go back to that night and she was on top. I remember that. I can picture you trying to swing your arm, but my brain didn't compute any of that." She sobs, pressing her lips together to detain another wail. "I didn't want to believe it because I could never understand why someone like you wanted to be with someone like me." Her eyes beg me to understand. Hearing her insecurities cripples me now as much as it did then. Nothing I said would placate her, and Sarah's actions that day were the nail in the coffin for Holly. It was the physical proof she needed to confirm her doubt.

I had no doubt about my love for her.

Because she had made me a better person, what had at first been lust and curiosity soon catapulted into an obsession and then quickly love. "I think I stayed in Richmond all of these years because I knew, at some point, you would return, and it was the final step in my grieving process," I continue. I have no idea what she wants to say to me. What do you say to someone when you discover you were wrong after all this time? "Seeing you at the fair that day was like lighting a firework in a closed box. Everything came to the surface, and I realised I hadn't dealt with it all like I thought I had. And I need to, so this is me dealing with it," I admit shakily. "Taking control of my trauma. I never understood what my therapist meant by that, but I do now."

Surprise flits across her face. I offer her a smile and shrug a shoulder lightly. I had a therapist. What does she expect? I was barely an adult and my life fragmented, in the most horrific way.

"I don't feel like there are enough words to express how sorry I am." Small hands lift my larger and rougher ones. Holly dips her head and kisses my clenched fist. "I'm sorry for doubting you and myself. Sorry for leaving, for not coming back sooner. I'm truly sorry I wasn't there to support you." She lifts her head, and as soon as she sees my tears, she bursts into another round of sobs. "Oh god." She shakes her head. "Cameron, you may never forgive me, but I will do whatever you need to help you through this. Whatever you want."

I cup her face and give her a mournful smile. "You don't

need to do anything. You came home, and I needed that more than I ever realised. It gave me the push I needed to finally lay this all to rest. I stayed because I needed to have this moment with you. You're the only woman I loved, and losing you in that way only added to the trauma of Sarah and my parents cutting me off. Now, I can let go. I've decided to let go of you and Richmond."

Her eyes widen. Regret and disagreement swim through her pain. She doesn't want to lose me, but I've finally come to recognise I never found myself after everything happened.

"You're leaving?" She snaps out my hold. "Cameron, I don't want you to leave because of me!"

"I'm not. I'm leaving for me. I've put an offer in for a place by the coast. I'll be renting my house out, and Dan has plenty of space if I ever want to visit."

She stares at me, astonished. "I don't know what to say." She sniffs. "I thought we could...I don't know, try to be friends." Beautiful eyes plead with me.

"I could never be *just* your friend, and I know you haven't moved on and met someone because of what you thought I did." I rub her hand with my thumb. She drops her head and I sigh. "You used a donor to gain a child because you were too scared to love again. Holly, that's not normal," I whisper. "I don't want to watch some other guy father Beau when we made all these plans. I know it was years ago, but my life has been at a standstill since then, and sometimes it feels like it was only yesterday when we were sneaking off to make out behind Grayson's barn." She chuckles sadly.

"I know. And you're right, I haven't let myself move on because I was heartbroken. Apparently for no reason. What a stupid idiot I was, huh?"

"Stupid and most beautiful idiot." I wink and stare at her face for a long time. She does mine too. Cataloguing. "I do forgive you, Holly. We were young, and it wasn't your fault. Stop blaming yourself, I can see it in your eyes."

"If I had just come home…" she whispers.

"Then you would have had to face the wrath of the village and all the hell that followed. It's taken me until now to realise, but I would never want that for you. Not really." I sit back and her hands drop away. Holly leans in and wipes my cheeks dry.

"When are you leaving?"

"I'm nearly done renovating the old rectory, so once that's complete and the other house goes through," I tell her, and she bites at the inside of her cheek. "I'm really proud of you, though." I say gruffly.

"You are?"

"Beau is amazing. She's smart and cute, and a credit to you, Holly, you're an amazing mother, but I always knew you would be. The shop too. I've loved having a small insight into your life, and meeting your daughter."

"Beau really likes you." She picks at the rug and sighs. "Thank you for being so kind to her."

We sit in a restrained silence. The tension is thick because we know what's coming. We need to get over that last hurdle. "Look, I really ought to get going, and I appreciate you letting me come round." She nods and bites her lip. Panic flashes in her eyes, but I don't allow myself to acknowledge it.

"I'm sorry for what you've been through." Her raspy tone alerts me to more possible tears.

I tap my chest. "Stone heart." I give her a lopsided smile. "Don't worry about me." Her pointed stare tells me she most likely will.

"Can I give you a hug before you go?" Her cheeks stain bright red, and I smile at her. Always so shy when asking for what she wants. God, she's so beautiful.

"I'll do you one better." I cup her face, bringing my lips flush to hers, and like I knew she would, she gasps in shock. I dive right in with my tongue. There was no way in hell I was leaving Richmond without kissing her goodbye. She is the love of my life. My old life, admittedly, and I'm sealing the door closed with a kiss for good luck. Holly grips tight and tangles her fingers into my hair. I want nothing more than to push her against the nearest available surface and sink into her, but I keep it to just a kiss. It goes on and on. All those times I kissed other women, this was what I imagined—trembling hands, soft lips and hard passion. Holly effortlessly pulls off a sexual innocence that triggers something in me. Something I'm programmed to reciprocate in the only way she needs. I clasp her face as tightly as I can without hurting her and feel every brush of her lips against mine. After an age of losing myself to the one vice that has grounded me to an unshakeable calm, I drag myself away.

"I hate that I still love you," she confesses. She wasn't supposed to admit that. I see the regret in her face.

"Back at you." I give her lips one last chaste kiss and stand. "I'm going to go," I say, for both our sakes.

She stands and follows me silently to the door. "Goodnight, Cam."

"I have a gift for Beau before I leave."

"Thank you." She wipes under her eyes and pulls her sleeves down over her hands and hugs herself. "It's her birthday in two weeks, so if you're still here, perhaps you can give it to her then?"

"She'll have it for her birthday." I step out of the door.

"Thank you." Her whisper becomes swallowed up by a passing car, however I see her gratitude and it fixes me to the front step. Her understanding rankles me slightly. I thought she would beg and plead for me to stay. She's too accepting. Too selfless to voice her true feelings, not that it matters. I've made up my mind and chose to heal myself without her.

"Goodnight, Hol." I turn finally and begin down the drive.

"Cam!" she calls after me. When I turn, she is shaking her head tearfully.

"I know." I know, and it fucking hurts like a bitch.

This is it. It only took us a decade, but we finally got closure. I told Dan I would head to his after, but I'm not in the mood for company. I get in my car and drive home. I've got a gift to make.

I STARE AT DR PETERSON, who has aged well over the last decade, her once blonde hair now pinned back in a grey bun, and her face is slightly wrinkled. I've spent the past forty-five minutes giving her a rundown of my life. How Holly is back and how I've handled my grief and taken control like she said to do years ago. The guys would be sickened to see me bleating like a goat to some shrink, but I'm satisfied with the outcome. For some peculiar reason, I need to hear from an outsider that I've done the right thing.

She smiles at me over her iPad, and I throw her my most charming smile. I am a little smug with myself. I took control. Goodbye, bullshit past. "Cameron, I suspect you want me to commend you for your efforts. Or, at the very least, reassure you've made the right decision." My smile slowly begins to drop away at her tone. What else is there to say? "Would I be correct in thinking you believe after all you've been through, both yourself and Miss Matthews cannot resolve this whilst being intimate?" This is why I hated coming here. Every thought I had deflected is gouged out and slapped in front of me to dissect. I swallow and stare silently at her. "Given your history with Miss Matthews and your tendency to sabotage..." I grit my teeth and shift in my seat. "Is it likely that you are choosing to run from the situation as you feel it's too big an obstacle to overcome?"

"It is," I grind out, furious at her for not giving me a pat on the back and sending me on my merry way.

"How would you know? Have you tried?"

"I... We're not the same people."

"And yet you are. You've both been living in the past. Sure, the world has continued moving and you've aged, had an experience or two, but the root of that night has tethered you both. I would like to see Miss Matthews at our next appointment, if she is willing, of course."

Who the fuck is this lady, and why isn't she supporting a decision she expressed I needed to achieve! Okay, it was years ago, but she could at least commend me.

"I'm not having a next appointment," I spit and stand. Fucking fuck! This was not supposed to go like this. "I'm moving away. I already told you that."

"You stayed for Miss Matthews to return so you could tell her that you have loved her all this time and quite likely still do?" She tilts her head at me and my damn eye twitches. I don't like this older Dr fucking Peterson. "I'm just reaffirming what you have told me. Is this correct?" she hums in that same fucking tone.

"Yes," I snarl quietly. I hate this place with an absolute passion.

"You both declare your love and you state you're leaving her and Richmond for good?" Her stylus clips the iPad, bringing my narrowed eyes to hers. I'm starting to doubt myself now.

She purses her mouth, and I get the distinct sense she is disappointed with me. Ditto. I want to tell her she is shit at her job, but she continues on despite my obvious discomfort. "Would I be right in saying that you're punishing Miss Matthews for all the years of heartache you endured because of her disappearance?"

And there it is. I'm a class-A bastard.

I hang my head and close my eyes. Guilt swims in my gut,

cooling my veins and making my limbs heavy with remorse. Did I feel satisfaction at Holly's hurt? Yes, I did. I was hoping she would be a little more theatrical and throw herself at me, but the result was the same. She is hurting because I made sure she knew she was at fault. She cheated us, not me.

"Cameron, I feel it's crucial that Miss Matthews attends your next meeting."

"Don't bother, you've made your point."

"And what point would that be?" Dr Peterson asks lightly.

"That this is the only way I know how to hurt her, and I'd rather cut my nose off to spite my face than risk being hurt again."

"You're still struggling to trust."

"My parents disowned me, half the village still ignores me, and I hate that I care." My voice filters into a frustrated whisper. Angered, I begin to pace her office.

"You want to be acknowledged and respected for the man you are, not the man from the rumour." I pin her with a look that says she is stupid for pointing out the obvious. She tilts her head, still expecting an answer. I nod and blow out a stream of air. "And on the other hand, I think fuck them. They'll need me before I do them." I verbalise one of my many thoughts on the subject.

"I believe the only person's opinion that matters to you is wondering how she is going to cope when you leave her after she hoped she might just get you back." Dr Peterson stands with a practised smile, and I curl my lip, insulted. She isn't supposed to be giving me such a hard time. I'm paying her to help me, not make me feel like a loose fucking cannon again. "That does, however, bring us to our hour." The sneaky fucker, I narrow my eyes at her. "Are you hoping lasers will shoot out your eyes?" she muses, and I bark out a laugh.

"It's a pleasure, as always, Dr Peterson." I let myself out before she can suggest a little get-together with Holly again.

Chapter Nineteen
Cameron

The electric sander whirs therapeutically as I smoothen the edges. I raise the measured piece of wood and blow off the remaining sawdust. It bursts apart under the harsh puff of air and dances like falling snow before me. It's one of my favourite smells, and being in here is exactly what my mind is demanding. I can never quite remember what made me pick up my first block of wood, but I had, and a small part of me relaxed. It had become a hobby, something to quieten my mind in the evenings. Nighttime was, and possibly still is, my least favourite time of the day after Sarah. Not only had the assault happened in the evening, but each time night came around, I was left with the stark and haunting realisation I was isolated, alone and left with too many thoughts to bring me any peace from the horror my life was. The love I had experienced in my childhood was nothing more than a dirty memory. They'd just left. My parents had packed their belongings and fled in the night, leaving an already devastated and terrified son to the unreasonable clutches of the law. I had never stood a chance. No one had believed me. It was her word against mine, and my cocky arse attitude had given me a middle finger. Despite the years that had passed, it's something that fills me with a sickness I can't fathom. My own parents, two people I was proud of, who I loved, had abandoned me in my hour of need. Another reason I hated the onset of a darkening sky. Back then, I'd exhaust myself each night. I honed my skills making small ornaments, soon I progressed to bigger pieces until I was designing unique furniture and selling them from my own workshop to customers who had no affiliation with Richmond. I look around the space and my eyes rest on Beau's present. This isn't the first time I've made a wooden playhouse, but I'm putting my all into giving her the best I can offer. Knowing that in my absence, she will have a small part of me is fulfilling in a way I hadn't realised I required.

My phone rings and Dan's name flashes. "Hey, man," I answer.

"I thought you were coming round?" He yawns.

"Nah, sorry, I just needed to clear my head." I've blown him off almost every day this week, and he hasn't pushed me once.

"I take it things didn't go so well with Holly the other night?"

"Things went fine. I saw Dr Peterson."

"That's good. She's still alive then?" he jokes.

"Barely. She's a mega bitch now." I scoff, blowing the wood clean once more.

"I take it things went better with Holly than the shrink?"

I hum and add the wood to the growing pile and pick up my jumper. The main body of the playhouse is done. I have affixed the flower boxes under the window and added the door and shutters. It's the smaller, intricate details I need to add on.

"You could say that." That kiss. I blow out a short breath. It was everything I never wanted it to be. Sweet. Soft. Hot. Kissing Holly was a step short of placing my lips against the sun. As a teen, I'd been shocked by my reaction to her. We'd been electric together. Now, we'd be explosive. I could feel it right down to my very bones. My skin had buzzed under the tremble of her fingertips. My spine had rippled and any traction of thought had dispersed into particles no bigger than the sawdust clinging to my damn hair.

"You're really sure about all of this?" Dan questions.

No! But it's what I need to give myself to recuperate from a life of self-hatred. Holly had left to fix what she thought had been broken. Now it was my turn.

"You should be celebrating. No more Cam drama."

"I'm ecstatic." He hates it as much as I do. We're as good as brothers and not having my best friend a few streets away is giving me anxiety. It's the one thing I'm still battling with, walking away from him and Grace. They are my family. Grace has been this little but bloody bright light in my life for the last five years. I'll only be a couple of hours away, but I'm still leaving her. Dan is yet to tell her, as he knows I want to be there when he does. I'm going to break her little heart. She deserves better and I want to be better for her. I'm sure this needs to happen. It's best for everyone. I'm no good to anyone in this state.

"Emily can fill up your time now." I close the workshop and head across the garden to my house. "I hear she's good at mopping up issues?" I snigger.

He laughs. "I'm seeing her tomorrow."

"You need me to have Grace?"

"If you don't mind?"

"Sure, no problem. The last pieces of furniture arrive tomorrow so I'm in all day," I remind him, stopping for a beer on my way to the shower.

"Thanks. Look, get some sleep and we'll catch up tomorrow." His pity causes me to grind my teeth. It's another reason I have to get out of here. My friends are watching me with the same pitying glances I witnessed when I first got dragged into Sarah's lies.

It's only because Sarah's friend had walked in on us after Holly ran out crying that the allegations were dropped. Trina had seen Sarah on top of me. Saw me out of it on drugs and trying to push her off. She pitied me and was willing to give evidence against her friend. That and the toxicology reports proved my innocence. Sarah's vile lies had come crashing down around her, but lies form rumours and rumours ruin lives.

I drag in a shuddering breath, pushing the memory away.

Those that believe her cross the street.

And those that believe me pity me.

I don't want their pity. I want their respect. "What are we, married?" I mutter, shaking my irritation off.

"You wish. Fucking perv." He disconnects on a snort. My laugh is short-lived because I'm left alone once more, alone with my chaotic thoughts. Screw Dr Peterson and her bullshit theories.

OVER THE LAST WEEK, I have taken to following the same routine every morning. Sleep eludes me, and despite the lack of it, I'm unreasonably full of energy. My shoes beat against the wet pavement. Torrential rain slants its way across my path, blurring my vision, the freezing cold water pouring in through the fine material, leaving my feet sodden and my shins splattered in grit. As soon as I'm rounding the bend and moving towards Holly's home, I slow. Her house comes into full view and through the open curtains, I see her with Beau in her arms. Dancing. It's barely seven in the morning and she is shimming her way around the living room. She dips Beau and swings her round and the only thing I can hear over my heartbeat is the high-pitch squeal of her little laugh.

This is what I'm giving up.

They're not losing anything because the evidence of their happiness is in front of me. They have each other. Dr Peterson's dagger sharp remarks have kept my mind full of doubt.

They can't miss something they never had.

They can't miss me because they never had me.

No one did. Not even me.

I lost myself ten years ago.

They dance their way across the window, then up on the sofa, jumping and giggling. I knew she'd be a fantastic mother. Holly always handled herself with a dignified calm. Where parents would falter, becoming flustered in certain situations, Holly takes it in her stride. Being a mother is a journey for her. One she is enjoying with her whole soul. You can see it in everything she does with Beau. Fuck, she makes most decent parents look bad. She's the purest woman I've ever known. I carry on, doubling back through the village, and round the memorial towards home.

My steps falter, and my gaze narrows at the car parked out front. Nadine. She cuts the engine and gets out as I near. "Hey." I've not heard or spoken to her since I ended things at Holly's shop. Shame engulfs me, but I meet her head-on, regardless. Her eyes are dull and cold.

Fuck. Yes, you're still an arsehole, Cameron. How many women have I seen look at me like that? Too many.

Swallowing roughly, I meet her beside her car. "You okay?" The words slip right out of my mouth, and she lifts a brow.

"I came to get my things." Tension throbs between us and not the good kind. Her jaw is locked, and when she finally meets my eyes, I can see she's close to tears.

"Right." I nod and give her a strained smile. "Come in." My walk is brisk. I can't deal with tears. Call me a prick, but unless a woman is crying because I obliterated all sense of being in the bedroom, then I'm as good as useless. I'd run if I wasn't already at my own fucking house. Nadine follows me in. She looks pathetic and, for a moment, I dabble with giving her Dr Peterson's number because something tells me she needs more than whatever support she is getting at the moment. An image of her slapping me hard stops me in vocalising my suggestion.

"You finished the house." She sounds impressed. It's hard not to be affected. The main living area is complete with two large and wide sofas facing one another. The coffee table crafted by my bare hands sits centre on a thick rug and the antique fireplace has been restored. The kitchen was ripped out and moved to the back to allow for an oak stained island and the long chunky sideboard I found second-hand, which I carved my own design into. I've used the sideboard to split the areas and define the living spaces. I'm thrilled with the end result. The snug is sporting a new L-shape sofa, artwork and mini bar. All the bathrooms are top range. Next to Dan's snobby mansion, my house is the next best thing in Richmond.

"It was completed last week," I tell her, moving to empty my pockets and flick the coffee machine on. "Drink?" I grab some water from the fridge and glug it back.

"No, just my things, please."

Fucking hell, this is awkward. "The house has been in a state, so I haven't really had a chance to put your stuff aside," I admit. Nadine rolls her eyes and kicks up her hip, leaning into the counter.

"I can wait." Her insincere smile gives her a menacing quality I had never seen before. Even when Holly was willingly hating me, she never once had the look Nadine is giving me. She's out for revenge. Frowning, I nod her towards the sofas.

"Do not say make yourself at home."

"Wasn't going to." I sigh, holding my hands up in surrender.

"That's right. This place is reserved for another woman

entirely." She curls her lip and disgust swirls darkly in her eyes as she looks around the immaculate place.

Nadine wanting to make my life hell is nothing more than I expect or deserve, but if she even considers diverting that anger at Holly, I will be forced to show her a side of me she doesn't want to meet. A side that I don't like myself. "I was aiming for more of a family," I bite back, angered by the possibility of me leaving a kind and unsuspecting Holly to Nadine's childish antics. I heard through the grapevine she'd been making unsavoury comments to her clients whilst we were still together.

She laughs disbelievingly, paling at the impact of my words. She shakes her head at me and slaps her palm down on the sideboard. "Could you at least pretend to care that you hurt me?" she hisses, her face contorting unattractively.

"I do care."

"And yet you throw your readymade family in my face!" Her voice raises, and her eyes fill with tears. I grit my teeth and lean onto the opposite side of the counter, getting her full attention.

"I don't have a readymade family, Nadine. I'm leaving and renting the house out."

"What?" She gapes. "You're leaving, why?" She walks closer, searching my eyes frantically. "Where are you going?" Her lip wobbles, and I get the distinct feeling she will beg me to stay.

Unlike Holly, who calmly accepted my decision.

"Just away." I raise my hand to rub the back of my neck when she moves to touch me.

"Cameron, you can't go, please!" She cups my elbow and stares longingly at me. "We were good, weren't we?"

"Nadine..."

"Do not say my name like that." Narrowed eyes meet mine as she drops her hand away. "I need to know I wasn't just some way to pass the time. I love you, I just don't understand. We were doing so good, until she came back."

"Good, yes." I swallow. There, that should do it.

"Just good?" She pulls back, insulted.

"For me, yes. I enjoyed your company, and it was good—" I struggle to think of the right words to give her the closure she needs, but she picks up on the tension in my body and the tone of my voice. "I thought I was ready for more, but then Holly came back, and you and I were—"

Shaking her head, she walks away and plops down on the sofa. "I just want my things, Cam. Please."

"Okay." I leave her on the sofa and go upstairs to retrieve the few things I know are up there. Twenty minutes later, I make my way downstairs to a puffy-eyed Nadine. "Anything I could find is in this bag, but I can drop other bits off if I come across them before I leave."

"And when will that be?"

"Trying to get rid of me?" I joke, but she looks as unimpressed as she did when she first arrived.

"I don't get it. Even if Holly wasn't the one who accused you, she still left you Cameron," she says spitefully.

"Look, Nadine. I'm sorry. I really am." My hand lifts to give her shoulder a squeeze, but when her face twists in anger, I drop it quickly. Awkwardly, I step away, giving her a look I hope she recognises as apologetic. I am sorry I hurt her. But I'm not sorry for putting my mental health first.

"I know you had it handed to you shitty, but it doesn't give you carte blanche to wreak havoc on other people's lives. You need to sort your head out." And there it is, her parting shot, another one for the stone heart. Does she think I haven't faced constant disregard from others before? I'm a pro at deflecting.

"That's why I'm leaving." I need to get away from all the speculation and constant emotional bombardment. I lead her to the front door. "Take care, Nadine." I raise my eyes and give her a blank smile. I take hold of the door as she steps through.

"Go to hell, Cameron!"

"Been there all my life, but thanks for the suggestion."

"You arsehole!"

I slowly close the door when she makes a move to scream another insult, but stops herself when she catches me wincing sympathetically.

"I don't want your pity."

"Affirmative." I nod. My response aggravates her further and when she points her finger at me, I hold my hand up. "Nadine, I'm the fucking worst at this. I don't know how to say what you want to hear, so please stop trying." I shrug. "I can't make you feel better."

"Isn't that the truth. You should see a therapist. I actually think you enjoy hurting others. It makes me wonder if the rumours were, in fact, true!" I slam the door in her face, my gut spasming with fury and something akin to disgust. Dr Peterson will have a field day with all this material.

"Fuck you!" she screams and storms down the drive and into her vehicle, slamming the car door loudly.

I drop my head forward until it meets the wood with a thud.

Well, that went well.

Chapter Twenty
Holly

All week, I have been preparing for Beau's party today. I have been left with an odd sense of guilt at dropping her to school this morning. Usually, we'd have the day together, but that will no longer be the case now she is in education. I'm just glad tomorrow is Saturday. Emily and Keeley have agreed to help run the shop, so Beau and I can have a day out. Danielle has made Beau the most stunning unicorn cake, which she is delivering when I finish work at lunchtime. It will give me a few hours to prep the last bits before her friends from school arrive. Most of the food is ready, all I need to do is decorate.

Being the first birthday for Beau without her Pop Pop here, I had a photograph of them printed and framed so she could enjoy his presence. I know she misses him, but school and Grace have kept her distracted. We have visited his grave several times since our return, but Beau doesn't understand what that means. I stared tearfully at the photo all night before I wrapped it up, covering their bright smiles with glittery unicorn paper. After Cameron's confession, I wonder why my father had never vocalised any of it with me. Had he thought

Cameron had hurt me too? We'd all wronged him. Me and his parents especially. No matter how long it takes, I will earn back his trust.

My only defence is I was unaware of the rape or any trial. His parents, on the other hand, they believed the lies and abandoned him. How could they believe the bullshit Sarah had spouted!

I want to make Cameron stay.

But what I want isn't relevant. Making sure Cameron heals and is happy is my only goal now. He was always determined, so I know he has given moving away careful deliberation. He's giving up so much to remove his past from his life, and having been through something similar, I know his mind is made up.

Seeing his vulnerable side the other week has left a shard of shame jammed in my gut. I abetted in his downfall. Unknowingly, I helped others to hurt him. All these years, I've held him accountable for something that seems so minuscule in the face of the truth. I hope Sarah is out there somewhere fighting against karma's capable hands. She deserves what Cameron would have been subjected to had she not dropped the charges. She perverted the course of justice and falsely accused him of rape. She should be charged!

"Hey, you okay?" Emily asks, startling me out of my dark thoughts. I snap around and throw a bright smile. "Thought you were going?" she asks, leaning into the doorframe. She admitted earlier she is seeing Dan. I'm not sure how serious things are or if it's official, but she looks a little brighter around the eyes.

"Just getting my bag." I lift it up and pull my coat down off the rack, tugging it on. "I really appreciate this."

"Yes. Yes, we know. Go, be with Beau!"

"Thanks."

"I'll be over tonight to give her my gift."

"Okay, I'll save you some cake." I peck her cheek, and she

blinks, startled at me. She is yet to realise that she will be my rock when Cameron leaves.

"Are you sure you're okay, hun?" I nod, hooking my bag over my shoulder and hightail it out of the shop. The cold air chases around my neck, and I huddle down, rushing to the car. The traffic is quiet, so I'm home within minutes, but coming back to find Cameron's car in my drive has me almost stalling my vehicle.

"Dammit!" I snap and wiggle the gear into place and park up beside him. I climb out and head towards the door when the echoing of someone drilling and hammering has me backing up and taking the side gate to the back garden. "Hello?" I call, but it's drowned out by a drill loudly splintering through the quiet neighbourhood. What on earth is going on? I round the back of the house and gasp, cupping my mouth when Cameron comes into view. He stands back with his hands on hips and grins happily at the wooden playhouse situated under the willow tree in the back garden. It's painted a delicate pink with a white trim. White shutters and pristine flower boxes finish it beautifully. Tilting his head, he moves in and adjusts the colourful bunting decorating the roof. "Cameron," I whisper, in shock. He spins round and frowns at me. "I-It's so beautiful. She's going to love it." I could never afford to give her anything as unique and charming as this, but that doesn't bother me. I'm astounded by his generosity after everything I have subjected this man to. He keeps on giving.

"I've upset you."

Shaking my head, I smile gently and walk towards him and the house. "This is incredible. You're so talented," I whisper, peeking inside to find it painted white, a small table and two chairs in the same light pink filling half the inside. I step back and stand beside him. "It's... Beau is going to be in awe. I'm in awe." I laugh lightly and smile up at him through my tears. I run a hand over the window and shake my head in wonder.

Cameron shifts uncomfortably and I flick a secretive look at him. He has no idea how gifted he is. "Thank you. Truly. No one has ever done anything like this for Beau. I can't even begin to think how I can repay you." I don't just mean the magical little playhouse he's built in our garden. As I hold his stare, I hope to convey that message.

"I don't need you to repay me," he mutters, using the hammer to scratch at his eyebrow.

When he said he had a gift for Beau, I thought he would turn up with a unicorn book or something else, but not this! "Cameron, I'm in shock. I'm not sure who is going to have more fun, me or Beau."

His laugh hits a chord deep inside me. Lit up, I turn around and smile at him. He flinches, stepping back and puts ample space between us. What the hell happened? I frown and wait for him to say something, but he clears his throat and drops his hammer into his toolbox. "I'm done here, so I'll get out of your way."

"Are you not going to pop in to Beau's party?"

"Probably not a good idea." He gathers his other tools and flask up from off of the grass.

"Why? Beau would love you to be here. Don't you want to surprise her with the play house yourself?"

"I didn't think I'd be welcome."

"You're welcome."

He nods and clips his toolbox shut. His jaw working as he averts his eyes momentarily.

"Beau is going to be thrilled."

"Maybe I can just pop by before I leave," he suggests. His response tells me he is leaving soon. I look at the house and notice the intricate swirls in the trim along the roof and flower boxes. So much thought and time has gone into this. Too much thought. Cameron Stone loves my daughter. "If you love my daughter like I suspect you do"—I raise my brow—"then you'll come to her party and celebrate her birthday with her." Selfishly, I want to spend a little time with him before he disappears from our lives for good.

His head drops, and he nods, looking down at his trousers littered in dirt. "I need to clean up," he mumbles, collecting his things up.

"Party is at four," I inform him and check my watch. I have plenty to be getting on with. "I need to crack on." I make my way to the back door, and he follows, walking out to his car.

Rushing inside, I open the pantry where balloons spill out. I begin kicking them into the living room and drag the bigger ones, spelling *Beau* so I can place them against the back wall. I'd cleared the sideboard free of photographs last night, and I plan to put Beau's birthday cake there when Danielle arrives, which should be any minute now. I peer out the window as her car pulls up.

"It looks great in here," Danielle tells me as she enters. "Where do you want this?" She lifts the box slowly.

"On the sideboard, please." It's big enough I can put the party food on either side of it too.

"You can keep it in the box until people arrive, then just slide the box off." She quickly dismantles the box and shows me before slotting it back into place.

"Great, thank you. This cake is gorgeous." It's a giant unicorn with clouds and rainbows round the outside. Smaller unicorns are on prongs flying mid-air and fake grass and flowers all cover the cake board. "It smells incredible." I inhale deeply.

"It smells like love handles." She grins and I laugh.

"It smells worth it. Beau is going to be over the moon with all of this."

"I bet. I need to get back to the shop. Have a great afternoon."

. . .

AFTER SHE LEAVES, I spend the next hour putting up bunting and arranging the party food and presents. I made a party playlist on my phone and get that set up so I don't forget when people arrive. I check my watch and leave to collect Beau. She is so excited when I collect her from school. She runs towards me with her birthday badge on her uniform, Grace in tow. "Hey, boo!" I scoop her up and give her a big squeeze and a kiss. "Happy birthday again." I laugh and kiss her little scrunched up nose.

"Grace has two parties today!" Beau tells me, wowed.

"Two parties! My word." I grin and wink down at Grace.

"Yes, because my Uncle Cam is moving to a new house." She rubs at her face and smears what looks like paint on her cheek.

"That's exciting," I say around the thick ball in my throat.

"Yes. He is going far away and we won't get to see him, but he still loves me."

"I'm sure it isn't too far," I dig further, smiling at Beau playing with my hair.

"He is going to the seaside tomorrow." I blink at Grace and stare at her sad little face. Tomorrow. I've not had a chance to right my wrongs.

Dan approaches, pulling me from my worrying thoughts. "Happy birthday, Beau." I ask Beau if she is ready to go home. She nods, and Dan looks at me. "We'll be round soon, four o'clock, right?"

I give him a quick nod and find I'm repeating the same reply to other parents as they check to confirm the time.

"Yes, four. See you soon. Say bye, Beau." I smile at another parent and buckle her in before I get in and we head home. With the school traffic, it takes a little longer to arrive home, but when I do, both my mother and Marcus are waiting on the doorstep for me. I park up, and Beau hops out as I do.

"It's my birthday!" she squeals excitedly, running to give

them both a hug. Marcus looks stiff and uncomfortable, but after a few tense phone calls, we were able to move past the awkward moment when he tried to ask me out.

"Hi!" I call, as Cameron pulls up, blocking us all in.

"Yay!" Beau jumps up and down when he exits his vehicle. My mother's eyes bug, and Marcus sneers at him. "Cam!" Beau is like a squirrel on steroids, flitting from one place to the next. She runs at him, and he swings her up.

"Hey, boo." He smiles softly at her, and she grasps onto his collar. She's out of breath, but it doesn't stop her from panting that it's her birthday. "I know, and I have a big treat for you in your garden." Her eyes go wide, and he reciprocates. *"BIG."*

"As big as your car?" she whispers, her face pressing close to his. He laughs at her overbearing excitement.

"Maybe."

"Come in," I say to him and lead the way, coming face-to-face with my mother's annoyance and Marcus's distrust.

"Can I have a word, Holly?" My mother purses her lips, looking Cameron up and down.

"Not really. It's Beau's birthday. Today is about her," I say and see her eyes narrow. "SURPRISE!" I beam, and Cam carries Beau in. She's soon wiggling free when she sees the decorations, cake and presents.

"It's a unicake!" she squeals, running at it, and both Cam and I move quickly, suspecting a mess is about to occur.

"How cosy," my mother sneers. Marcus hums his agreement and knowing Cameron is on child watch, I walk over to them with anger brimming below the surface.

As quietly as I can, I glare at them. "It is my daughter's birthday. You will not cause a scene, and if you cannot accept that Cameron is here as a *friend,* then leave. This is about Beau, no one else." My eyes well up. Marcus's eyes flare with guilt, and he moves to pull me into a hug. I hiss tearfully at my mother. "He made her a damn playhouse and he is moving away tomorrow. He came to say goodbye to her."

"Leaving?" Her keen stare is over my shoulder, as she's asking him directly.

"Cornwall," he says, and I turn to look at him. "I came to give my gift, then I'm heading out. I don't want to intrude." He gives them a polite smile, and although I can appreciate their suspicion with him after everything that happened with me, they don't know the truth. And that's my fault, not his. I'll update them this week. I'm not doing it now. I'm simply grateful he isn't moving abroad. "Ready to see your big present?" Cam drops down to Beau's level and winks at her.

"Yes!"

He walks her to the door, then covers her eyes. "It's a surprise so you can't see until the last minute." My little girl nods. So trusting. I'd been the same. The gentleness I see when he is around Beau is what he used to grace me with. Once outside, he walks her into the middle of the garden.

Beau giggles. Quickly, I turn to Marcus and ask him to film her reaction. Begrudgingly, he gets his phone out, and Cam nods. I give him the all-clear and he whips his hands away.

Silence.

I move to bend and look at Beau. She is staring wide-eyed at the playhouse. Her eyes are as big and as glittery as stars. Cameron kneels down. "Happy birthday, Beau." His voice quivers, and I bite my lip to stop my own tears from splashing my cheeks. Slowly, she turns her head, and they stare at one another. My heart thuds painfully, and there is no mistaking the connection we all share. Beau may never have known Cameron all those years ago, but we are all fused together in a way I could never expect anyone to understand.

She has never been attached to anyone like this.

"I don't want you to go!" she wails. Cameron's panicked eyes meet mine. Oh no! I rush to comfort her, but he envelops her as she grabs his collar fiercely.

As she hiccups, he picks my daughter up and holds her tightly. "I'll still see you, boo. Me and you will always be friends."

"Because you're my Cam?" she asks on a sniffle.

"Yes, I'm your Cam, baby girl. And I love you lots, okay." His face dips into her little neck, hiding the unshed tears I briefly noticed.

This is killing him. Why is he going? Why can't we try?

Aren't we worth fighting for?

Does he hate me that much? My head is a mess, but I hold back my tears for Beau.

"And Mummy?" Beau cries.

I can't watch. I make a small but painful sound. Cam's head snaps up, and he gives me a sad smile.

"I really need to go, baby girl. But you can write to me, send pictures. I'd love to hear what you and Grace have been up to," he suggests, wiping her damp face. "I want to hear all about your adventures in your new playhouse, okay." His big thumb scoops under my little girl's eyes and Beau nods at him.

"What do you say to Cam for your present, Beau?" My voice is shaky and I'm barely talking. I'm trying to hurry this along. Not only will guests be arriving soon, but Beau and I are both emotional wrecks.

"Thank you." She smiles the brightest I have seen in a long time.

"No problem, boo." He pecks her cheek and puts her down. "I've got to go now." He nods and Beau's eyes flash with worry, but she soon copies his nodding when he winks at her. "Good girl."

He walks over to me and pulls me to his chest. I choke out a sob and his lips press roughly against my hairline. Closing my eyes, I soak in every sensation, the feel of his arms, the calming heat of his body, his soft but firm lips in my hair. His smell. I inhale it like it's my last lungful of air. "Goodbye, gorgeous." He barely finishes, his voice breaking. He lets me go suddenly. "Ms Matthews, it's a pleasure to meet you. Marcus, nice to see you again."

And then nothing.

He's gone.

Chapter Twenty-One
Cameron

"This music is shit." Cole laughs under his breath.

"Grace chose it," Dan snaps and hands me another beer. I take it willingly and stare around the room.

My farewell party.

I'm still trying to dislodge the ache in my throat from earlier. Grace returned from Beau's party with a bag of treats and high on sugar. She does a forward roll along the sofa and ends with a proud 'ta da' at Emily who laughs.

"So, it's serious then?" I ask Dan, nodding at Emily.

"Not quite."

"So why is she here?" Cole wonders and smirks at Dan.

"Because she is." Dan laughs and shakes his head at our questioning. I stare at him, forcing him to acknowledge he has feelings for Emily. "Grace invited her, and I didn't want to let her down, as she was upset this morning." He clears his throat, and I squeeze his shoulder.

His eyes meet mine briefly, regretfully, and what I see reflected back at me is pain. Fuck. "I know you know this, but I love you," I tell him solemnly. He knocks his forehead to mine, and we stand quietly for a minute. He's losing his best friend, a prick of a friend who has taken up too much of his time with bullshit.

"I know, man." Dan swallows roughly.

"I want a hug," Cole huffs and swings his arms over our shoulders. Brant joins in with a small whoop, and I shake my head with a laugh. My chest fills with emotion, and I grit my teeth to stop from getting emotional. These men have stood by me through the most unimaginable of situations.

"You guys put up with some shit, I know that." I laugh lightly.

"You're worth it," Dan murmurs on a quiet breath. Little hands prise their way in, and we all stare down at Grace's toothless grin.

"Hello." She giggles.

"Hey, stink." I wink, and she takes her dad's hand. "You lot best come and visit me," A small part of me is worried I will up and leave and, like that, I'll be forgotten.

"Free holiday. Sign me up!" Brant chuckles and breaks away, allowing some light in.

"You can't get rid of us that easily," Cole croaks.

"To Cameron!" they bellow together, and my gut tightens.

A chorus of glasses clinking fills the room. "To Cameron."

Two hours later, I make it home, and I'm not ashamed to admit I cried in the car. I asked that no one wave me off tomorrow. I plan on leaving in the early hours to save myself the pain of saying goodbye twice.

I spend the rest of the evening packing my car. Most of my belongings were shipped earlier this week or are at Dan's garage in storage. Closing the boot with a loud clunk, I head inside and grab the last beer out of the fridge. I raise my bottle. "It's been emotional," I mutter to the empty room. Fuck, hasn't it just. Fucking Sarah Daniels deserves the worst of the worst. I shut off the lights and lock the doors. Tomorrow, this will all be over, and I can start a new chapter in my life, a healthier one.

I'M HALFWAY up the stairs, when a light tap on the door stops me. I take the stairs backwards and lean to see who it is. Holly's timid and ashen face stares at me. Discarding my beer, I cross the room and unlock the door. "Is Beau okay?" Nodding, she slips inside and bites her thumbnail. Nervous eyes watch me. God, she looks gorgeous, and seeing the slight stain on her cheeks, I suspect I know what's brought her here. "Why are you here, Holly?" I know why, because I've battled with the same thing constantly since I told her I was leaving. The desire to share one more night with her before I leave.

She sucks in a breath and blinks at me. "I don't know," she whispers.

"I think you do." She squirms under my gaze, and her eyes dart to the door.

"This was a mistake. I'm... I don't know what I was thinking." She moves quickly, but I block her path.

"You do know. Tell me." I search her gaze. She needs to be the one to cross this threshold. "You need to voice it, Holly."

"You're going to leave, no matter what, aren't you?" Her whisper stings my very skin. I hate seeing her so cut up like this. I nod, and her head drops. She shrugs and tries to move away, but I stop her again. "What's the point if it won't stop you from going?" Her light voice reminds me just how inexperienced she is. Only me. It's a hell of a thing to know that.

"I need this." I hold her dejected eyes with my own pleading ones. "I'm not a person I like, Holly," I admit gruffly. "I need time and space to sort myself out."

"I understand."

"Tell me why you're here?"

"I can't." Her cheeks are a dark shade of pink. I lift my hand and tuck a strand of hair behind her ear.

"Still the shy woman I fell in love with. You never could vocalise these things." Something has always stopped her from voicing her sexual desires outside of the act. It's one of the things I loved about her. "Would I be right in thinking you came here to see if what we shared all those years ago is still there?"

Big blue piercing eyes stare innocently up at me. "Yes."

"We didn't dream it up, Holly, it was real. No woman made me feel like you did. Not in all these years," I confess shakily. I cup her face and let my eyes convey my sincerity.

Her smile is sad, nostalgic, but determination swirls in her pupils. Her shoulders straighten and she sucks in a breath. "I want one last night with you."

Thank fuck.

"Are you sure?" I search her gaze. Her hand splays on my chest, her fingers shifting ever so slightly. When she nods, I say, "Good, come and dance with me." That shocks her. She blinks but follows me out into the back garden and I instruct my soundbar to play some music. It's late, and above the sky is velvet black, dotted with pinprick stars. "Do you remember that night at the lookout at Hill Top Farm?" I ask, taking her hand and twisting her into me so her back is to my front.

Her breath leaves in a rush and the back of her head rubs against my chest when she nods. "We danced," she whispers.

"Until the stars wore out. That's what you asked, for me to dance with you until the stars wore out." I angle my head so I can whisper directly into her ear. She shivers, and I smile, knowing this alone is enough to make her desire me. I begin to move my body slowly to the side, and she moves with me, her head twisted to look up at the stars.

"Do you ever feel like something, or someone, is working against us? Otherworldly?" She laughs lightly, but it turns sad.

I bring my arms around her, holding her close. I shut my eyes and inhale. "Every damn day, Holly. For years, I asked myself what I did so wrong for this to happen to me, but it just is. It's done and we can't change it."

"No. I guess not."

I grasp her wrist and spin her out and back in so she is facing me. Her face is split into a grin, and I have every intention of taking advantage of what's in front of me. I cup her chin, and she bites her lip in anticipation. "One hell of a love story, though?" I smile, and she nods, her eyes tearing up. "You're so beautiful."

"So are you."

"I was going for a more manly vibe." I pout, making her giggle. I stare at her mouth. "I'm going to kiss you. Are you ready?"

"Very."

I bloody hope so, because I'm not sure I am. I know without a shadow of a doubt this woman will knock all previous conquests out of the water. I'm not ready for the intensity, but I crave it. I'm not ready for the pain of walking away from the best moment of my life, but I need it more than my next breath. I drop my mouth and dance my lips across hers, trailing them back and forth. As soon as I press my lips to hers, she gives a little sob and I sweep my tongue in. Home. Can someone taste of home? Holly does. Her arms move up to hook around my neck, and we kiss our way through the next song. I'm not rushing this. I want her, every inch she will give, until it's all mine to take.

"It's getting cold," I hum against her swollen lips. I tug her back towards the house. The music is louder now so I turn it low and rest back against the island. "Come here." She moves and presses up to kiss me. "Do you want a drink?" I ask out of politeness.

"No. Just you." Her finger runs along my lower lip. I take

hold of her hand and kiss her fingertips. The song changes, and Holly's eyes blaze into mine. I pull her close and tuck her into my shoulder, dancing with her. Our fingers twine, and she watches as I run my fingers and thumb all over her delicate palm, taking a physical inventory of her. Her other hand is twiddling with the fine hair at the base of my neck. I sigh, feeling a sense of soul deep calm.

"I dread nighttime," I whisper over the music. "This is the first night I haven't felt like the walls are closing in." Holly brings our hands to her mouth and kisses my palm.

"Take me to bed, Cam." Turning her head, she keeps our hands close and awaits my answer. When I don't respond immediately, she uses our connected hands to pull me towards the stairs.

I go without a word. She walks down the long hallway and slows at a door. I shake my head and we carry on. Each door she slows at, I shake my head until we reach the furthest doors. "Left."

Holly clicks the door shut behind us and lets out a shuddering breath. She's nervous. When her shaky fingers move to unbutton her dress, I act quickly and stop her. I want to do that. Sensing the tension in her, I begin to undress first, slipping my shirt over my head and unbuttoning my fly. She watches me with big, glazed eyes. As soon as I'm down to my boxers, I move towards her and grab her dress between my thumb and forefinger. "Cameron." Her hands dance over mine.

"Trust me, I know." I smile slowly.

"Please."

I'm unhurried in my actions. Slipping each button through the material of her dress in a slow but accurate move. As soon as I have enough buttons undone, I slip it off her shoulders and take in her creamy skin and lace bra. Dusky nipples dare me to remove her underwear, but I want to savour her. Her dress slides off and her hands lift to cover her lower stomach.

"Hey." I pull at her hands, but she lifts anxious eyes to me. I drop my gaze and see the silvery lines snaking their way past her navel. "Holly, it may come as a shock to you, but I actually find you sexier with stretch marks." Her hips are wider, her breasts full. She's grown into a beautiful woman. Her thin, gangly teenage frame filled out to be something exquisite.

"What?"

I stretch her arms wide, revealing her stomach. She tries to fight me, and when she realises she can't win, she tries to move into me to cover her body.

"We all have scars. You just can't see mine. Yours tell a story that I want to know. Beau is incredible. I knew you'd be a phenomenal mother," I utter softly. "Don't hide from me."

She lowers her arms, and I help her step out of her dress and over to the bed. Cupping her face, I lower mine and kiss her lightly.

"Cameron, I never thought I'd see you again."

"You and me both." I really want to ravage her until her creamy skin is red with the scratches of my stubble, swollen and pulsing, but she wants slow right now. She needs something from me that I'm all too happy to give. I'll give her what she needs, then take what I want.

Laying her down, I peel her lingerie off and run my fingers all over her skin, kissing my way across her collarbone and right down to her toes before I move back up and latch onto her panting mouth.

"I need you," she whispers.

We've barely touched, but I'm aching to sink deep inside her, and she is glistening from the light touches of exploration. I know it's been a long time for her, but I don't want to fuck around with foreplay. I want to be inside her. I crave the blissful pleasure I always felt with her. I grab a condom out of the top drawer and rip it open with my teeth.

Sheathing myself, I spread her legs and stare down at her

pussy. She squirms, and I slide my palms along her inner thighs, moving back into position. Heat emanates off of her, and I shiver, knowing any moment now she'll be wrapped around me. I catch a look of worry in her eyes, and I know at that moment she is fighting the same fear. What if this will break every preconception we've ever had, and this fizzles away into nothingness. We might get closure once and for all. I don't want this kind of closure. I hate the thoughts ping-ponging around my mind, and I do the only thing I can to shut it off.

I thrust deep. "Fuck," I choke, and she grabs me tight and draws me in deeper. I shake my head as her fluttery moan slides over my skin, setting it alight. "Holly," I pant, keeping still.

"Ouch." She bites her lip, and then giggles when I puff my cheeks out. I was not expecting her to be so snug. "I was hoping this would be a bit more romantic." She fights a wide smirk, humming in discomfort as my cock stretches her open.

"Same, I wasn't aware you'd been training your pussy for the Olympics." I grit my teeth as I fight the urge to come.

She bursts out laughing, and I shift. I allow her to become accommodated with my size before I slide back out and then drop forward on a deep groan.

"I can't believe you just said that." She chuckles. I rock my hips back and drop back in on a lazy thrust. Perfection.

"I can't believe I'm finally back inside you, gorgeous." I grip her hair and drop my mouth to hers. Her fingers find mine, and she stares up, vulnerable. Open wide and lost to the growing need flickering like a dying ember between us. It soon ignites, and I drive in. "God, I missed you." With a shudder, I sink home again and again. I don't think, not when my need is this great. I sate both her and myself with every roll and thrust. We may be joined at the hips, but I feel our connection right in my heart.

"I missed you too," she moans, her eyes filling up. Her legs twine behind my back, and I slam in, needing to claim something that was taken from me. Claim her. Holly's mouth drops open, and I repeat the action again, eagerly drawing low moans from us both. Her body moves with mine, matching me thrust for thrust.

"I want to give you slow, but..." I tilt my head when pleasure tapers down my spine and grips my balls. Fucking hell.

"Just give it to me. Anything," she cries when I slam deep. My mouth hangs open as I feel the first flutters of her orgasm massage my cock.

"Dammit, Holly. You're tight as fuck."

Slamming my mouth to hers, I begin to plough in and out in chaotic strokes. "Cameron!" Her skin is so soft, her body yielding, and yet, she takes the hard strikes I deliver with a greed I can sympathise with.

"Not yet, baby." I shake my head, trying to focus. I'll give her slow afterwards. I fuck her as though it's my first and last time because I'm almost sure it is. She shares the same sense of urgency and clings, riding me in hard strokes. Her moans turn more desperate. As her tone crosses into tear territory, we slip over the abyss. Her tears win and she sobs, holding me tight. "I know, Holly." I swallow my own heartache and kiss us through our pain.

She is the only woman for me.

"I can't lose you again, Cam."

"I'm not me. Not really. You understand?" I cup her face and her hands slide up my arms and cup my face back.

"Do you think you'll ever come back?" she asks tearfully. I dip and press a kiss at the corner of her mouth.

"I want to." I have every intention of returning when I'm no longer a prisoner to my past. Dr Peterson has put me in contact with a therapist, and I have every intention of getting my life back on track and for good.

But will she still be here, waiting?

Chapter Twenty-Two
Cameron

8 *Months later...*

THERE IS a lot to be said for the sea, but those things are never spoken of. In its danger, I have found a sense of unshakeable calm. I bob on the gentle lull of the bottomless expanse. My legs are submerged and the water laps rhythmically at the surfboard I'm occupying. My hand sits close to the surface, the salty fluid licking at my calloused skin. Greg, my instructor, gives me a nod, and I rise up as the swell of the sea carries us forward. Adrenaline rushes through me, the sea roaring through my ears before it drags me under, spinning me amongst a tornado of bubbles. It taunts me with the miniscule pockets of air I can't have. I'd laugh at its audacity if I weren't a victim to drowning. Forcing my eyes to stay open, I take in its beauty because I've never seen anything like it. Breaking the surface, I gasp for air, and Greg laughs. "You nearly had it!"

Chuckling, I pull myself back on my board and shake the

water from my hair. He doesn't know I enjoy the moment of sensory peace below the surface. "Next time." I grin and begin paddling again as we make our way back to shore.

Greg hits the sand before me and waits for me to untether myself so we can carry our boards back to the surf shop. "Chrissy and I are popping to the boatyard after we shut the shop, if you fancy it. A few of the guys are coming," Greg says, wiping his face dry with his hand. He offers at least twice a month for me to join him for a drink, but I always decline.

"Maybe another time. I'm FaceTiming my niece," I tell him truthfully. I live for those phone calls, not only because I get to see Grace's face, but because she is my informant. She fills me in on Beau and Holly. I barely have to pry for information, as she freely gives it divulging everything to me. When we reach the shop, Chrissy, Greg's wife, is waiting for us.

"Hi, Cam, you looked good out there." They are an older couple, born and bred here. Cornwall is the only place they have ever been and their astute personalities can tell there is something wrong. My sudden appearance didn't go unnoticed, that's for sure. After the first two months, I kindly asked them to let me find my own way. I need to heal, but on my terms and not on the watch of others.

"Nearly beat the wave this time," I say and put my board aside for her and Greg to sort out. Truth be told, I'm a hell of a lot better. The therapist has quite frankly been a blessing in disguise, the disguise being a grumpy, obnoxious bastard. He has no room for pleasantries and goes for the jugular each session. His methods are nothing short of antiquated, maybe it's that or his antagonistic manner, but he's made me face some pretty appalling demons and lay them to rest. "Have a nice evening. I've got a date with a bossy six-year-old." I laugh and get out of there before Chrissy can try to coax me into going for a drink.

Cleaning up, I grab my duffel and walk to my car as Sophie

from the local dive school walks up to me. "Hey," she says skittishly.

I give her a polite smile. "Hey, Soph, is everything okay?" Slinging the bag in the back, I close the door on a thud and pull my door open, waiting for her to respond.

Small hands press together, and she sucks in a deep breath, preparing herself. "Would you like to go out for a drink sometime?" Her pretty eyes are wide. "Like a date?" she adds nervously.

Ah, fuck.

"I'm in a relationship, Sophie," I murmur, feeling bad for her. Her cheeks are raw with embarrassment.

"Oh."

"Back home," I explain. "A daughter too." My throat closes around the lie I want with every fibre of my being to be the truth.

Her frown deepens, and she gives me a disapproving scrunch of her nose. Jesus, how quick is she to judge? "Hey, you asked me out," I cough, sending heat into her cheeks. "I'm here on a temporary contract."

"Right, sorry. Goodnight." She hurries off back to her car, leaving me to stare after her for a moment. I get in my car and drive home.

THE COTTAGE HAS DOUBLED as my workshop. The garage is a cyclone of sawdust and unfinished articles. I pass by it and close the door as I go. The rest of the place is homely and decorated as the perfect holiday home, fit for a young family. My family. It took me to leave Richmond to realise the old rectory was never for me, but for Holly. Just as this place is. I've created the perfect life for her without her ever knowing. A life neither of us has had a chance to enjoy. But we will, if she'll have me.

I'm eager to return home, to see her again, but I have a few jobs to finish up here first.

I stalk to the fridge and the picture stuck to it, and as always, I grin at the snapshot of Beau and Grace standing proudly next to the playhouse. A plaque now resides above the door reading 'Cam Castle.' My heart swells, and I kiss my fingers and pat the picture. "You girls kill me," I mutter, opening the fridge and grabbing a beer.

I'm expecting Grace's call shortly, so I head for a shower and prepare my dinner so we can eat together like I demand we do. I wait impatiently, staring at my cooling meal and my blank phone on the breakfast bar. Half an hour passes, and I try to call Dan, feeling an uneasy weight settle in my stomach. They are never late with their call. It's our Thursday tradition. An hour passes so I ring and leave a voicemail before trying the guys, but no one answers, and my stomach shrivels with a sense of dread I can't explain. Something is wrong. I can feel it to the very core of my being. Rushing upstairs, I grab my car keys, when my phone vibrates on the counter. I take the stairs two at a time and snatch my phone up.

"Dan, what the fuck's going on!" I pant.

"Cam..." He chokes. "I tried. I fucking did, I promise."

"Tried what!" I shout. He sobs and I drop weakly into a chair.

"There was a fire," he cries, and I hear Emily shush him through what sounds like a fit of her own tears.

"Where? Who?" But I know. I just fucking know it's her. My Holly. I shake my head and stand shakily, pacing. "Don't you fucking say it. DON'T!" I choke out.

"I... It all happened so fast," Dan whispers. "There was so much smoke. I couldn't see and..."

"Dan, please," I beg, shoving my palms into my eyes to stop the burn of tears streaming down my face.

"I pulled Beau out, but the fire just grew. I've never seen

anything like it, I swear. I tried." His confession shudders down the line, and my legs give way. Sinking down, I stare at the floor as his voice becomes muffled through the rush of blood in my ears. "The fire service pulled her out, but she was so lifeless."

"Stop," I choke, sobbing loudly.

"They started working on her the second they got her out... I don't know how much damage her lungs sustained, or if she is... We're on the way to the county general now."

"I'm on my way." I hang up. If he doesn't know how Holly is, then there's a good chance she is alive. What state she will be in when I get there, I don't know, but she's my girl and nothing will stop me from loving her. Nothing.

SEVERAL HOURS LATER, I force my way through the queue of people sitting aimlessly in the hospital waiting room. Dan stands, and my steps falter at seeing how pale and traumatised he is. I shake my head, begging him to give me the only news I want to hear. His arms slap round my back and he apologises to me over and over.

"Where is she?" I ask.

"Won't let us in. We're not family." Dan's shoulders droop and he sucks in a deep breath. "Cam, it didn't look good. No burns, but...the fire was out of control. I'm sorry." Tearful eyes meet mine.

"Beau?" Her name is ripped from me. He shrugs in despair. They have to be okay. Emily is sobbing quietly with a sleeping Grace in her lap. "I need..." I begin. I need to know how they are, but they will never let me in. Someone comes through doors labelled trauma ward, and I snap free from Dan and run to the doors, twisting to the side to squeeze through before they close.

They click shut, and a nurse comes to me. "Excuse me, sir!" she starts, but I rush past her and start looking in beds frantically. I scan every inch to find my girl, but I can't see her anywhere. Doubling back, I see Beau's tear-stained face through a windowed door in the children's department. I crash into the door, but it's locked. As I press the button, her little face comes up and breaks into tears. "Beau!" I shout. "Baby girl, get them to open the door." I bang and call through as she holds her arms up and cries for me. Someone comes to the door and opens it, and I barge my way in. "Beau," I pant, rushing to her. She is hooked up on oxygen, and I scoop her up. "Shush, baby. It's okay, I'm here now."

"Sorry, sir, who are you?"

"Father. Where is my wife?" I demand, knowing they won't give me any access if I don't lie. Beau sniffles and coughs into the mask. I kiss her hair. "Shush, calm down, baby girl. It's okay." I rock her against my chest.

"My mummy," she cries loudly.

"Holly Matthews?" I question the nurse, and her eyes widen. I grit my teeth and close my eyes, pain ricocheting through my chest.

"In the ICU," the nurse whispers and looks to see if Beau is listening. Her tiny hands are wrapped up in my collar, and I hold her tight. "She sustai—"

I shake my head, cutting her off. "I want to see her. My friend is in the waiting room. He'll come and sit with Beau, my daughter." I stutter.

"No!" Beau cries in panic.

"I need to go and find Mummy. Dan is going to come sit with you, just for a minute, okay," I tell her, wiping away the tears running down either side of the mask. She shakes her head.

"I'm coming back, I promise. I'm not going anywhere, ever again," I vow to her little head cupped in my hands. Her size sends a ripple of fear through me. She's such a dot. I'm eternally grateful to Dan for getting her out. The alternative isn't something I ever want to think about. I look to the nurse. "Daniel Ocean. Please, can you get him for me?"

"Of course." She smiles sympathetically and moves towards the doors.

I sag and litter Beau's head with kisses. "See, Dan is coming and I'm going to make sure Mummy is okay."

"Are you coming back?"

I nod and pull her to me, holding back my own tears. Dan soon arrives, and I quickly explain that I'm going to the ICU.

"Come here, Beau." He holds his arms out and she twists into his hold.

"You got me out of the fire." She sniffs, and Dan nods, trying to keep from crying. "It was loud."

"It was," Dan whispers, rubbing her back.

"I'll be back soon." I leave them and ask for directions. The same nurse offers to show me the way.

"It's just down here through those doors." We stop outside of them, and she turns to me and gives me a reluctant look, twiddling with her staff pass.

"What?" I ask, lifting my hand to the door and motioning for her to open it.

"We know that you're not the father or husband. On arrival, we asked your friend, and he mentioned her mother, that's all."

"Okay." All this family bullshit is irrelevant to me. She's letting me in those fucking doors. I glare at her. "I'm getting in here," I say forcefully.

"Mister?"

"Stone," I spit, irritated by her lack of urgency and placid nature. I want to shake her stupid.

"Matthews." She gives me a pointed look, and the penny slowly drops through the fog of panic. "Perhaps say you were away on business," she offers and swipes her pass.

"Yeah, yeah." I nod and rush in, looking for Holly's name. I find it quickly and run through the ward. When I yank open the curtain, my legs wobble on impact. Choking out a plea, I stagger to her bedside and stumble into a chair. "Oh god, Holly." Wires and monitors beep as she lies motionless in the big bed.

"Sir, you can't be in he—"

I cup Holly's fragile hands in mine. "Baby, can you hear me, I'm here, okay. I'm home. I love you. Beau's okay," I whisper, pressing a kiss to the back of her hands. I scan her for any sign of injury, and burns but she looks unscathed.

"Sir, I need to ask you to leave," the nurse says quietly.

"It's okay; he's her husband." The voice of Holly's mother has me twisting against my girl's hands, and I smile my thanks. She looks as devastated and as pale as I feel. "Oh, Cameron." She cups her mouth and picks up Holly's other hand, careful to avoid the needle disappearing into her.

"I'll just get the doctor." The nurse leaves, and I meet her mother's face with watery eyes.

"Where is Beau?"

"She's okay. Dan is with her. I just arrived," I tell her.

"Me too." After a heavy silence, she speaks. "She was a different person after you left." Her mother voices. "If it wasn't for Beau..."

"I had to go. I didn't want to, but I had to, for them. I needed to get better."

"Holly told me everything." Sympathetic eyes look back at me.

I smile in thanks and sigh.

"I'd never cheat on your daughter. She's the love of my life," I say to her passionately. "Biology won't stop me either from bringing that little girl up as my own."

She holds my determined stare. I don't back down. I want her to know nothing and no one, not even her, can get in the way of us. Holly and I did not come this far, become so lost to allow others to set restrictions on us now. "I know." She looks down at Holly and sniffles. "Oh, my beautiful girl. Come on, wake up, sweetheart." She strokes her hair, and I drop my head, clutching her lifeless hands and pray that she will be okay.

"Our story is only just beginning, Holly. You hear me. I'm home now," I whisper emotionally. She smells heavily of smoke and the lightest shred of vanilla. I cling to that vanilla smell as if my life depends on it. "I love you, gorgeous." As I brush my lips over her hand, her finger twitches.

"Hello, I'm Doctor Varni." A tall and kind-looking man approaches us both, picks up Holly's hospital notes and flips a page. "Holly has sustained some damage to her lungs and was found unconscious at the scene. Luckily, the fire was still in the lower part of the house, so any injuries are smoke related," he informs us tenderly. A soft sob sounds from the other side of the bed. "She has come round, but her lungs are struggling and she was frantic with worry about her daughter. We have sedated her to ensure she gets the rest she needs."

"She knows that Beau is okay, though?"

"Yes, we tried to reassure her, but she was adamant to see her daughter." Of course she was. What do they expect? "She was putting increasing pressure on her lungs, so we felt it necessary to sedate her. Hopefully, seeing you both when she comes round will put her mind at ease." I give a short laugh. They don't know my girl. "You don't think so?" he asks, looking at me in question.

"I know so. Is there any chance both can be moved to a private room?"

"I'm not sur—"

"You said it yourself; the increased stress is putting added pressure on her. I know for a fact if you don't do this, Holly will get up and go find our daughter," I tell him sternly. "Put them in the same room." I finish abruptly.

"I'll see what I can do."

"What do you expect recovery wise?" I murmur, staring down at her hoping for good news.

"A full one, hopefully. We're administering fluids and steroids, and she is likely to feel out of breath for a while and become tired easily, your daughter too. I'll imagine both will need inhalers and continued steroids due to the impact of the smoke on their lungs. Long term, Mrs Matthews may need additional medication, but we're hoping to minimise that." He offers us an empathetic smile.

"Do you hear that, Holly, you're going to be okay, baby," I say, placing her hand down and tucking her hair behind her ear. "When you wake up, we can all be together."

Chapter Twenty-Three
Holly

A burning ache sits on my chest, adding what feels like an extra ton of weight, my head pounds with each beat of my heart and my throat is raw when I attempt to swallow. Ouch. Twisting, I whimper when the pain increases. "Holly, baby, it's Cam, can you hear me?" Eyes closed, I nod and weakly clasp his hand back when he holds mine. Tears run hot paths along my cheeks. "Shush, it's okay. Beau's okay. She's here too." Lips press into my temple, and then little hands pat my hair.

"Hello. Mummy, are you okay?"

"H-hey, boo."

"Thank god." Cameron exhales, tickling my scalp. His face drops into the crook of my neck and I blink to see Beau smiling down at me through a mask.

"Oh god." I pull her to me. She wriggles into my hold, and I tuck her right into my chest and sob quietly. "What happened?" I don't recall anything other than coming round in the hospital without Beau and falling into a blind panic.

"A fire," Cam says. "Let me get the nurse."

What! Oh no, my father's house. I look round the room in a

panic, trying to search my mind for any memory of what happened.

"The house?" My voice is hoarse and uncomfortable. I raise my arm round Beau and rub at my neck.

"Let me get you some water." Cam slips free and presses a button beside my bed. He fills up a glass, puts a straw in, and gives Beau a little wink. "Mind out, squirt." He grins, and Beau grabs her mask and clambers between my legs and out of the way. Cam gently removes my mask and puts the straw to my lips. "Little sips." His brows furrow in concern when I suck deeply.

"The house?" I ask. Cam shakes his head. "Burnt down?" I tear up.

"Downstairs is pretty much uninhabitable. Faulty electrics in the kitchen," Cam informs me and pulls my mask even further down and leans in, pressing a soft kiss on my cracked lips.

"Our belongings?" I blink tearfully. It can't all be gone.

"Your mother is at the house with a few others trying to salvage what they can."

"How long have I been out?" I blurt, wheezing.

"Well, I hear Olympics deserve the most rest." He smirks, and I laugh hoarsely.

"Is that so?"

"Like I said, that's what I've heard." He replaces my mask and puts the water on the side. I'm still smiling when he turns back to me. "You were admitted yesterday, so only a few hours, really."

"Okay."

"From what Dan has said, it's mainly damage to the downstairs. It's just stuff, though, Holly." He smiles when my eyes well up. "You and Beau are safe, and that's what matters."

"And my Cam Castle," Beau chirps from the end of the bed.

"Most importantly." He winks at me. I can't believe he is

here. I grip his hand tightly and let out a shuddering breath. "You know, if you wanted me to come home so badly, you should have just said. No need to set the arsonist to work." He nods over his shoulder to Beau, who is twiddling with the hospital band round her wrist, oblivious to his comment.

I laugh and cup my throat in pain. "Where's the fun in that?" I whisper, my throat constricting painfully.

"Baby, no more talking." He pecks my cheek. "Where the hell is the nurse?" He presses the button again. "I'll be back."

A WEEK LATER, I'm sitting quietly in the passenger seat as we pull up outside Cameron's house. Apparently, the family who were renting the property are now going through a divorce, so the place has been empty for weeks. I hadn't even noticed.

I didn't want to see the burnt-out windows of our house, so we drove the long way home, coming into Richmond from the country lane and straight to Cameron's home.

"Hi, Mummy!" Beau waves at me from the front door, my mother standing at her side. I wave through the window and unclip my belt, getting out. Cam threads his fingers with mine, and I smile softly up at him. We haven't discussed our relationship or mentioned the past. I'm not sure we need to. I just know I love this man and he loves me too.

"Hey, boo." My voice is still hoarse, and any physical activity leaves me breathless. Even the short walk from the car to his door makes me worn out. "I missed you."

"Mummy, come on. Look at this big house," Beau says excitedly. I hadn't really paid any attention to the house when I turned up the night before Cameron left. I feel like I'm seeing it through new eyes for the first time. I recall coming in here as a teenager and finding the place dated and dark, but it's now open plan and furnished in fresh colours. "Cam made this." Beau hugs the sideboard, making him laugh.

"Not that one, but I did make those patterns." My little girl traces her finger over the swirls. It's stunning and so authentic.

"Cameron, it's beautiful," I say, looking around. My mother comes over and gives me a quick hug. "Hi, thank you for watching Beau." I hug her tightly.

"Of course. She's my granddaughter." She tuts on a playful eye roll. "You're looking better." She gives my cheeks a soft pat. I know she and Beau stayed here last night when my girl was discharged, but prior to that, she has been staying at a hotel in Barton not too far away.

"I feel it." I smile.

"Baby, sit down, and I'll get you a drink." Cameron had mentioned back in the hospital that our belongings had either been sent to Cam's or put into storage, courtesy of Dan. I take a seat and Beau scrambles up onto my lap. I smile and yawn, already feeling shattered.

"I've made a casserole, so once you've eaten, you can get into bed," my mother suggests and moves into the kitchen. I nod and rest my head on Beau's.

We all eat in the dining room, at a table she tells me Cameron made. I blink in amazement at him. "No end to my talents." He gives me a toothy grin, and I chuckle.

I run my hands over the smooth wood. "It's so beautiful. And the chairs?" I ask, seeing they are as intricate and unique as the other wooden furnishings. He nods, then winks at me.

"What made you get into woodwork?" my mother inquires.

"I don't know. I felt drawn to it."

I fight back a smirk and drop my head when he looks up. He doesn't remember, or maybe he never knew what book he gave me all those years ago. Either way, I'm going to enjoy telling him.

My mother leaves shortly after dinner, and I help Beau get into bed. "Cam says I can decorate this any how I want." I chew my lip at her terrible grammar.

"Did he?" I ask, tucking her quilt round her. All her bedding and toys are here. A picture of my father and her sits on the bedside and on the drawer unit is a picture of Beau and me.

"Yep, this is our new home now. We're going to be a family and I get a daddy now." Beau kicks her feet and grins at me happily. Cam has wasted no time in laying the foundations for what he wants. I don't disagree with him, but I wish we could have done it together.

"Are you sad?" Beau asks when I stare at the floor in thought.

"No, baby." I'm not, but Cameron and I do need to talk. "Go to sleep." I peck her forehead and lay her unicorn teddy by her side.

Slipping out of her room backwards, I pull the door, and she grins brightly at me, the little devil. Thick hands slide round my waist, making me jump. "You're mad at me?" Cam's rough voice sends a ripple of heat down my body.

"No." I shake my head. "I just wanted to talk first before we said anything to Beau."

He presses a light kiss to my shoulder. "We spoke in the hospital. No more time wasting. Star dancing and going forwards only. Sorry, I'm just so fucking happy."

"I just don't want people to think we're moving too fast."

"Yeah, you're right, eleven years is light speed," he huffs, and I laugh. "Who cares what people think?" He walks us into the master and my eyes sweep in awe like last time.

"This room still gets me," I whisper. It's my favourite room in the house. It has a new wide four-poster bed and twin barn doors on rails to a large ensuite with a freestanding bath. The last time I was here, we didn't leave these two rooms. Cam had made love to me repeatedly and simply made sure I wasn't going to forget him anytime soon. It had mocked our first sexual encounters and having him relearn my body had left me emotionally broken with a different kind of loss.

Cameron encourages us towards the bed and stops me. "Fit for an Olympic?" He grins into my cheek.

"One with dodgy lungs." I cough. He sweeps me up and deposits me on the bed. I run my hands over the bedding. "I hope this is new bedding." I scrunch my nose, thinking about the previous tenants who lived here.

"New bed and mattress." Cam drops down on a bounce. "Are you glad to be home?" He twists and tugs me to him before I can answer.

"Yes."

"This is your new home. You know that, right?"

"Beau informed me," I remind him, rolling my eyes. "Are you sure you want this, Cameron? You left to work on yourself, and if the fire hadn't of—"

"I was coming home." He tucks his chin over my shoulder and sighs. "I was always coming home to you and Beau. It was more a question of if you wanted me when I did."

"I do."

"Even after everything?"

"Because of everything," I say firmly. His fingers sweep up and down my arm, and each time I inhale, I get a waft of his manliness. "I do have a confession, though." Cam stiffens.

"What?"

"Do you remember the book you gave me back in the library the first time we spoke alone?" I'm chewing my cheek to stop from grinning, but it breaks free. Cam shakes his head, still tense. "It was about carpentry and joinery." His face is contorted in confusion, then concentration. "You said it wouldn't matter what it was, as I'd never read it." I laugh at his perplexed face.

"You kept it?" He smiles, tucking my hair away. "Does Richmond college know their favourite nerd is a thief?" His mouth twists into a smirk.

"No, just you." I lean in and press my mouth to his. "Thief and an Olympic." I widen my eyes for effect.

"So talented, babe."

I laugh and snuggle into his chest.

"Promise me the past won't haunt us." He cups my face, running his thumb along my lower lip.

"It won't," I swear. "Cameron, there are a lot of things I can't change, but I am sorry from the bottom of my heart. Can you ever forgive me?" For me, everything is as good as dust. It's gone, a thing of the past. For him, it's very different. He suffered multiple traumas.

"I forgave you the minute you found out the truth; I just couldn't forget it all." He sighs. "My therapist has really helped me work through my issues." Cam rests his head on his hand and stares at me. "He highlighted some personal faults. I've made some shitty decisions, Hol, and I can't blame others or my past, I've faced those too. I needed to sort my head out because I was a mess."

"You seem lighter," I murmur, tracing my finger over his brow.

"He thinks I need to contact my parents."

What for? They don't deserve to know Cameron after what they have done. "Do you want to?"

"No."

"So don't."

"He thinks it's the last step in recovery."

I want to find this therapist and tell him to shut up. "What exactly is he expecting you will gain from this?" It's a little late for their apologies. "Could you ever forgive them?"

Cam shakes his head. "Never. He thinks I need to forgive them to gain full closure, though."

"I suppose if you faced them, you might feel different."

"Hol, whenever I think of my father, I want to lamp him, and I honestly wish my mother would fucking vanish into thin air." Sighing, he shoves his face in my neck and inhales. "I don't need to forgive them. I have you and Beau and the rest I have come to terms with."

"I will support you, no matter what." Kissing his head, I roll back. "I'm going to get a shower, if that's okay?"

"It's your house too, Holly." He tuts. "And no, it's not okay."

"What?"

"I'm coming in too."

"Good." I grin, getting up. The hot water feels heavenly after the hospital shower, and as soon as Cam steps in behind me, I turn and hug him tight. "We missed you," I confess. My breasts squash against his abs, and I smirk, stupidly in awe of how fit he is. He is toned and muscular and bloody hot. I felt bereft when he moved away. I grieved him like I had done all those years ago, only this time, the experience and depth of emotion intensified those feelings, causing me to slip in on myself. Beau had been my life raft. I felt Cameron's disappearance as keenly as I had my father's death. Beau too had struggled. She asked me every day when he was coming back.

Grinning, he drops a peck on my nose. "To new beginnings."

"Kiss me," I pout, ready for his mouth to catch hold of mine.

"I love you."

"Only me?" I giggle, pressing into him.

A large hand slides down to cup my arse cheek, his fingers millimetres from the centre of my thighs. "I love your Olympic pussy too." He brushes his finger through my heat. "Very much, baby."

"Cameron," I plead, titling into his touch.

"You're not well." His face twists, pained.

"I'm home, aren't I?" I rock back on his hand, and his finger accidentally slips inside. I moan, and Cam grits his teeth.

"Holly."

"Please?" I beg shamefully, reaching to cup his heavy balls. His brow twitches, and I massage their weight. "Fuck me slowly," I whisper. "I missed you."

"Holly," Cameron curses and lifts me quickly to rest my back against the cold wall. His hand reaches down and his fingers slowly inch inside. "Maybe just a quick touch," he reasons.

"The health police aren't going to turn up."

"No, but my fucking conscience will," he mutters, pumping his fingers inside. My toes curl, and I press my face into his neck. "You're shaking already, Holly."

"Because you feel good. Don't stop." I rock my hips into his hand. "Oh, just there. Faster." Panting, I blink and find Cam watching his fingers disappear inside me. His thumb joins in, and I jolt.

"Fuck yes."

"I'm nearly..." I cough, and his hand tears away.

"No!" I cry. Cam drops his head to mine and closes his eyes. "Cam, I'm okay." I tug his hand and press it back between my thighs. "I'm so close. I need it."

"Holly, you need rest." He presses a kiss to my mouth and sighs, stepping away from me. He picks up some shampoo and squirts some in his palm. Pressing my thighs together, I bite my lip and stare at him, pleading silently. "Don't look at me like that." He's tense as hell and sporting a huge erection.

Moving close, I slide my palm down his cock and grab it at the base, making him choke out a groan. "Cameron Stone." I gain his full attention. I try not to smirk when his eyes widen playfully. "We're having sex," I tell him bluntly. His grin makes my heart falter. He's so handsome. I stroke him once, twice. His forearm hits the wall, and he leans into me, his head bent in pleasure.

"It's been months. If you carry this on, I'm going to come before I'm even inside you."

"As long as you admit you're going to be inside me," I hum, satisfied.

"Fuck." He laughs, lifting me once again. He positions himself, and I grip his face, watching as his brow distorts as he slides inside. "Holly."

"I need a second." I squeak and try to adjust to his size. Cam slides slowly out so the tip is kissing my entrance, then sinks back in. Yes! "I love you," I whisper, grateful to be alive, grateful he came home to us. "Don't leave us again."

"Never." Cam slants his mouth over mine and swirls his tongue in as his cock hits my cervix. He pumps in rhythmically, making me moan sweetly. He adjusts his stance and slides back in, making me cry out in shock.

"I'm coming," I yelp. He picks up speed and slams into me.

"God, you're fucking gorgeous when you're coming." He hisses vividly, watching my eyes.

"Oh, yes!" I mewl on a scream. My orgasm rips through me and clamps down, pulsing and suckling his cock.

"Dammit!" he growls and fucks me a little harder, pressing me into the wall. He kisses me hard, stealing what little air my lungs have left. His mouth rips away as his hips piston upwards, pulling another release from me. I cripple in his arms, sobbing, and Cam groans into my neck. "God, Holly." He shudders, pouring himself into me, his cock throbbing deep.

I cup his face and kiss him roughly. "Grind into me," I beg, desperate to feel more of him. Rough hands grip my hips, and he does as I ask, ensuring every inch of him grates deeply inside of me.

"Now you need to sleep because we have guests tomorrow."

"We do?"

"Yes, gorgeous, we do."

Chapter Twenty-Four
Cameron

Waking up to a giggling Beau and sleeping Holly has to be my favourite memory by far. After coaxing Beau downstairs, we make breakfast and surprise Holly when she wakes up. We eat, laugh and spend the morning like a real family. I have to take a minute in the bathroom because I want to blurt out how ecstatic I'm feeling. I want to fucking cry in relief that they are finally mine.

My family.

It's our first day in Richmond as a family, and I want to parade round the village with my girls, puffing my fucking chest out, because as far as I'm concerned, I won the damn jackpot.

"I'm nervous," Holly whispers. We're heading into Richmond to grab some bits for tonight. I haven't mentioned who, as I want it to be a surprise for them both.

"Baby, don't worry." I grip her hand in mine and check my mirror, finding Beau murmuring quietly to her toy.

"Yeah, baby, don't worry," her little voice chirps, and Holly laughs. She gives me a pointed look, but I smile internally, buzzing that I even have her in my life to give me pointed looks.

"Yeah, baby!" I sing, and Beau giggles, shaking her unicorn.

"Baby!" she joins in.

"Let's face it, after what you've been through, no one will dare say anything anyway," I tell her truthfully. Who would have the audacity to make a comment when she nearly died days before? No one, well, not any decent person anyway.

"I guess." Holly pouts, looking out of the window. I park up behind her shop because we're guaranteed a space, and it's a short walk to the small supermarket. I don't want them overexerting themselves.

"Right, boo, ready to get some party food?" I grin, and Beau whoops from the back, ripping her seatbelt off.

We're barely across the street when people stare at us. "I feel awkward," Holly murmurs, going red in the face. I lift Beau up and walk into the store with a massive grin on my face. Hol turns to say something to me and pulls back, then laughs, bewildered. "You're enjoying this?" she asks.

"Damn right I am." I wink and press a quick kiss on her stunned mouth.

"Cameron, people are talking," she replies under her breath, clearly concerned.

"They always did. At least now it's something I can be proud of." I hook my arm round her lower back and pull her to me. "Are you ashamed to be with me?"

"What? No!" Small hands run up my chest. "You've been through a lot. I don't want this to set you back." Her troubled eyes meet mine.

"We agreed it's done. I'm mentally in the best place I've been since you left ten years ago." I peck her cheek and whisper, "Don't shit on my parade." I utter quietly so Beau can't hear.

"I wouldn't dare."

Slapping her arse, I lean to get a trolley. I lift Beau in so she is standing in the deep cart. "Right, we need a big cake, so you're on the lookout, boo," I say, pointing my finger at her seriously. She nods and squints, looking at the shelves. Holly leisurely walks next to me as I push Beau along, picking up bits as we move round the store.

"What about a fruit platter?" Holly asks, lifting a grapefruit and leaning to see what else is available on the centre aisle.

"Sure." I shrug, happy with anything they choose. Beau hangs over the trolley and grabs a bunch of grapes. "What other fruit do you want, boo?" I ask, encouraging her to choose more. Nadine appears in my periphery, and I groan because she walks straight for us. "Incoming," I whisper to Holly, who twists round and drops the punnet of peaches she was holding in the trolley with a thud.

"This looks cosy," Nadine says. I bristle and step round the trolley to defend my girl to the fucking death when Beau holds up a box of figs.

"Hello," our little girl says simply, innocence personified. "We're having a party because our house died in a fire." She frowns at the fruit in her hands. "What's this?"

"Figs, baby girl." I take the box from her. "Do you want to try one?" I open it up and bite into the fleshy pear-shaped fruit, showing her the seeds inside. She wrinkles her nose. "I take that as a no." I laugh, swallowing it.

"That was your house?" Nadine inquires, seemingly shocked.

"Yes." Holly tucks her hair behind her ear in a gesture I know to be anxious.

I know from Dan that Nadine is already in another relationship, so I refuse to feel sorry for her. It's been months. "I'm sorry to hear that. Where are you staying?" Her eyes shift from Holly to me, digging for information. Holly's shoulders stiffen, and my hackles rise. I haven't forgotten what she said to me all those months ago.

"With me," I respond and decide before she can say more to

fill her in so she's up to speed. "We're together. A family." Her jaw clenches, and I ensure she has no room to comment. "I hear you're in a relationship now. I'm happy for you. We both are." Holly nods numbly, obviously feeling far more uncomfortable than me. "All the best, Nadine." I give her a brief smile and manoeuvre the trolley round her. "Baby, let's grab a cake," I say to Holly.

"I didn't like that," she hums in my ear, and I peck her hair. I fucking love her hair. It's yards long and the silkiest gold I've ever seen. Plus, it smells like vanilla.

"It's done now. Don't let it get to you." She gives me a strained smile. "We're looking forward, not back. That's what we agreed on."

Shopping wiped Holly and Beau out. I've left them sleeping whilst I prepare the food and clean the house. It's another hour before I'm expecting anyone to turn up, but I want everything perfect for Holly. Beau chose a unicorn cake and helped me fix the horn when we got back because it had an extra nose when we removed the packaging. Now, it's a wonky unicorn cake.

"Hey." Holly's hands slip round my waist and her ear lays flat to my back.

"How are you feeling?"

"Okay. A little sleepy." She yawns and laughs, pressing her face into my shoulders.

"Come here, I've got you a gift."

I twist enough to pull Holly round and place her with her back flush to my front. The parcel was on the doorstep when we returned home not long ago.

"What is it?" She stares at the cardboard box and cranes her neck to look over her shoulder at me.

"Open it." I hug her waist and drop my chin on her shoulder as she opens the lid, unsure of what to expect.

Shredded paper hides the gift, and she quickly delves her hand in and pulls it out. I grin when I see the image, and she gasps. It's a photo of when we were in our teens. Fresh faced and not battered by years of pain. "Turn it round."

She twists the cup and reads the personalised message, and begins laughing heartily. *"Cameron's personal Olympic trainer,"* she says, running her finger across the words, chuckling. "I love it and I am. You're my protégée." She grins, twisting to kiss me.

"God, I can't wait to be inside you later."

"I thought I was too unwell?"

Gripping her arse, I lift her onto the side and yank her forward so I'm wedged between her thighs. "If last night was anything to go by, you can handle more of me."

"Do you promise?" she murmurs, giving me big seductive eyes.

"What do you think?" I nudge my cock, and she smiles.

"I think you're already at Olympic standard, Mr Stone." She reaches to cup me and squeezes me when she says my name. She's right; I'm rock fucking hard.

I grip her thighs and slant my mouth over hers. "I love you."

"I love you," she whispers softly. "Kiss me again."

GUESTS START ARRIVING, and Holly looks to me emotionally when Jeremy walks through the door. He rushes over and gives her a big hug. "How are you feeling? How's Beau?" He looks round for her, and I point to the snug where she and Grace are giggling in the corner. "Jesus christ, Hol, you gave us all a heart attack." There is no doubt in my mind this man has feelings for my girl, but I'm confident enough in us to not let it bother me.

"I know, sorry. I'm okay. Cam's looking after us." She smiles lovingly at me, and I soften, pecking her temple.

"Remember what I said. If it gets too much for you or Beau, just say the word." I wink cheekily at her.

Jeremy frowns. "And what's the word?"

"Olympic," we say in unison, and he frowns.

"Drink?" I ask, trying to steer him away from Holly.

"Sure, what have you got?" He looks around, clocking the guys and Kerry, and stiffens. He was a rat in school and I know he was seen leaving with Holly the night of the party. His refusal to help me locate her only ensured our general dislike for him. We'd hoped finding Holly would prove my innocence back then, although my solicitor said it would still be Sarah's word against ours. Holly was my girlfriend at the time, so it would seem as though she was defending me on that basis alone. Both Jeremy's and Holly's dads refused to help me. It hurt at the time, but they were protecting her, and I don't blame them. Emily sees Jeremy and waves, making her way over.

"Beer okay?" I say to him.

"Please." As soon as I step away, I hear him ask Holly if we're an item. He's hardly going to fight me for her, the bloody idiot. I collect us both a beer. Emily is standing with them when I return, and they are discussing a book. I hand over Jeremy's beer.

"I've been meaning to read that," Holly says. "I know I keep asking you, but how's the shop?" She winces at Emily. It may have only been a few days that Holly was in hospital, but two people offered to help in the shop whilst she was unwell. I'm pretty sure with the number of customers she has, she will need to keep one on, or maybe both. It's something we discussed this morning. I'm so proud of what she is achieving.

"Honestly, having Claire and Rita has been a big help. I've kept up with the books and Danielle has helped me with small bits. Keeley has been amazing too."

"Okay, good."

"Hol, just focus on getting better. The shop is not going anywhere," Emily assures.

I slide my hand into the back jean pocket, using it to

leverage her into a twist to face me. "Baby, stop worrying," I say. She smiles and I drop my face in her hair. "You smell amazing."

"Stop." Holly shrugs me away, embarrassed, but I know she loves it. Her eyes sparkle, and she pinches my arse discreetly. I grin into my bottle and Emily marvels at our little moment.

"You two are glowing."

Holly shoots me a shy look, and I pull her into my chest and nip her earlobe. I can't get enough of her.

"She's the love of my life," I say with pride, not missing Jeremy's hand tightening around his beer.

"You soppy sod." Holly giggles, pressing a kiss to my jaw.

"Look at this, Daddy!" Beau runs over and holds up a picture of us with a unicorn on a lead. My heart thuds with a painfully ecstatic squeeze. Jeremy murmurs something, but I catch Emily elbowing him and swallow a laugh.

"Wow, baby girl, I love it. You're so clever. Go and stick it on the fridge."

"That's me and Mummy and you." She points at the stick thin me with eyes too big in my wobbly head.

"I know what big eyes I have." I smile down at her artwork. "Do you want me to help you put it on the fridge?"

"Yes."

"Did you call me Daddy?" I ask, sucking in a deep breath. I want to hear her say it again.

"When I was sick, you said you were my daddy." She looks from me to Holly, trying to gauge a response.

"I am your daddy, boo," I tell her. "Do you know when I first saw you at the fete, I knew I was going to be your daddy." I smile, recalling seeing her toddling about.

She nods, and I suppress a smile at her eagerness to please. "Give me kiss." Giggling, she smacks a kiss on my cheek and takes my hand. Grace runs over and jumps on me. I lift her up and walk them to put the picture on display.

My heart is full for the first time in a long damn time. It

feels better than good. Euphoric. I help Beau display her picture on the fridge. I stand back, appreciating her work and scruff her hair as Grace wriggles free. "Ready to give Mummy her cake?" I whisper. Beau covers her mouth and giggles. Getting her to keep this a surprise has sent me into a mild panic today, but hats off to her because she hasn't said a word. I pull out the ring box in my pocket, and with shaky hands, gently slide it onto the wonky horn that looks ready to drop on the floor. "Don't you dare," I whisper to the cake. "Remember the words to sing?" I look at Beau, who is shoving her finger in the buttercream. "Greedy guts." I laugh, scooping some up and dolloping it on her tiny nose.

"I'm a unicorn!" She laughs.

"That's right, and I've chosen you to sing the special words. Can you remember them?" I ask, but she frowns, confused. I whisper them in her ear and, thankfully, she nods enthusiastically. "Good, get ready."

I lift the cake and Beau breaks into song. "Happy home day to you!" The room joins in, and a few gasps erupt, but Holly is too busy smiling at me to notice the ring hanging precariously on the piece of shit horn.

"Happy home day, dear Holly!" We sing.

"And Beau." I wink down at Beau, who points to the cake.

"Look at the ring, Mummy!" she squeals with excitement. I was so fucking close to being the one to surprise her. I groan, laughing. Holly's eyes widen and glisten as I drop down on one knee, gripping the cake at my front.

She presses her fingers to her mouth and begins to cry. "A decade ago, I caught sight of a gorgeous nerd fumbling with her stack of books in the library," I whisper. "Her blonde hair and big blue eyes made my gut hurt. They still do."

"Like mine!" Beau exclaims, blinking her blue eyes at me and the room bursts into laughter.

"Yes, just like yours." I nod to her mum. "Focus." She gets

serious and nods, looking at Holly. "But fate wasn't so kind to us and for all your love for books, someone wrote us a different story. Words can be erased and rewritten. And that's what we're going to do. Write out our own version." Holly sniffles quietly, nodding. "Marry me, Miss Matthews?"

"Yes." Her voice catches, but her eyes say it all. She's ready to dive into creating our own story. I flick a look to Emily, who jumps into action. She takes the cake, and I slip the ring off the horn. It drops with a splat, and Beau grabs it off the floor and shoves it in her mouth, grinning at us. I laugh and wink at Holly, pulling her the short way to me and lifting her hand to slide the ring on her finger.

"And for the record, I'm going to be Matthews." My lip threatens to wobble, but she recognises my struggle and pulls me in for a kiss.

"You always were."

I rest my forehead on hers and close my eyes.

Holly and Cameron Matthews. I was so determined to have my name plastered after hers. I thought it meant something. Ownership on paper and in name—at the time it seemed like the most important thing, but I can't wait to shed my Stone heart and live again. Maybe we'll stay here in Richmond, perhaps we'll move a few towns away. I couldn't care less. As long as I have my girls, the rest is inconsequential.

Holly's mother strides over and pulls her into a hug. "Congratulations, darling."

"Oh, Mum. Thank you. Did you know about this?" She sniffs, picking Beau up, who is yanking at Holly's ring finger.

"I didn't." She keeps her face tight with feigned happiness.

"You don't agree?" Holly deflates before her mother, and I pull her to me, giving her the strength she needs.

"I don't know, Holly, it's just very sud—"

"He loves me and Beau."

"Yes, but—"

"No buts." Holly holds her hand up, halting her mother. "Just because you don't agree doesn't make you right. Maybe this isn't your idea of perfect or ideal, but it's mine."

"And Beau?" Our guests are trying not to hang onto every quietly spoken word, but the tense silence hanging over us all makes it hard to ignore. "Is *mine*. My child. Mother, you didn't agree with my life when I was in London. You don't agree with it now. What difference does it make? We're not the same people, and if you love Beau and I, you'll learn to accept this just like I did when you left Dad and I here in Richmond."

Margaret flinches and Holly touches her arm. "I never judged you. I didn't understand, but I accepted that *here* wasn't for you. That Dad and I didn't make you happy, even if you loved us. Something was missing for you. I gave you your happiness without an argument. You can do the same for me." Holly leans to brush a kiss on her mother's cheek and steps around her, moving quickly into a chorus of congratulatory cheers. I don't bother wasting my time with her mother. The only parent I give a shit about is the one clutching our daughter on her hip.

Holly chances a look over her shoulder at me, and I smile supportively. All I need now is for her to tell me she's pregnant and I'll be the proudest man to walk the earth.

"*I love you*," she mouths.

"*Olympic wife*," I mouth back, making her throw her head back in a husky chuckle.

Mine.

Fuck me, she's finally mine. After all this time, I won her again.

My Holly.

My love.

Epilogue
Holly

Three years later...

"Don't run too far!" Cameron's voice carries. I give his hand a gentle squeeze and watch as Beau spins to look over her shoulder, her hand gripping Noah's little podgy one in her own.

"We won't! I can see the park from here!" her voice calls back as she steers her little brother along the grass. The sea air whips her long blonde tresses round her face, and she yanks it into place.

Noah cries excitedly as the park comes into view and Cam laughs. "I'm going to go grab the gate." He slips his hand out of mine, and I watch as he pulls it open, bowing to let both of our children through.

We stayed in Richmond. Too fond of our house and happy to be close to our friends. Over the years, people moved away, others forgot about the vile stories, and we began to live the life we dreamed of. We married that year and started trying for a child of our own, and Noah arrived a little over a year and a half ago. We want more. Cameron is desperate for more.

I'm watching him carry our little green-eyed bruiser and assist Beau through the gate when someone calls my name.

Twisting, my smile drops away when I see Cameron's parents seated outside the cafe on the other side of the road. "Holly Matthews?"

Both have aged considerably, but the stuffy air of money and self-importance round them is as evident now as it was back when Cam and I first started dating. I swing to look for my husband, worried.

His father stands and walks towards me, using a cane. I shake my head and fight the bile swimming in my stomach. Cameron appears at my side, oblivious, because he dips to kiss my neck. "Hey, baby, come on, the kids are waiting."

"Cam," I whisper, but he doesn't hear me.

"Cameron?" My husband's head snaps up, and I grip his hand wrapped round my waist.

"Cameron, is that you?" His mother is also making her way over. Her simple linen dress and matching cardigan are prim and expensive. They look like they are still living a life of luxury. Rich, respected, and purposely unaffected by the past thirteen plus years.

"We can go," I whisper, and he nods. Turning, we start to leave. My eyes search out the kids, and I see Beau pushing Noah on a swing a few feet away, just past the gate.

"Cameron, wait!" his father says in a panic. My husband stops, and I bite the inside of my cheek as he turns back and walks towards his parents. My eyes flick between the children and my husband. "You're together?" Reggie asks, perplexed. His eyes jump between each of us.

"Any aspects of mine and Holly's life are none of your business or our children's, for that matter!" he seethes.

"You have children?" Martha blinks at me in shock.

"How could you?" I whisper sadly. "How could you leave him like that?" My voice grows angry, and Cameron turns to cup my face, halting the angry triad I can feel on the tip of my tongue. The gate clangs loudly, and Beau struggles over with Noah in her arms.

"Dad, are you coming?" she huffs, and I rush to take Noah from her and pull him into my chest. Cameron cups Beau's shoulders and stares at his parents.

"I never did it," Cameron states.

His father has the audacity to clench his jaw, and I take a step forward. "She did it. *To him,*" I state crossly. "He was the victim. Imagine leaving your child to fight for himself, to face that trauma alone. Sarah did it to him!" I cry, my lip wobbling.

"Holly, we're leaving!" Cam snaps, and Beau looks around, confused.

"What's wrong?" Beau sniffles, taking her father's hand.

"Nothing, baby girl. Holly, can you head back to the car?"

I reach for Beau, and she takes my hand, unsure but always so damn sweet. I don't want these people around our children. Noah blows a raspberry in my ear, and I begin to usher them away.

"Please tell me that isn't true?" Martha, his mother, gasps, and I flinch but keep moving. Beau is hanging back, worried about her dad.

"Why, does the alternative make you happier?" My husband's humourless laugh scrapes like nails on a chalkboard. "You left me. *Without. A. Word.* Not so much as a letter. Do you have any idea of the level of trauma Sarah caused me? You both caused me! I never even so much as looked at her. She *assaulted* me! You're not welcome in my life. Or my family's. Any attempt at contact will result in a restraining order."

"Mum, what's happening?" Beau croaks.

"It's okay, please help me to the car. Your dad is..."

"Holly!" Cameron's broken voice calls, and I see him

walking to me speedily. Beau whimpers and I watch as he picks her up, swinging her on his shoulders.

"Dadda!" Noah gurgles, and Cam smiles. I twist to see Beau looking back over her shoulder. She lifts her hand in what I expect will be a wave, but she must think better on it, so instead, she reaches for Cameron's hands resting on her knees and we walk away.

"Who was that?" she asks softly.

"We'll tell you later. Right now, Daddy wants to get back to the cottage. Build the biggest sandcastle and eat ice cream with my little horde."

"You're sad," she comments, and Cameron's shaken green eyes find mine. I rub his back as we reach the car.

"No, boo, I'm happy. But those people make me madder than Arabella Jacobs makes you in PE when she cheats." He helps her down and Beau pulls a face. "Yes, that mad."

"Are they your parents?"

I listen as I put Noah in his car seat and Beau clambers in beside her brother in the Range Rover. Cameron stands at the door, our eyes meeting briefly, and I look back down the promenade to where his parents stand stricken.

"Remember when I adopted you last year, and you asked why, even though me and Mummy are married?" She nods, resting back against the seat.

"Yes, you said that not everyone is lucky enough to choose their family, but we got to."

"That's right, baby girl. We got to choose. I also choose *not* to have them in my life," he says calmly. "It's a lot more complicated than that, but they do not make me happy."

"Are they not nice?"

"No, they're not." I pull the keys dangling from his back pocket, and Beau nods. "Fancy another surf lesson later?" he asks, changing the topic. "You're getting so good now."

"Yes, I can show Grace when she comes tomorrow."

"She's pretty good at surfing. She will be able to help you as well." Cameron winks and clunks her door shut.

He turns to me, and I wrap my arms around him. "Get me out of here," he pleads. I nod and get in as Cameron walks to the passenger side, his face averted away from where I see his parents hurrying to their car. No doubt trying to follow us. I drive away, heading straight for the cottage on the beach that Cameron purchased all those years ago. He is shaking, and I offer to take the kids for a walk to give him some space.

"No. I need you. All of you." He lifts a sleeping Noah from his seat and slings an arm over Beau's shoulder.

"I'm just going to grab some snacks and a blanket; I'll meet you down there."

I rush inside and prepare some drinks, snacks and make a quick call to Dan.

"Cam already reminded me to bring extra deck chairs!" Dan laughs.

"It's not that," I say in a rush. "We just bumped into his parents."

"Fuck!"

"Swear jar!" Grace hollers in the background.

"Yeah, yeah."

"Don't call him, but I wanted to let you know before you arrived." I chew my lip.

"How is he?"

"Okay. They noticed me first, then Cam. It could have been worse," I mutter. "He has taken the kids down to the beach."

"I'll make sure to go for a beer with him tomorrow."

"Thanks, Dan, I just don't want this to set him back. We came away to avoid being in Richmond at this time of year." I sigh. Cameron always goes a little quiet when the anniversary of the incident arises. He never talks about it, but we notice the shift in him. When Dan suggested going to Cornwall for two weeks, Cam practically loaded the car on the spot. We arrived two nights earlier than everyone else. Brant and Cole are joining with their families too.

"It won't. If anything, this will only solidify how far he has come. How lucky he is to have you all. It was always going to be a shock, Holly."

"I know. Thanks. I'll see you tomorrow."

I hear Emily call goodbye in the background. I remind myself how many people he has around him who love him. How much support he has. We both have. Our family is growing. Our lives progressing, as we succeed in our chosen careers. We have everything and more we dreamt of.

Dan is right; this only solidifies how lucky we are.

CAMERON

BEAU TAKES my hand and flicks glances my way as we head down to the beach. Noah is a deadweight in my right arm. "Are you okay, Dad?" She's so bloody grownup that my heart aches when she calls me that. I tug her to me and drop a kiss on her hair.

"I'm fine, kiddo, just a strange afternoon."

"Promise?" She tilts her head to look up at me, big blue eyes wary.

"Boo, I'm perfect." I let go of the anger that seeing my parents caused to fire up in me. "I'm here with my favourite people, in our favourite spot."

"Mum's coming now!" I twist, seeing Holly fight with the sand as she sinks into the golden dunes.

"Go and help her, please." I nudge Beau back and she races off to help her mum. I drop my gaze to Noah; his chubby cheeks and pouty lips make me smile. He has my eyes and

Holly's hair. I pull him closer and kiss the crown of his head. Emotion swells in my chest and it's nothing of what I expected. No hatred or shame. The anger is gone. I'm just grateful and so fucking blessed.

Holly is laughing when she reaches me. "Phew, I thought I was going to disappear in that sand."

I thread my fingers with hers, and we follow Beau running up the beach, the blanket billowing behind her. She drops it down and Holly finds several rocks to hold it in place. I lower with Noah, and Holly slots herself next to me as Beau begins digging at the ground.

"You called Dan, didn't you?" I lift my brow, my lips twisting lovingly. She has always got my back, anticipating my needs.

Her cheeks flush. "Are you mad?"

I frown, perplexed by her thought process. I shake my head. "But I don't need Dan, baby. I need you. Our beautiful kids, and I have that." I lift her hands and kiss them.

"Okay. Anything else?" She smiles softly, twisting to watch Beau.

"We need a dog."

"What?" Holly says.

"Can we!" Beau screams, overhearing.

"Really, Cam?" Holly shakes her head. "How on earth are we going to look after a dog when we have that little maniac running us both ragged." She nods at Noah, who blinks awake after Beau all but rendered us deaf with her piercing scream. He scrambles from my lap and toddles to his sister, his arms high and a loud babble rolling free.

"Please?" Beau clasps her hands together, begging with big blue hopeful eyes.

I look at Holly and pout. "You're on dog poop duty," she tells me firmly.

"Yes, ma'am." I wink and nod at Beau, who jumps up and down, screaming excitedly. Noah joins in, bouncing on his chubby little legs, and I drag Holly over my leg and tuck her between my thighs. "I love you. I love you for having my back and being an incredible mother and a perfect wife, but I love you for coming back to me."

Her hand reaches round, and she cups my jaw. I dip for a kiss as Beau makes a gagging sound. I smile against my wife's mouth and she smirks too. "I love you too, Mr Matthews."

We help the kids build a sandcastle and spend the remainder of the day on the beach. Later that night, after we are stuffed to the eyeballs with ice cream and they are sleeping, does Holly say, "Cam, you'd tell me if you weren't okay?"

"I wasn't. Not when I first saw them. Oddly, I don't care now. I don't care if they still think I did it or are struggling to comprehend that I didn't." I drop my head on her shoulder, our legs entwined in the bath. The sea glistens under moonlight and the light swish of water from outside is a calm hum through the open window. "I think I just needed to say it to their faces, as an adult. Face them once and for all, you know. I have no control over what they think."

"What if they contact you?"

"Then I will make good on my threat. I don't want them in our lives, Hol." My chest inflates, and she rubs my thighs, before twisting to straddle me. Her full breast peek through her ridiculously long blonde hair and her soft hips tease at wanting more children between them. She's fucking stunning. Sexy as sin and I love her with every goddamn breath I own.

"Me either."

I cup her arse and tug her to my stiffening cock. "You look good," I moan as she shifts to line me up and then sinks down. "Goddamn, Holly." My hands shift to her hair. I grab big handfuls and grunt as she rides me as fast as the bath allows.

"I want another baby," she whispers.

My eyes flash to hers, and I grin. "Ah, the real reason you didn't want a pet." She snorts and runs her hands over my head, kissing me. She bounces quicker, her moans short and sweet. Her breasts rub against my chest, and I groan as my spine tingles and my balls tighten. "You know I want that too. Fuck, I love seeing you pregnant."

"Now, oh god, now." She trembles, and I growl possessively as she comes on my cock. My own orgasm rushes forwards, and I kiss her. Moaning into her mouth, telling her how perfect she is.

"We need a bigger bath." She sighs.

"And a bigger house, where are we going to put all of these children and a dog!"

"I don't care." Her arms find a place around my neck. "We could live in a shed, and I'd still be happy."

"Me too, gorgeous. Be a bit of a squish, though."

"I could just live on your cock?" She giggles, wiggling purposefully.

"I'll start looking at sheds."

She laughs throatily. "I'm so happy, Cameron. I love our life, our friends. The family we have made."

"Making," I remind her. "Maybe we'll have a little girl next time. Or twins. That could be fun." I snort when she snaps back in shock. "No?"

"You're crazy!"

"Crazy in love with you, Holly Matthews." I wink, and she rests her head on my shoulder. I envelope her in a tight hug and she sighs.

"Twins could be fun." She whispers and I nip her neck and groan as she begins to slide all over me again. When she lifts her head, her eyes are burning with desire and love. I cup her face and she bites her lip, eyes filling with emotion.

"I know, Holly." I sigh, shifting to slide back inside her again. She doesn't need to say it. We are both overwhelmed by our connection. She loves me as fiercely as I do her.

Holly nods and presses her mouth to mine, and I hold her tightly, a deep breath shuddering through me.

"I love you too gorgeous," I vow softly, and her lips tremble against mine.

It's not just love, it's gratitude, relief and every other emotion in between that has torn its way through our lives and pulled us back together.

It's us.

But most importantly, she's mine.

The End.

Also by A. R. Thomas

The Whiskey Promises Series

Portrayal

Betrayal

After Hours

Stolen Hours

Escape The Light

The Panel Novella

Join My Reader Group!

Confessions Of A Smut Addict

If you Want to be updated with upcoming releases, subscribe to my newsletter here.

https://dashboard.mailerlite.com/forms/436452/87905851521632159/share

About the Author

A. R. Thomas is an Author from England who writes contemporary romance with an edge. After being an avid reader and soon she realised she needed more than to be on the receiving end of a good book, she wanted to deliver one. What started as a hobby soon became an obsession, and as they say the rest is history.

She has a weakness for alpha males, edgy romance and loves a good twist.
Angsty, edgy, romance heavy . . . the perfect recipe for any love story, right?

A. R. Thomas lives with her son, and when she's not supporting him from the sidelines at his latest sporting event, she is usually, lost to the thought of a book.

Find A. R. Thomas on her Social Media

Acknowledgments

This story has been sitting, gathering dust on my desktop for a very long time.

I'm not sure why I kept it hidden for so long. I initially wrote Stone Heart for myself, and I never felt the need to share it. After a while, I realised I was doing Cam & Holly a disservice.

Thank you to my incredible readers for pushing me to release this, and my alpha & beta readers for helping shape this into the story it is today.

So many people have given their time and talents to this story, either in the form of covers (Thank you Jess! @forgetyounot.designs) or graphics, I am still obsessed with the map of Richmond (@designsbydanielle is amazing to work with!)

None of this would be possible without your support so I appreciate, every page read, every post shared, every review and message sent.

So thank you!

A. R. Thomas
xx